The Trials of Sylvie DaSouza

Lark Holden

Published by New Generation Publishing in 2024

Copyright © Lark Holden 2024

First Edition

The author asserts the moral right under the Copyright, Designs and Patents Act 1988 to be identified as the author of this work.

All Rights reserved. No part of this publication may be reproduced, stored in a retrieval system or transmitted, in any form or by any means without the prior consent of the author, nor be otherwise circulated in any form of binding or cover other than that which it is published and without a similar condition being imposed on the subsequent purchaser.

ISBN
    Paperback   978-1-80369-439-9
    Ebook   978-1-80369-440-5

www.newgeneration-publishing.com

 New Generation Publishing

To Toby and Ollie, with love

This book was published through
The Book Challenge Competition part of
The London Borough of Barking and Dagenham Pen to Print
Creative Writing Programme.

Pen to Print is funded by Arts Council, England as a National
Portfolio Organisation.

Connect with Pen to Print
Email: pentoprint@lbbd.gov.uk
Web: pentoprint.org

Chapter 1

Across the road from the entrance of the Very Important Criminal Court, a gathering of dishevelled looking women in bright coloured cropped tops, their downy arms gleaming in the soft spring sunshine, are holding up a plethora of placards, already furled and battered at their early morning corners. One placard hollers a message in red paint: 'SAY NO TO SLAVERY,' and another bawls its outrage: 'PARTRIDGE: GET STUFFED.'

In amongst this group, a chubby woman with copper-red curls, the ringleader no doubt, cups her hands over her mouth and whoops like a banshee. Some people in the crowd smirk uncomfortably, and look away at nothing in particular as if to signify they're not part of this display of female disorder. A collective female cheer breaks out and carries overhead to clash with the narrow strip of cloud-streaked sky, before settling in bright unison on a song, jeering, defiant and –to my ears at least—as alluring as ditch water!

> *'He's no-one special, just an old has-been*
> *Da doo-Ron-Ron-Ron, Da doo-Ron-Ron!*
> *Now he's off to prison, never to be seen*
> *Da doo-Ron-Ron-Ron, Da doo-Ron-Ron!*

It's not for a bunch of shi**eads to decide—it's the jury that counts. I'd like to swat the whole lot of them like flies, with a giant newspaper, crush their ugly little heads on the bleach-white pavements.

A group of photographers nearby, with multiple straps crisscrossing their flabby chests, steady extravagant tripods, fiddling earnestly with their camera lenses, comparing them with each other's as they tease, smile and gesture over an event that should never have been allowed to happen. The air round me seethes with false rumours and reports, and although I'm outnumbered, I'm here to set the record straight.

To my right, a young man, with a nose that wrinkles up at the end, looks up in surprise at a battered-looking older man with a wad of tissues in his hand. 'Not going in?' he asks.

'Nah' says the other. 'Right proper scrum in there. Besides—didn't get a bl**dy pass, did I?'

'Never bl**dy stopped you before,' and they snort in unison, whinnying like horses, showing tobacco-stained teeth.

I turn my back firmly on them, taking my place near the head of a bemused queue that snakes languidly outside the Very Important Court.

Ahead of me a stout, red-headed woman tightens the belt of her canary-yellow jacket that makes her flabby sides spill over. I'd seen one such jacket on a television travel documentary, which I now devour with my eyes for a second time. I take in each pleated pockets of perfection, like giant envelopes, the dazzling sunny buttons, and the silver-white stitching that makes the outline of the garment stand out. It must have cost a fortune.

'Day out for me,' wheezes the woman in a festive mood as if she's wandered in from a funfair. She has a gap in her upper front teeth, a gap wide enough to push a piece of macaroni through it. She winks at me, patting one of her yellow pockets. 'I'm sneaking in a snack,' she says in a conspiratorial whisper, making me an instant accomplice. She offers up her bag for inspection to the security guard before her sturdily packaged frame plunges through the somersaulting horizontal arms of a turnstile. I press down hard on my moustache and beard, as I copy her actions with my rucksack, and follow her through. After gathering my keys from the electronic conveyor belt, I hear the woman chatting to a white-shirted security guard, his hair styled in intricate rows resembling a chessboard.

'His hour's up, Cap'n!' she tells him in feigned solemnity, and follows this up with a dazzling mock salute. 'Let's hope they hang the s*d!' she trumpets to the rest of us with a familiarity which makes it clear that she's been here before and not too in the distant past.

'Now, now, Annie,' says the security guard, wagging a playful finger at her. 'You know better than that!' At which Annie emits a babyish squeak: 'Sorry, Jevon!' and enacts a series of exaggerated gestures: the cowering shoulders, hand over her mouth in mock trepidation; eyes darting from side to side before her left-hand bears down to smack her broad backside several times. When this display of humour comes to an end, the woman straightens to full height, 'zips' her mouth with her fingers, and assumes the sober expression of a monk. She is familiar with the rules, as we all are: that once the commoners' garden gates (court turnstiles) clank shut, you relinquish all traces of cosy, familiar chat and easy gait and replace them with more formal modes of speech and stuffy respect. That's what courts do to you. Turn you into a breeze block, indistinguishable one from the next, silent, your character expunged.

I'm glad to see the end of this woman's—this Annie's dire little pantomime show. I can't abide women who think they're the life and soul of the party, wherever the party happens to be, clamouring for attention from strangers as if it's an entitlement to which they were born.

I press down on my beard again, the tips of my fingers rubbing the unending torment of chafing skin that threatens to flare up underneath. My glasses—the ones I've borrowed from Melanie—are steamed up and I rub them with my fingers. It was a spectacular discovery to find that bat-like eyesight could be cured by two pieces of glass, throwing everything into sharp focus that I'd never experienced before. I head inside the cavernous building where marble pillars sprout like headstrong tree trunks; the fiery gleam of the ochre-patterned, burnished floors makes my eyes water. A surface as smooth as ice is very easy to slip on. I'm just saying.

The Very Important Criminal Court. If you, like me, have never had cause to come to this vainglorious building, and have only familiarised yourself with its sensational history from secondary sources like television dramas and documentaries, the real thing is, by far, spectacular in comparison.

The place echoes with the cries of 'lost souls' who had never escaped the place, who had lingered a little too long and got left behind. Am I the only one to hear them, slobbering like teething babies, snuffling like hogs on a truffle hunt?

Am I the only one to feel their presence, as they run and swirl around in the hazy ether of the spiritual world that runs parallel to our own?

I'm not being fanciful here, but if you listen with your full attention, you might glimpse a flicker of movement, or detect a light, hollow sound through these walls. These hapless scrag-ends of the spirit world, beggared unfortunates who sigh and sob uncontrollably, shivering and lamenting a plight they can never escape or undo. They had once started out as substantial beings that had become distracted walking down the palatial corridors of the court, or who had told untruths in the witness stand, and stayed afterwards in the hope of correcting them, but had never got around to doing due to the ceaseless volume of court cases. Over the years, although accustomed to staying, they also yearn to leave. Listen! You can hear the chattering of teeth from behind the stuccoed antique walls or above every grand arch as they approach, pleading with me to end their misery, to snuff them out, but I don't know how! 'God**mnit! I've got problems of my own!' I scold them. 'Ask someone else!'

I'd give my eye teeth not to be here in this detestable space where blankets made from the weave of shadows descend over my mouth and eyes, making it hard to breathe. I'd much rather be buried in fresh manure in an open field than face the surging clamorous crowds, but my situation—his situation—dictates otherwise, and I must be here for him.

******

I tell myself that I've got a conscience prone to work overtime, an unbending loyalty to my friends, and a strong sense of justice. That's what's brought me here, to the implacable walls of the Courts.

And so far so good.

With groping fingers, a court official in navy-blue uniform furtively adjusts her laddered tights under her waistband. Her shoulders stiffen, her arms fall to her side. 'Hoodies must be worn down, sir,' says the official, bristling at me for watching her.

As I make a half-hearted attempt to pull my hood down, I shove a scrap of paper under her nose. Her eyes narrow as her lips move slowly to read it. 'Ah yes, *that* one,' she says with a gleam in her eye, of one looking forward to a prawn salad for lunch. 'Court Number Three. Please use the public gallery—and the hood, sir...!' Her eyes bulge slightly as she nods at a wall painted with letters, numbers and red arrows pointing in different directions. In the past I'd have to get two inches close to the writing to even begin to see it, and even then I'd need to squint. But not anymore. Not with these glasses. I can see everything clearly from where I stand.

******

I'm pleased with myself. It's amazing how you can get by without having to say much; although by this time, with the horsehair in contact with my sensitive skin, and my nerves creeping up on me as never before, the urge to scratch my face to the bone makes my fingers itch. I'd spent the early hours of this morning making myself look presentable, smoothing and kneading my face and head all over, putting every nylon strand, every layer of adhesive where it should be according to the instructions that came with the kit. I had to sneak out of the house this morning and catch my taxi two streets away—and away from Melanie's prying eyes.

As soon as Miss Droopy Draws, with the frayed tights, turns to help a member of the public with their enquiry, I pull my hood further over my head and gingerly walk in the opposite direction, up the majestic wide staircase to Court Number Three.

Along the way I rehearse for the umpteenth time what I have come to say. The way you dress up words is what matters most, more than the actual words themselves. As you would clothe a mannequin to feature its best points, say, with a gay scarf, a pretty belt, or a striking gold bracelet, so the well-judged use of stress, pitch and intonation are the high fashion accessories in the world of words. I bound through the building on the balls of my feet, slipping on the shiny floor in my haste to get there. I go over in my mind what I'm going to say so that I don't dry up in the witness box—who would have thought it? Me in a witness box! I wonder how I'll manage the whole army of them, their eyes boring into me, making me a figure of fun, rolling their eyes: 'Oh yes, she would say that!' A flicker of anger flits through me: who are they to judge me? I want to turn and run but I can't.

I've prepared my lines like an actor on opening night. My legal and army training have sharpened my skills, given me the confidence to express myself in a coherent and succinct way; to sound spontaneous and sincere and, most important of all, not to cause offence.

To establish the right amount of indignation: 'Whoever said *that* is mistaken, Your Honour!'

To establish credibility as a witness:

'...I should know— I was there for forty years!' *To accept the frailties in others:*

'....they were grasping women ...and who wouldn't concoct a whole bunch of fairy tales in exchange for a new home and a fat monthly cheque?...'

Oh, I'm going to be better than good. I'm going to exceed all expectations.

******

In the midst of a sea of elbows and hard-packed bodies in the high ceilinged, oak-panelled walls of the courtroom, I shoulder my way forward, past the snoopers and purloiners of privacy—the body of people called the general public. Some wigged barristers are sitting on benches, some standing as they flick through thick arch-lever files; a grinning man holds up three fingers as if confirming a bet. '…old Hollerton will be out of order at least three times; she won't be able to contain herself! Mark my words!' he says.

A few uniformed policemen, hands in pockets, pace up and down with members of the press. The press! The saddest bunch of people you could ever meet. Give them a press badge and they will give you a world drained of joy and colour, life and meaning; relying on pleasing homilies, second- hand stories mined from the ashes of the dead and tormented. They've been hounding my family for years in pursuit of a good story, with their intrusive questions: 'Any news of Sylvie?' 'Where is she now?' They don't know I'm here—under their very noses! Just thinking about it makes me nervous and jittery so I bite my tongue.

As I shuffle forward, mindful of stepping on toes, a surge of cool air blows over the left side of my face, almost lifting me off my feet, blowing down my hood –and all the other bits and bob – so that I must hold down my face with my left hand. I look to see where it's coming from, and am confronted with the sight of a wraith-like figure of a man with sunken cheeks, flanked by two white-shirted custody officers, in the dock. The man stands squinting under the harsh lights and looks about him as if he's just landed on an alien planet; he rubs his thin wrists which are marked with crimson blotches, the size of rosehips. A scorched scowl is embedded across his caved-in face as if dug deep with a spiteful spade.

Out of his eye-line, I stare at him in confusion and wonder for a few seconds. A luminous light shrouds itself about his neck and shoulders with the ease of a silk shawl. There is something familiar in the way his shoulders slope, the slant of his forehead, and even in the sour and surly expression that doesn't care who sees it. My upper lip prickles, my mouth runs dry. An explosion goes off in my head, blurring my vision, and sending shock waves down my spine. I clap my hand over my mouth—but am too late to prevent the low squeal that half-escapes my lips; I turn the same gesture to hammer down the beard and moustache around the mouth, swallowing hard to keep it all together... literally all together!

It's him! It's Ron Partridge. The one I know as well as myself and call my friend. His eyes are darting from ceiling to floor, to the barristers in the front row, then back to the ceiling and floor. Looking every inch a cornered animal, he squirms from one foot to another, although I can't see his feet. Flecks of bloodied tissue glinting like pomegranate seeds, line his chin. And his hair—ah, his hair!—once gold-spun and abundant like a lion's mane—is thin and greying like the frayed end of a well-worn blanket. With lips, sore and cracked, his face puckers as he chews.

At that moment a harassed-looking man with a goatee beard, satanic black robes flying behind him, swoops down like an ungainly crow next to me. Breathing hard, he points to the swing doors I've just come through. 'The public gallery,' he sniffs haughtily. 'And if you don't mind, sir...' he tails off to indicate his own head with a twitching forefinger, meaning for me to lower my hood.

I hold out a folded piece of paper, expecting the bearded man to take it. I try to press it into his hand but he's formed a fist, hard and unyielding.

I nod towards Ron in the dock who, had he looked up, wouldn't have recognised me due to my altered appearance.

I turn to the bearded man, and gleaning my knowledge of courtroom dramas, I surmise that he's a court usher. 'Please...could you make sure his barrister gets this?' I avoid his gaze, cross with myself. My voice sounds thin and shrill like a woman's which catches me off guard. The usher's brows knit in surprise. I swiftly revert to a low, gruff voice. 'Please, it's important.' I think I've fooled this CrowFace as he takes the folded piece of paper from me without looking at it.

'I'll see what I can do,' he replies, scrunching up the paper with one hand while placing the other in the crook of my back. People scatter as he propels me towards the heavy swing doors as if I'm a wheelie bin.

Then between gritted teeth, in the last seconds of my exit: 'I'll call you if they need you,' he says and with that the door swings back and forth, until it stops, with me bent double outside Court Number Three. The imprint where his fingers have been, starts to throb like a flesh wound, and I wonder if I should go back inside the courtroom to have it out with him. To cause a scene. No, I'll deal with him later. My heart thumps against my ribcage like a drum, syncopating with the gravel-like breath that explodes in spurts through my nose and mouth.

I'm the only person he's thrown out. I straighten up, dab the palm of my hand over my face— all's well!

******

At first I can hardly see the back of my hands in the public gallery that overlooks Court Number Three from where I've just been unceremoniously thrown out, my back still throbbing, and my pride out of joint. But this only strengthens my resolve to be here. Was there something they didn't want me to know? Were they hoping I wouldn't turn up? That I'd simply go away? They sure picked the wrong gal. They'll never get one over on me. That's all I'm saying. As my sight adjusts itself in the dimness, I can make out the outline of other people's heads and shoulders as they sit in rows of tiered seats. A faint smell of peanuts wafts through the air. Toughened glass muffles much of the vibrancy of the court below making all sights and sounds anaemic and washed out. Microphones fixed to the walls and ceilings squeak or ring out, setting my teeth on edge.

Yet the intensity of the voyeuristic gaze of the viewers, the lust for titillation, the desire to be thrilled with salacious titbits of squalor and scandal is equal in measure up here just as much as it is below in Court Number Three.

I can't see Ron. Not a scrap of him. I go down a short series of steps to the front, craning forward to press my forehead against the cool glass but I still can't see him. The jury box on the left is as desolate as an abandoned bird's nest and I assume the jurors are on their way.

'Sit down, Bighead!' someone calls out behind me, but there are no spare seats. Every seat is taken. A woman yanks a canary yellow bundle off an aisle seat next to her and tugs my sleeve.

'Sit there, love,' she whispers to me, indicating the now vacated seat, her luminous jacket spots yellow in the dark; the smart, ponderous white stitching around the pockets is familiar. 'Ooh, hello, young man,' giggles the woman next to me who had shown me an empty seat. 'You aren't stalking me, are you?'

When I don't respond, she adds, 'I'm Annie.' Her right hand moves as if to shake hands with me but veers course and dives into a giant pocket of her yellow jacket, now on her lap, to ferret out a handful of peanuts. I can make out her features, her gleaming, prominent teeth.

It's that ridiculous woman from the turnstiles at the entrance to the court; her face is flushed with pleasure, shiny with excitement. 'I hope they hang the s*d!' she says.

I avert my head, and approach the front of the glassed up public gallery, kneeling there; forming a 'gun' with thumb and forefinger, I track the bearded court usher below. With the air of one approaching a royal Empress, he carries a document to a self-important looking female court clerk who sits below where a legal grand-dame, swathed in purple robes is enthroned. I 'shoot' the usher at this point.

This Judge fits the negative portrayals of female judges in courtroom dramas like Kavanagh QC: grim and constipated-looking; a wig that's been dropped on her head as if fixed there from birth.

An impatient voice asks me to sit down, and to not 'hog the view.' So I slowly return to my aisle seat.

Just then, a portly man, aged about fifty, and buttoned up in a serge suit way too small for him, hovers above me waiting for me to move my outstretched legs to let him pass. He carries a spiral bound booklet and as he slows down to get past me, the title of the document flutters past my eye-line: 'Pre-Sentence Report: Ron Partridge.' I stare at the attractive letters in bold, letting them wash over me as you would a pretty picture of a beach or country scene that you might see in a book or magazine; the 'Report' bobs out of sight still clutched by the man in the serge suit who takes an empty seat two rows away, one that I hadn't seen.

******

It's as if someone's punched me in my stomach; all breath sails out of me, and the sound of my gasp fills my cavernous hood. I've not felt such palpitations of terror since I last saw yellow police tape festooning the New Horizons house where I'd last lived, the only happy home I had ever known. The reason that has brought me here— to be forced in the company of strangers, to face their unwanted stares....I...I...

Watching police and legal dramas on television has taught me that a pre-sentence report is used solely for the purposes of a sentencing hearing, *after* a guilty verdict at trial. A pulse beats in my neck and a wave of cold sweat drenches the entire length of my back... my head throbs.... I'm about to pass out....a voice calls me back...

'Are you alright?' whispers Annie through crunching teeth. 'It can get a bit claustrophobic in here...I'm melting...'

My eyes are misty with tears as the sense of impending doom sweeps through me. I'm trembling all over and can hardly get my words out. 'The jury…the jury…but...?'

'The jury?' echoes Annie. 'Ooh, no!' she says, forgetting to whisper, and a stern "shush" goes up behind us. She lowers her voice after a pause. 'This is his sentencing hearing. He's going away for a *very* long time!'

'But the trial?' I insist, peering at her from under my hood. My eyes burn like hot embers, that I'm sure are glowing in the dimness of the public gallery. 'The trial…the trial…' I say stammer.

I catch a glimpse of Annie's large upper teeth, slightly sticking out, that give her the air of an expectant child looking to pass a dull afternoon with some jolly entertainment.

I lean forward in my seat, my head towards my lap, gulping quietly like a fish out of water. The more I brush away the tears, the more they spring up and fall like a drip from a leaky tap, before disappearing into the quicksand of a bushy beard. As I press down on my facial hair, steadying the arrangement on my face, a seed of stabbing desolation slumps in my heart, until I have to breathe through my mouth. It's all been for nothing. My being here makes not one jot of difference— and nothing I can say can change anything now.

Annie's eyes are crawling over me.

'Aww! Don't you live in this neck of the woods? It was all over the news,' she says.

'You see, he's from abroad... that sort of thing's second nature to them over there…' she adds. 'You can't come over here...doing *that*...then deny everything when you're exposed to the world.' Then pausing, Annie lays a sweaty forefinger on the back of my hand and presses down. 'Aww! You came to give evidence, didn't you?' Her whispered tone of sympathy flutters soothingly over me. I remember to speak in a deep voice but it comes out as if I've got laryngitis making me wince at myself. 'Dates....got my dates mixed up,' I say. 'Why! You came to help those poor women...' Annie says, her eyes full of wonder.

I nod just to shut her up, waves of nausea floating upwards from my stomach, and I feel a sudden urge to get away from her.

'Never mind,' she continues, amiably, 'They got the old devil in the end!'

Someone from behind pipes up. 'Give it a rest Annie! I can't hear what's going on if you keep gabbling on...'

I tug my hood firmly over my head, away from prying eyes, from those who might be wondering how I got it so wrong.

In the courtroom below, a female barrister, sophisticated and slender, straight as a candle, stands at a lectern that holds her papers, to address the judge with the screwed-up face.

But all meaning in her words escapes me. I'm transported to the days when language had not been invented, when people grunted, squealed and slapped each other to express themselves. Her words rise and fall, dangle, then pirouette in the air before leaping into a muddled heap of discarded words labelled 'INCONSEQUENTIAL.'

Annie turns to me confidentially, sneakily. 'His trial was in Court Number Two. They've got some juicy murder in there now,' she whispers, still chomping on peanuts. The sound of a slowly released balloon—'Shhhhh!'—comes from the direction of the man in the serge suit. My hands are itching now—not from the horsehair and acetate—but from a fervent wish to get my hands on his sentencing report; it might give me a clue about what went on in the trial. I take a peek at where Serge Suit sits, his back firmly turned on us. Blonde curls, mixed in with a little metal-grey, drape over his stiff shirt collar. I glimpse the report peeping out from under his upper body, the plastic cover squashed and askew as it's become firmly wedged between the back of his seat and the armrest.

I lean back in my chair and close my eyes. Ron's name appears in bold letters in my mind's eye, growing fatter and fatter before exploding into a thousand little pieces. I slide my hands under my hood, cupping my ears to blot out the world. The smell of salted peanuts, mingled with musk cologne, circulates through the air, releasing a merciless pang of hunger from the pit of my stomach.

******

I don't know how long I drift in and out of consciousness but when I next open my eyes, a male barrister is now on his feet, addressing the judge below. I straighten up in my seat, accidentally nudging Annie who gives me a quick recap of what I've missed.

'That's *his* defence lawyer, Mr Pemberton,' she hisses in my ear. 'He's always on the judge's bad side, that one!'

Ron's defence barrister is well-spoken, unctuous: 'My Lady...Mrs Helier, in her pre-sentence report, states that Mr Partridge accepts he was a man who lacked judgement...a man who didn't ask too many questions, a man—'

At this, the judge sets her pen down sharply, folding her arms to stare down at Mr Pemberton.

'Her Ladyship doesn't think much of his plea-in-mitigation,' chuckles Annie, licking off the beads of salt from her fingers.

The barrister continues: '...Mr Partridge, a man of previous good character, admits his naiveté...and he has asked me to say on his behalf...that as the sole male individual in a household predominantly made up of women... it was probably not a good idea to place himself amongst them.... and that in the long run, his intentions...his *very* well meaning intentions, in all likelihood, would have been open to misinterpretation...'

'He comes over as impenitent —' says Annie. 'And the judge doesn't like that...'

I clasp my knees to stop them trembling. I tug my hood down and slump back in my seat.

'Pathetic—absolutely pathetic!' she whispers tersely as Mr Pemberton continues his mitigation....

******

The hawk-like judge –Old Hollerton– peers over her spectacles towards the dock as if surveying a rotting carcass in her courtroom. Her antics seem to both amuse and inspire awe in my garrulous companion. Then the judge's brutish mouth quivers dramatically before she spits out what everyone's come to hear.

'Had it not been for that one telephone call for help that alerted the authorities to your grave misdeeds, I'm sure your abuse would have continued indefinitely. You've been shown during this case, and even at your own admission, to have lived a life of considerable dishonesty—'

At that moment, a voice rises to interrupt the judge, croaking feebly at first, in a lilting American drawl. 'There's a name for all this where I come from, lady—and that would be "hogwash!" Cos you, Your Go**am*ed Almighty Highness, don't know a go**am*ed thing!'

A wave of frantic murmurs ripples through the court and the public gallery.

With pursed lips, Judge Hollerton lowers her head, waiting for things to calm down before continuing. 'The manner, in which you gave your evidence, was one of complete callousness. You have shown no shame or remorse for the many lives you've—'

'Baloney!' This from the dock. 'It's a load of bull!— a travesty! This is what happens when you put a fox in charge of a chicken coop…!'

'…I've come to the conclusion, that you are devoid of any morality and not fit to be part of a civilised society…' says the judge tersely, her words drowned by the wild shuffling and stomping of feet coming from the dock; the clink of metal and shouts from the guards: 'Calm down, Partridge!' and 'Don't make me— don't!'

Helpless to do anything for him, I cover my head with my arms and rock back and forth in my seat; but the man I've known for forty years is having none of it. His roar charges through the courtroom – in full battle cry, heroic, unyielding:

'No! *You're* not fit to be part of civilised society! You've no idea what a fair trial is—you—you dried up old t*t!'

His choking fury makes me jump to my feet as if my legs are fitted with coiled springs. I press my forehead against the glass screen much harder than intended, expecting it to crack. I pull back, nursing my face with the tips of my fingers, then lurch forwards again, but this time it's as if an invisible force field lies in my path.

The space in the public gallery shrinks around me and, if I stretch my arms, I can touch the walls and ceilings with ease. The air is dry and stifling.

'You animals! Get your filthy hands off me!' This from Ron, followed by the sound of punches and slaps, of bodies slamming against hard surfaces.

A tickle starts in my nose, a mere flicker at first, then flutters down my throat, churns through my abdomen, before travelling back to explode through my mouth. I'm overwhelmed by a fit of the giggles, right there in that peanut-smelling public gallery overlooking Court Number Three, No one can see me in the dark, bent double, laughing fitfully, a lapse in self-control.

Just as I'm about to walk back to my seat, I lean over some bemused looking people in their seats, and in a gannet-like swoop, I scoop up the Pre-Sentence Report from the back of the chair where Blue Serge sits; he doesn't notice a thing.

'Wait for me, won't you?' Annie says, squinting up at me as the skirmish below continues. I give her an indifferent 'thumbs up' sign, throwing off all remnants of my involuntary giggles.

******

I kick open the door to a cubicle in the Ladies' bathroom, just in time, as a cup measure of bile floats to the top of my throat and lurches into the toilet bowl, some of it sloshing onto the floor.

'Why me, God?' I scream. 'I like a quiet life—so why me?'

A low half whistle that sounds like a nervous 'Jee-zus!' floats from the direction of a cubicle a few doors down from me.

'Why am I the one who has to sort it out?' I bellow, not caring who's listening. I am angry with God, with Melanie, with everyone, but most of all with myself, for losing the opportunity—that one chance I had to speak up for him at trial–that surely would have set him free!

Seized by a coughing fit, my innards are ready to turn inside out. Then from the occupied cubicle, the sound of bustling nylon, the twang of elastic on firm flesh; the metallic ride of a zip. The toilet flush throws a hissy fit, and the squeak of metal scraping back e-ver-so-slo-wly; a two-second pause before the clackety-clack of heels make good their escape across a brittle floor.

I survey my ravaged face in the only full-length wall mirror there. Looking back at me is a pair of grey eyes, the whites criss-crossed with fine, blue-red threads that would defeat a painter's hand. My moustache, now unattached on the left side, flops about like a piece of wilted spinach; the beard, too, is dislodged but not in an unattractive way. My skin, in its perpetual state of red-raw disrepair, makes me long to dig in with my nails for a jolly good scratch. My eyelids start to droop, my arms grown heavy. I sit on the toilet, lid down.

I begin to review the situation. My military training has taught me that if things are beyond your control and the situation becomes irretrievable, you need to think strategically, to work out the steps to reverse defeat. It's like reading the first and last paragraphs of a military exercise outlining a tactical mission requiring stealth and cunning, with the middle section missing. With a clear and logical mind, you must retrace your steps (the middle section), retrieve certain facts, previously unascertained, before deciding what you need to do next.

I must now find out why a bunch of spineless, unconscionable women would pretend to befriend a man who had fed, watered and sheltered them—a man who would've given you the shirt off his back unasked—and had put the needs of others before his own. But instead, they had sourced a secret horde of bullets, polished them and lined them up to aim at him. They had plotted assiduously every step of his downfall. And I hadn't suspected a thing!

I scrape off some of the foul-smelling glue used in the lining of my wig to re-attach my facial hair. No sooner have I fixed this when the leathery smell sets me off again and I re-enter the cubicle. Two heaves of the stomach make the fake beard and moustache fall off into the toilet bowl. I should've taken them off first...but in my haste.....

By the time I clean the bristly hair with pink soap from the hand soap dispenser, and finish it off under the hand drier, all the glue has washed away. In the end, I clutch the whole hairy caboodle into place; it looks as if I'm nursing a toothache. There could be people out there who know me, who would want to... see me get my comeuppance.

I arrange my hood like a gladiator affixing their helmet, calm, noble and reinvigorated; chin thrust forward, nostrils flaring. As I open the door of the ladies' restroom, a woman about to enter stops abruptly in her tracks and, on seeing me, holding up a braceleted hand in apology. She shuffles back a few paces back before muttering a fleeting, 'Sorry— thought this was the ladies!' She bows her head and quickly turns in the direction of the men's restroom instead.

******

Try as I might, my mobile phone doesn't want to switch on. Perhaps I'm not doing it right, pressed the wrong button. I'd hoped to ask Melanie—aka the Glass of Water— to come and fetch me. Before I can sort out the phone, I feel two stiff prods in my already sensitive back where the court usher had lain into me.

A voice pipes up. 'I was worried about you—I didn't want to say... but are you alright?' I turn around to see Annie; her cheeks look as if they've been slapped, and her eyes gleam almost prettily, her upper teeth sticking out more than usual.

'You sounded...a bit emotional, dear,' she says, staring at me.

'Just needed the loo,' I say, without looking at her.

'I sensed a tear or two…?'

'I guess…I screwed up…'

'What? Because of…no!—they didn't need you in the end! He got twenty-two years!' she booms, chuckling loudly so that people slow down to stare at us.

I shrug, making a face, unable to absorb her meaning. 'The judge only went and gave him twenty-two years!' she crows.

Annie waits for me to respond but the words stick in my throat. I nod and manage to shake out a smile. My legs start trembling again, and I slump against a marble pillar that I'm sure right now helps to prop up this section of the majestic court.

'I've got an aspirin if you like,' says Annie with concern. 'Aspirin?' I echo dully.

'Well…the way you're holding your face—I thought you must have a toothache…take your hood down…you must be hot.' So I do.

Then an idea comes to me…she is, after all, a mine of information! Annie had attended the trial! She could tell me a lot of what had gone on, instead of my having to piece it all together like a patchwork quilt. She might even lead me to one or two of the…witnesses.

'We could get a coffee and talk if you like…?' I say, the words bolting from my lips with the speed of a freight train, and my invitation sounds all jumbled up at once. 'A …coffee?' I say again more slowly.

'Aww!' she sounds disappointed. 'I'd normally say 'yes', dear heart, but right now, I've promised to take someone home.'

'Call me,' she says, slipping a small gilt-edged card into the breast pocket of my hooded sweatshirt. She pats my arm in a motherly way, and as she walks away, she gives a half-turn to wink at me. This stops my breath. I'm not used to being winked at. Does she know who I am? Hasn't she figured me out yet?

'But I feel like talking now!' I want to scream at the top of my lungs, but instead I smile and nod some more.

Just then my heart skips a beat, for at that moment, a foreign-looking woman with an unruly comb-over hairstyle where the scalp shows through, is descending a palatial flight of stairs with the help of a walking stick. As I squint through my steamed-up glasses, I can only make out some of her features. She looks familiar. I run my fingers over my lenses, still holding my fake hair in place.

The female prosecutor and the defence barrister—Mr Pemberton, bl**dy QC— from Ron's sentencing hearing are following the woman with the stick; the pair glide down the stairs like Fred and Ginger, their heads leaning in, chatting away as if at a school reunion. The light catches Mr Pemberton's signet ring that has a blue centre stone, the size of a gull's egg, and I can't take my eyes off it.

As the woman with untidy hair reaches the bottom step, Annie throws her arms around her so that the woman stumbles and must steady herself with her walking stick.

I squeeze my eyes trying to focus better on her face. Can't be! Yes….it is! Can it be? It's her alright! Bunchee Golding! I haven't seen her in eighteen months, and she ends up looking …like that! She must weigh as much as eight bags of TeePee Basmati rice, each bag weighing ten kilograms—far out of proportion to her five-feet-one inch stature! Tears stream down her leathery, bloated face and into the folds of her double chin. People nearby stop conversations in midstream, lower their phones or avert their gaze from the wall maps depicting the court building. They stare open-mouthed at Bunchee Golding, seeking confirmation to questions from anyone who happens to be near.

'Izzat her?'

'She was one of *them*? Really?'

'I expect she'll write a warts-and-all book about it. I know I would…'

'Well done, her—to come out on top like that!'

I creep behind the stone-stout pillar, clasping its coolness to my chest, my racing heart thudding in my ears. Annie croons soft words of encouragement to this woman—this Bunchee Golding—hugging my former friend heartily.

'It's all over now, sweetheart! *He* is no more!' says Annie, punching the air, an action that provokes even more glistening tears in my now sworn enemy's eyes.

Fred (Mr QC Pemberton) is pulling a face at Ginger. 'Better head down to see him, I suppose,' he mouths. Ginger winces in sympathy, touching the tips of her fingers with her lips slyly, and flicking them towards him before they part ways.

Lawyers like to spar, they like nothing better than to beat the sh*t out of each other, bloody a nose or two on behalf of their clients because the one thing they crave most of all—is winning! Lawyers are wrestlers or boxers who enjoy shuffling and skipping around their opponent (another lawyer) ducking and weaving before landing their deadliest blow. But if you're rubbing palms with your opponent, like this pair, how can you properly butt heads with them?

******

The events of the morning make me feel dizzy and lightheaded, as if after a morning's exercise in the hot sun: a montage of disordered images in vibrant colours, some out of focus, flood my mind: cheering women waving placards with abandon, photographers with flashing cameras that can blind you; a cornered friend in the dock full of loathing; a bearded crow in black robes circling the high ceilings of Court Number Three; a door swinging shut; a female hunter in a canary-yellow jacket who won't stop eating; a pair of legal lovebirds!

And Bunchee Golding! A powerhouse of snot and tears who must have melted a jury's heart!

I take out the gilt-edged card from my breast pocket:

Annie Lederer (Director)
Unchained

And this woman has within her grasp, the one person in the world I'd most like to kill. The one person in the world who doesn't know that by tea-time Thursday, she's going to be dead.

******

Just then I spot Crow-Face! (the court usher)…the one who had flipped me out of court. His over-sized robes flap between his legs and, as he mounts the stairs two steps at a time, moving like liquid gold, I can't help wondering if he'd look just as elegant on his way down. And as I hold that picture in my mind, I can't stop smiling.

******

Chapter 2

Leaving the clatter of noise and shrieks that's not long erupted behind me, I trip over my feet in my haste to get past the security guards, and the turnstiles to exit the court building. I pass the same reporters I'd seen earlier, their group now multiplied, jostling for position on the steps of the court entrance. They chatter like sparrows, looking up at the narrow strip of blue sky streaked with tentacles of blond clouds, as if interpreting its message. I toss my false wig and beard into a passing stranger's gaping shopping bag.

I turn to face the light. The moist air feels bracing to the skin. The words 'Twenty-two years!' are still ringing in my ears. Murderers who chop up their victims with meticulous planning get far less!

******

Who said that?

'You'll figure it out, Sylvie. You'll find a way'

'Is that you Ron?' I'm panting and laughing at the same time in feverish excitement. I walk in circles, tripping and bumping into passersby who stare at me. A man, with a briefcase, rolls his eyes at his companion, enacting a quivering motion with his hand as if to signify drinking.

As I've just spent the morning strapped to the anvil where bad dreams are forged, it's natural that my mind should start playing tricks on me, and that perhaps none of this has happened. Then like an unwanted guest, a scene pops into my head, pulsating before my eyes, to play like a silent film: a vision of me as a child, bony and angular, splashing at the sea's edge where the briny water caresses my toes, snuggling my ankles. The sight of my grinning father picking me up...throwing me into the sea. The rolling water surges above my head, bubbling...frothing, its cold, powerful wet breath pulls me down, blinding me with its saltiness.

'You'll figure it out, Sylvie. You'll find a way,' says a voice.

And now— as back then, aged five, trying to throw off a watery shroud stitched out of foam and air—I wonder if I'll ever find a way out. And somehow, I know that I will, because back then I had found a way to escape the watery grave my father had dropped me into, because I'm here— aren't I?

******

The journalists have been joined by sober-looking men and women speaking to camera; all around a bubbling cacophony of voices are offering up their creative outputs that not even a troop of jackdaws can outdo.

I fandango my way through the swirling crowds, scanning hostile faces, one by one—and my mouth runs dry as none of them look like Melanie. The streets, the buildings all seem the same to me, full of foreboding...I'm on my own! Where the hell is she?

The demonstrators from this morning have now mushroomed in size, forming splinter groups up and down the pavements. Throwing back their heads, this squadron of lusty vocalists pour out snatches of nonsense-songs which boom overhead like cannon balls. Their once proud and libellous placards, oozing messages of ill-will in an untidy hand, are now limp, and soddened by the jittery air; my heart gladdens at the sight; their wooden stumps lean discarded against the leg of a trestle table where two women stand each with a lanyard emblazoned with the word, "Unchained," dangling from their neck.

I imagine these panting thrill-seekers as having day jobs as drab as a pile of uneven bricks, spending their time stealing stale food out of fridges in the kitchens of tall office blocks. I'm sure they are here to catch a glimpse of the innocent man they have helped to bind hand and foot before throwing him to the lions.

I cross the road towards the two women at the trestle table, standing under a burnt-orange banner that reads 'UNCHAINED.' The table is crammed full of magazines and booklets. There are colouring pencils, pens and blue rubbers, badges and stationery—festively scattered. For Sale. A girl, aged about twenty, with a bruised left eye and inky black hair spiralling down to her waist, accosts passersby, explaining and informing, answering questions with emphatic nods of her head: 'People's support can make all the difference in saving lives...' she intones with empathy.

Her companion, who has a liberal sprinkling of freckles on her nose, and a brown fringe that looks as if it's been hacked at with a penknife, addresses me with the warmth of an oven left on overnight. I take a step back, give a forced smile, feeling clammy under her gaze.

Freckle-Face breathes hard as if she's just arrived there running. 'Would you like one of our badges?' she asks, her gapped upper teeth slightly projecting. I'm sure I've seen their design before.

I screw up my nose, flicking my hand to murmur, 'Just looking...'... with a fixed grin. I pick up a burnt-orange leaflet from a burnt-orange pile, and begin to read it under the burnt-orange banner. 'We're giving them away today,' adds Freckle-Face, as she wipes something with her expansive thumb before handing it to me. It's a silver object twice the size of a fifty-pence piece. A woman's burnt-orange head is embossed on the surface, a hand, delicately poised, fans across the lower part of her featureless face. A tiny chain—a real one!— made of miniscule silver links dangles from her neck; the chain is broken, however, and as it catches the sun, I have to shield my eyes. The word, UNCHAINED, in bold vermillion letters, appears around the edge of the badge like crimping on pastry. Had it not been a freebie, I would have secreted this stunning little bauble between finger and thumb before making off with it.

I bring the badge up and down in my cupped hand, surprised at its weightiness. I stare at the eye-catching design, the intricate chain link, the splash of vermillion against silver. It must have cost a pretty penny.

I trace the lettering with my finger: UNCHAINED, staring at it like a person obsessed. My eyes alight on a pile of newsletters and I pick one up. A photograph of Annie Lederer fills the front page. Annie smiling as if she's reached the Promised Land, every crevice of her face steaked with euphoria, her cheeks dimpled with pride. She's wearing the same canary yellow jacket in the photograph that she had on today.

'Who's this?' I ask, holding up the newsletter.

'That's Annie. Annie Lederer,' says Freckle-Face.

'What's her business here today?'

Freckle-Face frowns at this, busying herself with re-arranging the merchandise on the table. She didn't like my tone, perhaps, and I admit that there had been just a tinge of a left hook with a dash of bitter lemon. I try again.

'I had a nice chat—with this lady—with her earlier—a funny lady!' I say, focussing on Freckle-Face's front teeth that catch the sunlight, giving them a gloss-white finish.

'Oh, do you know Annie?' she breathes, tapping a burnt-orange pen playfully on her wrist.

'She was in there,' I say, lifting a finger towards the Very Important Criminal Court.

'She's the Director of Unchained'

'Oh?'

'She got me this fundraising job, you know.'

'Did she indeed?' I say, gripping the badge. 'That's ree-al mighty charitable of her.' Then working on a hunch, I look at her fully in the face. 'You're related, aren't you?' I ask, holding up the picture of Annie. 'You could be sisters.'

Freckle-Face's smile turns flaccid, the tips of her ears growing crimson. She is about to turn to a tall man approaching us; he wears an expression as blank as a whiteboard, ready to be written on with a permanent marker, for the sake of learning something new.

'What y'all do here?' I say, blocking off Freckle-Face's path, so that the woman with inky-black hair must deal with the tall man.

'We fundraise for Unchained...we're a charity.'

I hold up the badge. 'But what's with the chains around the neck?...all this stuff ... the placards from this morning...'

'We help people living in servitude...'

I feel hot under the collar, rubbing my cheeks that have started to sting. 'Any jobs going?' I ask.

'What?'

'No, really. I'd like to help...raise funds and stuff.'

Freckle-Face's eyes never leave my face, and pausing briefly, she asks in a faltering voice, 'Have we got any, Jess?'

'Have we got any what?' asks the other girl looking up, her forehead wreathed in fine wrinkles.

'Vacancies?'

'Yours was the last one.'

Freckle-Face takes up a newsletter from the pile, opens it up and taps a page with an aubergine-painted fingernail. 'If you write to this address— or go on-line at www.unchained.bt.world.uk, you can fill in a —'

'If I sign up for membership,' I ask, 'how much of my donation will actually go towards the victims you save? How much does Annie make...as a Director?'

Her eyes widen, her arms flop to their sides and, at first, her mouth quivers vaguely but no words come out; and then in a brisk snapping tone, 'You can find everything you want to know on our website!'

With a sulky mouth she continues to tidy up the charitable bits and pieces.

'I hope you're licensed to sell your wares,' I say, indicating the trestle table, and pointing to a random woman in the crowd wearing a smart copper-red coat.

'See her? That's Gallows Greta. She works out of one of those little council offices across the road from here...' I tail off to point to my left before continuing: 'I'd pack this gear up if I were you. Otherwise she could stick you with an almighty fine!' And with that I turn on my heels and walk away.

******

A crowd begins to form further up the street. A woman in a powder blue suit, with teeth the size of pearl barley that matches her pearl necklace, prepares to give a legal statement to the press who are pushing microphones under her nose. She speaks in the tone of someone recovering from the shock of winning the lottery, but doesn't wish to crow openly about it. 'On behalf of the survivors in this tragic case, we can say today that justice has been duly served. We applaud the courage of these women in coming forward...'

The sun disappears. I don't stay to hear the rest.

I pass a figure wearing a cape, a checked deerstalker perching on his head that shadows one side of his olive face. With one leg folded under him, his back leaning against the side of the court building, he writes in a notebook, his phone tucked under his jaw. 'We need something else...different...a different angle to pep things up...' he says.

As I walk in the direction of a taxi firm that's signposted, I hope that the semi-louring skies will unleash torrential rains to sweep everything away in wild eddies and whirlpools. Instead, a strong beam of light pokes through the clouds, daubing the pavements and the sides of the buildings in strips of mellow yellow like melting butter.

I wonder where Melanie is—she was meant to pick me up! I shudder inwardly as the sourness of my breath seeps through my mouth, clambers up my nostrils and curls up to lay there.

I bend forward, hands on my knees, gulping breaths of air, glad to be away from the strident crowds who are, no doubt, jubilant at my failures today; celebrating the whole thing as a jolly day's outing.

I am deep in thought, hunched over when a sharp tug at my sleeve pins me to the spot as if a stake's been driven through my central core.

'Don't Melanie!' I snap, slapping away the offending hand.

'Ow!' says a voice, and I stumble forward to see the man I'd passed earlier in his flashy cape and Sherlock hat, sucking the knuckles on his right hand. Close up, he's a good-looking man of forty except for a battered nose that looks as if he's suffered one round too many in a boxing ring. A flap of triangular skin is flattened down one side of his cheek.

'Sylvie…Sylvie DaSouza—?' he breaks off, wide-eyed, as an involuntary growl flies from my throat. I don't know what fills me more with heartfelt terror; the fact that he's a stranger, the fact that he's a man, the fact he's a strange man who thinks he can tug my sleeve to which he is still attached. It unscrambles my equilibrium—even more so—in that he's waving a photo under my nose. I push my glasses up, squinting at the palm-sized black and white studio photograph of me aged thirteen. Lank, dark hair, uneven skin tone; beady but alert eyes. Unsmiling in school uniform. I take it from him, peering at it.

'How the hell did you …?' I choke, giving my sleeve a vicious yank that sends him lurching forward. I am determined not to be manhandled a second time that day. A sky-blue ink stain blooms on the pocket of his white shirt visible under his cape. I plan to make my escape when he's distracted. He plucks the photograph from my loose fingers, his eyes darting from me, then to the photograph and then back at me again.

'This is you!' says the man, his shining eyes boring into mine. 'You're that woman…the one from the sex cult!' he says, adjusting his cape over his shoulders. The corners of his mouth are upturned and creased, revealing blue-white teeth.

His words makes me stop dead in my tracks, as the sun quietly heats the top of my head.

'It *is* Sylvie, isn't it?' His eyebrows rise a good inch or two above their normal position. 'We thought you were missing!'

I shake my head. 'I think you've got me mixed up with…' I want to break away, and run back to rejoin the crowds but his powerful thigh blocks my path.

'The Argos Express,' he says, as if we have an appointment. He thrusts a scrap of card under my nose, with a foreign-looking surname that's unpronounceable on it. His first name's Nathan. I glimpse the word 'Senior Crime Reporter' in homely-grey letters underneath his name.

I rub my arms feeling a chill wind that flies up. 'I hate newspapers,' I say, as coldly as I can.

With folded arms, an involuntary sigh dribbles from my lips. I scan the tall buildings with vacant windows across the road— to avoid looking at his battered nose.

'Someone's got to write 'em,' he says with a shrug, hoping to deflate the situation with humour.

'You're in my way,' I say between clenched teeth, his sturdy leg still in my way.

'You are Sylvie though, aren't you?' he asks.

I close my eyes, with heart pounding. I feel sick.

His eyebrows threaten to disappear under his hairline. 'You lived in New Horizons, didn't you?'

I dive under his arm and run back into the crowds that have formed into disparate groups, haphazard and sheep-like, speaking in reverential tones as if waiting for a sign, a miracle to appear.

When I'm sure I've given the journalist the slip, I sneak a peek to see where he is. He is talking to a stout photographer who wields the largest camera I've ever seen— poised and ready for action. The air is hushed, palpable. Transfixed like statues, people stare at the side entrance of the court building, their eyes wringing with anxiety; then their mouths in their sullen faces move slowly, creating a hubbub of primitive noise.

Just then, a boxy gleaming white prison van scuttles out from under a bricked arched entrance, like an unwieldy, coughing beetle; it kicks up clouds of dust from under its wheels. The van edges tentatively through the swarm of people who follow as if hypnotically held by its blinding white light, magnetised and pulled along. One or two individuals run up to hit the sides of the van. Shouts of 'Fu**ing scum!' and 'B**tard!' ring out, each torment twisting my guts, and I blink away tears that cloud my vision.

Some men grasp the lower corners of the prison van, and, with whitened knuckles, try to wrestle it to its side; others bang futilely with their fists. It's a scene I've seen in many a television drama, where a disgruntled public thinks it's entitled to bare its collective breast in the name of civilisation.

A pock-marked man, in mud-stained wellington boots, is wielding a crowbar above his head. He follows the van at a brisk pace, aiming to connect a good blow.

A woman wearing a red scarf, vigilante-style, lines herself up with a skip-and-a-jump, to lob an object she carries surreptitiously in her rounded fist. With nimble tread, I follow, tapping her on her right shoulder, and as she turns on that side, I move in the opposite direction to snatch the object out of her hand. It's a smooth flat stone, the size of half a roof slate. I hurl it with contempt, glad to have prevented damage as befits my training in the protection and safety of others.

However, 'Pockmarks,' with the crowbar, gets in the path of the stone's trajectory which strikes him squarely on the back of his head; his legs buckle, and he plops to his knees, the crowbar dangling from his hand for a full two seconds before it bashes the ground with a metallic thud. 'Pockmarks' draws himself up, stumbling around in circles, stomping the ground, groaning. He clasps the back of his head with a look of astonishment, his fingers tapping for damage. He examines what he's touched, rubbing together red-stained fingers. The photographers, interspersed amongst the baying crowd, run amok like furious schoolchildren, raising their cameras to the height of the van windows to unleash an explosion of shock-white light. The van speeds up and tears away.

Red Scarf, displeased by my sleight of hand with the stone, indicates me with her head to the others, squealing, 'She did it!' She appeals to the group who have gone to help Pockmarks. They turn towards me with hardened fists and harder mouths that make my chest tighten like a piece of over-wound string.

A youthful, assertive voice pipes up behind me to address the mob. 'It was an accident, folks—an accident! She didn't mean to do it, did you?' The man turns to me as he says this. It's that ridiculous journalist—Nathan-something-or-other: the man in the cape with a foreign-sounding name; he scrapes his fingers through his thick glossy curls, gloating, as if enjoying my predicament. His stare tells me "to apologise"—'Go on!' he murmurs as I hesitate. But pride gets the better of me, as a lump fossilises in my throat so that I can hardly speak. My apparent inability or unwillingness to make amends, or throw myself at their mercy provokes the crowd to come after me.

Nathan grabs my sleeve and drags me to a path away from the court building, and we run until the public clamour falls away. I hold my side gulping for air, while he holds both palms against the side of a building as if propping it up.

He gasps like a chronic asthmatic. 'I can help you,' he wheezes.

'You've got the wrong person!' I yell.

He clicks his tongue in irritation.

'You're not the type to say, "thank you" or "excuse me," are you? You know—all the little things that get you by in life.' I shrug, not knowing what to say.

Nathan holds up his bleeding knuckles. 'Like saying sorry' when you caught me with your nail back there. And again just now... that man was actually bleeding—'

'—But I do know how to say "please,"' I interrupt. 'Now *please* leave me alone!' and I surprise myself by stamping my foot like a child.

He puts up his hands at this. 'Okay, okay! Forget it!'

His voice, warm and soothing, sinks into the far reaches of the neural potholes that have built up in my brain. Shame about the nose.

Nathan points to his face. 'I did that when I was sixteen—went through a car screen window.'

'Not interested, Sherlock,' I say

'You keep looking at it,'

'Looking at the weird costume'

Nathan tugs his cape. 'Oh, this? I'm in character.'

'So you're not a reporter?'

'Ever heard of The Caped Crime Crusader?'

'Nope'

'It's the persona I use in my work for The Argos Express.'

'You told me your name's Nathan'

'It is…Nathan Chudasamar... a humble reporter,' he says, and then pointedly, 'At your service,' and with a flourish of the hand, he bows dramatically, his head almost scraping the ground.

'What d'you mean, "service?"'

'I mean we can help each other.'

'Can you get me a gun?' I ask, pushing my spectacles up, looking him squarely in the face.

He scratches his head, squinting as he takes me in, and decides that I'm joking

'Ah, no…' he puts up a finger.

'Not much cop then, are you?'

'I only deal with stories of the heart, life stories that people will be interested in… I'm always after a story that'll make people think…make them reflect on the best and worst of human nature…it's my specialty, if you like.' Then after a pause, he adds, 'I *do* know who you are.'

I regret having discarded my fake beard and moustache. Da**nit! How could I have been so stupid? I should have tried to find some adhesive or used my own sh*t to glue the bits back on!

'I covered Ron Partridge's trial.'

My heart skips a beat. 'So you know Bunchee Golding?'

'Who, the sex slave?'

I glare at him. Nathan straightens to full height, a smile playing on his plump, ruby lips.

'You're really beginning to bug me—'

'So, she wasn't a sex slave…?'

'Say that again and....you'll see chalk dust,' I snarl at him, adjusting the rucksack on my back.

'Alright, alright…' he puts his hands up, 'I won't say 'sex slave'—'

'D'you want me to thump you?'

'Sorry…sorry,' he says, grinning like an idiot.

'How can I get hold of her?' I ask.

'Who?'

'Bunchee Golding'

' "Get hold of her?" ' he asks slowly, and his eyes narrow as his head cocks to one side.

'I need to speak to her'

'I wouldn't think she's speaking to anyone right now'

I was going to give him another nasty look but, instead, concentrate on controlling my ragged breathing.

'She's an old friend of mine,' I say

'She's in a witness protection programme.'

'I need to speak to her'

'You're never going to get hold of her—'

'Why not?'

'I told you…someone might have it in for her'

'I don't have time for this,' I say, swatting the air with impatience, swinging round to leave.

'Why? Have you got something terminal?' I'm finding him tiresome.

'Alright, alright!' he says, and I turn to look at him. He pats his breast pocket, his eyebrows playfully moving up and down, as if he has something I want. 'I've gathered some names here of people connected with the case. Now…' The rest of what he says is drowned out as a heavy goods lorry trundles past us… '… just might know where she is,' is the end bit I manage to hear him say.

Reaching into his inside pocket, Nathan takes out a small pocketbook decorated with blue and pink peonies, and as he holds it tantalisingly over my head, grinning widely, I stretch out my arm instinctively like a street beggar; but he yanks the book away, and slides it back inside his pocket. 'Ah-ah!' he warns. 'You've got to do something in return.'

******

Nathan's eyes shine like a trapped mine shaft worker who sees a chink of light from the other side. 'So, we have a deal?'

'Unbelievable! Un—fu**ing— believable!' I say, shaking my head. Young men are so…so starved…they'll ask anyone - even me!

'You don't have to decide now…mull it over for a few days…a story… that's all I'm asking!'

I let out a long sigh – the noise of the traffic had drowned out most of what he'd said.

'My number's on the card I gave you,' he reminds me.

I don't seem to be getting through to him. I look up at the clouds that are rolling away like a white bridal train smoke. Who would've thought I'd be negotiating my way through the big wide streets like this? Mingling with strangers…all by myself? Then when he's least expecting it, I give this fraudster a hefty shove in the chest. His eyes widen in surprise, his smile disappears like a bolting rabbit down a hole. I square up to him again, shouting at him.

'Who d'you think you are, you low-life? You ape!' I follow this up with a couple of stronger jabs, and a soft slap across his face. 'You think, yeah, that you can just walk off with my life story…tell lies about me?' I feel my scalp prickle, the blood gushing through the tubes in my ears and down my nasal cavity. Nathan puts his hands up, stepping back against some wrought iron railings that stand fixed behind him. His arms and legs are all over the place, and it looks as if he is in the middle of a primitive dance that morphs into a traditional marriage proposal– down on one knee! He tries to take a lunge at me, but that shi**y cape of his catches the railings, and draws him back like a piece of elastic. He goes down again—properly this time, legs up in the air! I take off into the busy lunchtime streets. A weight lifts from my shoulders, and I swear my feet leave the ground a good foot high with each bounding step, under a dull urban grey-blue sky streaked with pink. My glasses are steamed up but I somehow manage to outrun the wind, not knowing what's in front of my nose.

In time, the pounding between my ribs subsides as the euphoria wears off.

I don't know where I am; it's unnerving not to know where I am. I clasp Nathan's 'Book of Contacts" to my chest as if a stranger may yet pluck it from my grasp. The pink and blue peonies that seemed earlier to dazzle in his hands, now appear as if the colours have been drained from them—washed out and ordinary. So insignificant and unremarkable to look at, I'm convinced that Nathan may not even miss the dam*ned thing at all.

******

Chapter 3

Sinbad, the pit bull terrier, fixes me with his full attention, his pupils circled with hellfire. Propped up on his huge haunches, smooth and solid like a horse's rump, he refuses to budge from my side. Shooting pains run down my legs, but there's no a chance of rubbing or flexing them in case any sudden movement startles him. I've heard that pit bulls can be temperamental, and this works up a sweat in me. Sinbad's boxy head cocks to one side, and his unblinking stare can unnerve even those who have no fear of death; his two-hole button nose quivers with wetness, and his tongue flaps about like a celebratory flag in his permanently fixed smiling mouth. His jaws look as if they can snap in half a butcher's prize bone at the first attempt.

I have a sweeping view of the kitchen from where I sit in the living room. I glance up to see The Killjoy engulfed in billows of steam. She takes off something from her face (her glasses I think), rubs them with her fingers and puts them back on. She looks up and is about to call out but changes her mind.

We used to call her The Killjoy as she was prone to report us on the slightest pretext, and went around spoiling our fun by getting people banned from going on outings or enforcing early curfews. The Killjoy and I go back a long way. I'd forgotten her real name was Rosemarie until I saw it in Nathan's address book.

I'm convinced she's trained the dog to keep me in my seat, so I don't have an opportunity of rummaging through her stuff. A mobile phone, encased in pink-lilac, lies on the coffee table amongst pretty knick-knacks and curious objects, including snow globes. I want to touch them, see them up close as I appreciate fine objects.

The Killjoy had asked to see my identification when I rang her front doorbell. And as she led me into an overheated sitting room, she had mentioned something about the need to be vigilant, about unscrupulous people trying to pull the wool over people's eyes for their own advantage.

The Killjoy no longer has those firm red apple-cheeks she once had, and the beautiful aquiline nose that used to make the rest of us green with envy, now resembles a bloated acorn.

But after forty years, she doesn't recognise me. Her name and contact details are the only names of two people I know from a list of five in Nathan's phonebook. She is listed as number three. Number four is Irene Cotter, Ron's solicitor. I'm reminded to see that manipulative legal b**ch asap. There's no mention of Bunchee Golding in the book. She's the one I'm after.

The elegant gilt chair I'm sitting on is rotten to the core… riddled with woodworm, no doubt, —as the bottom of it is gradually sinking under me. Five minutes ago, I could see the kitchen sink behind The Killjoy as she gets our tea ready; but I can no longer see it, as my backside has slumped down a further couple of inches in my seat. I'm wedged fast. My eye-line falls to where Sinbad now stands guard, and I'm only an inch away from his bulging, staring eyes. I can smell his stale-liver breath, feel the wetness of his sloppy jowls.

The dog lets out a top-throated growl as The Killjoy comes in with the tea tray; my hands clench themselves to resemble rock-hard fists, ready to strike different parts of him should I need to: throat, top of head and nose. Why a woman in her seventies should want to own a hundred-pound pet that's usually paraded around by anti-social men, with bits of metal dangling from their ears or bolted onto the surfaces of their tongues is beyond me.

The Killjoy trills in her best English sing-song voice: 'Are we ready for a spot of tea?'

But her English accent is second-hand. She's picked it up in the UK, her adopted country, and underneath the prim tones there's a distinctive honey-coated American twang. She wears loose-fitting, elasticated trousers that come up to just under her breastbone, and a low-cut embroidered top; both items are straight out of the sales catalogue intended for ladies who can never keep warm either during the day or night. She wears pink bunny slippers with floppy ears that jingle as she walks. A string of large purple beads sits low on her flat chest. Hydralike, straw-yellow locks—that I figure must be dyed—fall about her shoulders; the tips lift and dance in the breeze of a rotating table-fan that's turned full tilt in her direction. The fan whines like the hum of trapped bees, alternating every ten seconds with the rattle of a builder's drill. Sinbad's tail bangs ceaselessly to its staccato rhythm.

A side table is ladened with a multi-piece dinner set decorated with gold rims and splotches of damask plums. A mound of Jaffa cakes, oozing gleaming orange jelly through hairline cracks in the chocolate, sit haphazardly on a plate decorated with cheerfully bright purple damsons.

Out of the corner of my eye, The Killjoy—Rosemarie—pours the tea and places my mug next to me. My attention is still on Sinbad, and while the fan continues to play with The Killjoy's hair, her fingers hover over her mug as if over a campfire in a room where the temperature hits thirty degrees. I wonder if different parts of her body tolerate different temperatures.

'Is the dog bothering you?' she asks, trying to sound concerned, but knowing perfectly well that, in all probability, the dog's doing exactly what he's been trained to do.

Then The Killjoy does something foolish. She leans forward and holds out a Jaffa cake, clicking her tongue and slapping her thighs. 'Sinbad! Come here, boy!' As Sinbad steps onto my left boot, and launches into flight, his "chandeliers" on full display, his whip-like tail slaps my nose with alacrity; in one bold leap over the coffee table, he pounces on the chocolate treat like a lion on a gazelle. And it's whoops-a-daisy to The Killjoy's mug of tea. She also knocks the plate of biscuits off the table, scattering them across the floor. As the dog 'hoovers up' everything within seconds, white-hot drool splashes from the corners of his wide mouth.

'He's very excitable', she says with a nervous laugh, patting herself dry with a paper napkin. 'People think they're dangerous, but this one's a pussy cat… he's absolutely adorable,' and as she flicks the dog's nose, her voice turns thick and syrupy.

'Yes, you are…goob-boy! Yes, you are…my honeybunch! Who's mummy's boy, then?' She picks up the dropped plate, continuing: 'People label things they don't understand. They believe all the bad stuff in the papers…on TV, and then they tar the entire breed with the same brush. Pit bulls make life-long friends; they're faithful and loyal to a fault. They'd do anything for you, absolutely anything…wouldn't you my darling, boy?' and she lands Sinbad an almighty 'thwack' on his rump that continues to tremble long after contact. The dog's now lying at her feet, his doleful face slumped on the ground in folded brown curtains of jowl, his eyes darting all over the place.

The Killjoy cautiously sips her tea from a Rule Britannia mug, the label underneath showing '50p'. Her flat is crammed with battered, antique furniture. A guitar with one string stands propped up against the wall. Every inch of floor space is piled waist high with newspapers, books, records and children's toys. It reminds me of the basement room I had exclusive use of while living at New Horizons.

The smell of antiquity, fusty and life-affirming, invades my senses.

The Killjoy offers me a cigarette, shrugs when I refuse and lights up. The smoke makes the dog's eyes water, and he scurries to the kitchen.

She stirs her tea and offers me cream and sugar which I refuse. 'So you're with the Daily Argos?'

'That's right' I say. 'Nathan might have mentioned ...?

'He's never mentioned you at all. What's your name, again?' 'Sharon,' I say

'He never mentioned a dam*ned thing...and that's so-oo unlike him...'

'Sorry?'

'To send a stranger to my home...'

I try to laugh it off. 'He's got a lot on his plate, ma'am...'

'You'd think he'd let me know though,'

She's watching my lips closely as if lip-reading.

I hold out my hands, palms upward, always solicitous, always accommodating. 'Miss Whittington, I only follow orders. Now if you'd rather I go—'

'He has my number... all he had to do was ask,' she says glumly.

'As our chief crime reporter, he wanted to do your story himself,' I tell her, '....but he had to follow some other line of enquiry...' 'But I don't know what I could tell you,' she intones.

'Ron Partridge...' I say, as a sensation of tiny hooks claws up my spine.

As soon as I mention his name, her gaunt face screws up, and grooves and wrinkles sprout from each corner of her thin mouth. Her voice turns shrill, grating to the ear. 'Now, why would I wanna talk about that as**ole? Huh? It happened—' she pauses to take a long drag of her cigarette and blows out a wispy train of smoke, '— a long time ago. Let's leave the past in the past. Can we do that please?' Cigarette in mouth, she frowns as she pours from the teapot, stirring in some sugar into her mug.

'Well, the piece we want to run won't show him in a good light' 'Oh?'

'It's what we in the business call, "The Nail in the Coffin" piece.'

The Killjoy squints in puzzlement. 'What the hell izzat?'

'It's to ensure he never gets out of prison'

'Papers can do that?'

'I can't remember if Nathan told me...but did you...um...go to Ron Partridge's trial?'

Her eyes widen in horror. 'Are you fu**ing kidding me? Wild horses couldn't have dragged me there.'

'And that's why Miss Whittington, it's even more important to give an account telling your side of the story!'

'But why?'

'To give your version of ...um ...events'

'But who'd be interested in *that*?'

'The public would want to know what happened, you know... your experiences...as you...um...experienced them.' She peers at me over her glasses.

I lean forward, rubbing my cheeks; the chafing is flaring up again.

I take a sip of tea to find it's stone cold. My lips stick fast to the rim. 'Well, Sharon, I don't know what good that would do?'

'From what Nathan tells me, he wants to know about your life in New Horizons...you have such a unique, unique...'

'Perspective?'

'Perspective...that's right! I just wondered if you could tell me about some of the residents you remember when you were there, you know, a little bit about their background...and um...where they might be right now.' I pretend to adjust my glasses near the bridge of my nose.

'All I can say is that he da*n well deserves to be where he is—in prison!'

'I'm sure that's....um... right, ma'am'

She looks up at me, and as she searches my face, she takes another drag of her cigarette before stubbing it out in an overflowing ashtray.

******

In the pose of a psychic acting as a medium for the long departed, hand resting over the bridge of her nose, The Killjoy pulls out the names of the spirits of the past: Jo-Jo... Light-Fingers... Shivers, Scooter ...all the women she had spent time with in New Horizons. As for me, I had long discarded these characters like so much debris after a party, expunged them forever from my mind. They don't count as anyone. Rosemarie recalls that the kitchen had been a place to nourish body and soul; a hub of noise, chatter, bad jokes, and endless gossip; a place where water seemed to stream forever: the endless washing and rinsing of pots, mostly in cold water, the draining of soggy vegetables.

'That's great—that'll go down well,' I nod enthusiastically, jotting down notes in my blank notepad

'No it didn't go down well...we hated watery vegetables'

'I meant for our readers—'

'It's a joke,' she says, and I laugh until my sides hurt.

She continues after I calm down. 'I remember just how funny they were, smart and warm...and tender.' She wipes her hands on a green tea towel with the map of County Sligo on it.

Then like a pair of squelching boots in the rain, ready to come off, it's time....

'D'you remember a Chinese girl...?' I ask nonchalantly, trying to get up to pour myself another cup of tea, but I've sunk all the way down to the boxed part of the seat, and am stuck fast. 'The girl I'm talking about looked like a porcelain doll... couldn't speak a word of English. We're talking forty years ago, mind...' I add, my eyes roving over the coffee table.

The Killjoy squeezes her eyes shut; her face blooms into a network of wrinkles that connect and intersect like a street map; she shakes her head slowly, caressing her earrings that are the shape of purple honeybees. Finally, she opens her eyes. 'I left after a year or so... perhaps she came after that, 'cos honey, I sure don't remember no Chinese girl.'

'No, please think about it! Just for a second!' I swallow hard, trying to ease my shallow breathing. 'You were paired up with her as her house buddy in her novice year—she asked you to write her ...to keep in touch,' I say, remembering to smile between clenched teeth.

The Killjoy taps her dry-as-a-desert forehead.

'This lump of meat's not what it used to be,' she says ruefully, pulling on her purple beads. On hearing the word 'meat' Sinbad scuttles in from the kitchen, his tail wagging vigorously, working all the packed muscles of the lower half of his fat, kickable body.

The Killjoy strokes the dog until his eyes bulge like sparkling watery orbs; she slaps his sturdy haunches that quiver like a waterbed. The dog whimpers and scampers off, his tail pointing downwards. A gloom fills the room. She gets up, and the bells on her bunny slippers jingle like an alarm clock, startling me.

As her eyes bore into me, I make fanciful flourishes with my pen.

'How d'you know all that stuff?' she asks, her tone sharp, prickly.
'What?'
'The buddy and novice system—nobody knows that stuff!'

I reach for my rucksack at my feet and shove my pen and notepad inside.

'I think you'll find it was in the newspapers…'

The word shoots out like a bullet to penetrate the sombre shadows of ghosts past that had settled on us. 'Bull**it!'

She turns morose and unfriendly all at once; bright red and white splotches spread across her chest.

'What do you want with this Chinese girl?'

'Her parents are looking for her—'

The Killjoy glares at me intensely and after a long pause, she lets out a grunt of exasperation.

'You're not from the Argos Post, are you?' she says, pulling at the beads around her neck. She points at me with her chin. 'Anyone can see that's not a real press badge!'

I jab my forefinger in a downward direction. 'If you wait, I can show you my driving lesson. It's in my car... I can get it—.' I grip both armrests, and with one enormous heave, a popping explosion of air sends me in an upward trajectory... and I'm out! The chair's drenched with sweat and the smell of sour-dough rises from the seat.

The Killjoy starts to lift up a flurry of objects from the coffee table, swatting them aside on not finding what she wants. 'I don't know who you are, lady, but I don't believe a word you've said!'

Her lower jaw juts out, exposing orange-yellow teeth. A purple haze scalds the air as the beads around her neck cascade to the floor, trundling in all directions like skittles.

I decide not to ask to use her bathroom. I take all necessary precautions before I slip out to find a taxi.

******

Chapter 4

Melanie is waiting for me at the door leading to the basement room where I've lived for eighteen months.

'Sylvie…where *have* you been?' Her voice, normally muffled and panting, is slightly sharp and raised which surprises us both. It's her sense of entitlement to know my whereabouts— that whiny, rasping voice she uses to show concern—that makes me recoil from her. She is, after all, a complete stranger, and I hate being rebuked by a stranger—especially her.

'Did you get to where you wanted to go?' she asks, taking small, even breaths, her watery eyes creasing around the edges. Charcoal lines double-scrawled under her eyes are more fitting to a Victorian child labourer working in a boot factory than to a modern day art student.

Such a nosy cow she is too! Always poking around in my business, to find out what I'm doing, who I'm seeing, how I'm feeling, what I'm eating and would I like anything. I think she's obsessed with me, and I wouldn't be surprised if she kept a diary of my daily activities, or used her mobile phone to relay reports about me like the little spy that she is.

But then again, had it not been for her, I would, no doubt, have been sheltering under the trees in the local park, or hunkered down in some cramped doorway where drunks splatter their shoes with their own p*ss. But I've avoided all that, thanks to Melanie, who I bumped into in the town square (I can't remember exactly how we met) but I remember lying face down somewhere. Images from that time, float to the surface, unsavoury, animalistic and I try not to think about the past....

Melanie's got one of those faces you can't pin an age to, but I know she's too old to be the art student she claims to be, and too well-spoken to be squatting in an elegant three-storey house in _____ Street where she's brought me. She's a petite brunette with a bouffant hair style, similar to how I used to wear mine when I was younger. Sometimes when I catch a side view of her, as she's handing out toothpaste, shampoo and soap, she could almost pass for a younger version of me.

And in all the time I've lived in the squat, I've never seen any evidence of her artwork: not a glimpse of a canvas, paint or brushes, palette, easel, pencils, chalk, sketchbook, charcoal stick…. nothing!

Melanie dispenses painkillers, soothing balms and medicinal lotions, yet her own drab and sallow complexion clamours for roughage and vitamins. Her forehead is sticky and a sickly pallor pervades every scrap of her skin. I once went into the kitchen unannounced when she was making a snack, and she visibly jumped out of her skin; then she kept apologising to *me,* over and over again! On another occasion, and for my own amusement, I stared at her— just stared at her. I focussed on a spot on the bridge of her nose— just staring until she started to fidget with her hair and wring her hands. Then her mouth started to quiver like a vibrating saw, her eyes were shimmering with tears. Everything about her reminds me of a Glass of Water, the way she talks and walks—drab and …and watery! Uninteresting. I take to calling her 'Glass of Water' in my head, and sometimes 'Glass' for short. I once blurted out, "Hey, Glass" to her but she just gave me a watery stare and carried on as if nothing had happened.

I imagine how The Glass of Water would have fared in a place like New Horizons. The female residents would have hated the way her long skirts flounced prettily as she walked, the delicate way she ate her breakfast with dainty matching utensils. They would have put salt in her food or worms and frogs in her bed to get shot of her. Or they would've just ignored her until she slowly went off her head.

******

The Glass of Water is waiting for me after my visit to The Killjoy. I hear the rapid succession of tiny breaths that makes her necklace, fashioned out of gold coins with cherubs on them, jingle on her chest. 'Can we…d'you think we can have a chat, Sylvie?' she asks in the dark, boxy hallway. The faded lights from the street and neighbouring houses poke through the stained-glass in the front door to resemble scattered beads on the floor. A gleam of red light bounces off her mouth that's poker straight and determined. Two resident squatters come in soon after me, giggling and chatting. They stop in their tracks when they see us, and looking me up and down as if I were a stranger. The tantalising smell of fish and chips and vinegar fills the air, making my stomach rumble sorely. One of them carries a bundle of rags which turns out to be newspapers with their dinner wrapped inside.

The taller of the two asks Melanie, his eyes still fixed on me. 'Have you told her yet?'

'I was going to—' The Glass tells him.

'Now's not a good time,' I snap without looking at them. 'I'm exhausted...so *if* you don't mind—' On seeing that I am determined to go down to the basement, Melanie plucks up her bohemian skirt and steps away. I notice a scrap of paper in her clenched fist. It isn't until I get downstairs that I realise that she was actually blocking my path—and that requires some bold pre-meditation on her part. What could be so important?

I clamber back up the basement stairs to find her still there, alone in the cold gloom.

My tone is curt and incisive. 'What is it?' I ask. 'Has someone eaten stuff out of the fridge again?'

No sooner has she given me a creased piece of paper, than her clenched hand disappears under her wide sleeve, and she turns to go. I catch a glimpse of a blurry grey-orange figure through the glass door behind her, of someone lurking in the main shadowy space there. The Glass of Water goes to join whoever is there, shutting the door firmly behind her.

I make my way to the kitchen. I take out half of a leftover cheese sandwich, still in its packaging, a strawberry flavoured yoghurt, and a chocolate bar; I spend the next minute or so washing it all down with a can of diet-Coke.

******

All my possessions are crammed into countable bags after sixty-three years of living. In the corner of my basement room, a litany of shopping bags are piled high. There's a lockable briefcase with documents dating back to the late 19__'s: my school certificates, letters and photographs that curl up at the edges, yellowing bank statements, and all sorts of odds and ends that the police didn't steal after they raided New Horizons.

I unfold the piece of paper from the Glass. It's a court interim possession order dating back a few weeks, demanding squatters to vacate the property within...oh, I don't know! I calculate the time remaining...forty-eight hours to go...

I screw the paper up into a tight ball and hurl it on top of the bags.

******

With each breath I take, a smoke-like mist appears and disperses into the air. Hands deep in pockets, I kick the radiator once or twice in the hope of igniting a miracle. Kicking off my boots I dive under the bedclothes; my body absorbs the shock of the coldness, and I squeeze cold air through my teeth which hurts my gums. As I lie there, numb with cold, I remember Ron's sentencing report in my rucksack. The sound of a leaky tap can be heard from the other side of the room where the ground around an old sink is stacked high with remnants of old carpets; old crates full of odds and ends: drip, drip, drip, drop, drop, drop....

******

It's been ten minutes. Ron's Pre-Sentence Report lies on top of the counterpane. I can't bring myself to read it. How can a few A4 sized pages, stuck together in a plastic cover, make you quake so that your fingers stop moving?

I walk slowly around my bed like a shark circling its prey, never taking my eyes off the gleaming cover. I walk in the direction of the dripping tap and stare at the report from there. When I balance my glasses on my hairline, the report disappears, and all that remains is the blue blur of the counterpane. I slide them down my nose and –hey presto!— it appears again. I stroll over to the elegant lattice plaster work on the farthest side of the room, rubbing my hands, staring at the report from there.

I recall childhood Christmases and birthdays when I left my presents unopened, not through apathy, but in my childish belief that my parents had conspired to spoil any festivities by buying me useless and unattractive gifts. They had a poor track record: a world atlas, a German dictionary, encyclopaedias, a chemistry set. And now, as I toy with the idea of reading the report about Ron, the feelings are just the same and, like my unopened and unlovable presents, an act of defiance.

Then before I know it, I've picked up the report and I've started to flick through the silken pages, the whoosh of air blasting my face.

I glimpse a few words and phrases: 'Texas', 'British citizen', 'cult' 'distortion,' 'remorse,' 'in plain view,' 'New Horizons,' 'sincere...'

I lie on my bed like a piece of wreckage in a salvage yard, misshapen, bent, waiting to be untwisted and smoothed back into shape.

I turn to the last page of the report after the Appendix. No offensive material here.

But unlike the rest of the white glossy pages, the last page is of a matt texture, grey and drab, out of keeping with the rest of the report. Perhaps, they had run out of paper and used a different batch for this section? I hold this page up to the one stark, dim and dusty light bulb in the room, turning to scrutinise the report from all angles.

My heart starts to pound. I don't know why. A few inches from my face—and it appears! –in printed letters, the size of a grain of rice: I can make out her name— "BUNCHEE GOLDING" followed by an address! All nine words – all in a tidy row— appear like a shimmering spectral streak across the dull grey page, as if propelled by a ghostly breath; the grand swell of music, the beautiful singing of a Sunday choir rises to a crescendo inside my head.

My heart turns somersaults inside my misshapen chest. I clench my pillow, waiting for my breath to catch up before I'm overpowered by a coughing fit that's been creeping up on me– the moment her name materialised ethereally.

I recall a high-profile murder case from a few years ago where the names and addresses of prosecution witnesses had been published in a public court document— in error— and which had placed those witnesses at serious risk of harm from those with a grudge who might hunt them down!

The ghostly address is seared forever in my mind. I next pull apart the report's pages from its plastic cover, and tear the loosened pages into long bendy strips, before shredding each one again. And now I'm whole again.

******

The next day The Glass of Water is loitering in the hall waiting for me! Her eyes spring open when she sees me, as if she's just woken up. 'Have you seen it?' she trills, meaning the eviction notice. 'We haven't got long to leave, you know.' Her face looks as if it's been mauled by rough thumbs, and a sliver of pain crawls into the pit of my stomach.

'It's okay,' I say with a wide smile. 'We'll find a way.' She shrinks from me a little, and scans my face, a curious habit of hers, as if she's missing out in life, that somehow life has passed her by and she hopes to experience it through me! Her upper lip is moist, and I can smell the soap on her. Her hair is bushy and tangled as if she's washed it in a hurry. It occurs to me that I still don't know where her room is within the squat, where she lays that scratchy, bouffant head of hers each night.

The Glass hesitates. 'Where will...you go?' She pats her upper lip with the back of her sleeve. 'What'll you do?' She holds out one of her breakfast packages wrapped in baking foil as she is wont to do. I take it and slip it into my rucksack and give her a little salute. I know I will wolf it down in the taxi that's waiting outside.

'The Lord will provide,' I say cheerfully. Saint Glass of Water! It's the only one of a handful of scripture I know. As a churchgoer, she's tried to persuade me to go to church with her, saying it would be 'good' for me. She's also pleaded with me to see a counsellor, saying that Doctor Buchwald— someone a friend of hers had used in the past — would be good for me.

The use of scripture has an immediate effect. Her eyes brighten at once, her lips a drizzly smile that's far from her usual wary or forced one. She's observing my every move, giving nothing away. Does she want to tag along, perhaps? I give her a three-finger-up-in-the-air wave and bang the door shut behind me.

I step outside to a resplendent, nurturing sun that nuzzles my face and lends me an invincibility that warms my bones. A thunderous roar that's been welling up inside, explodes in my ears, and I bend at the knees, my hands gripping the top of my thighs to steady myself.

I breathe in the crisp, cold air that reinvigorates me. I must stand tall and glorious:

'"Vengeance is mine; I will repay
In due time their foot will slip; for the day of disaster is near,
And their doom is coming quickly!"'

It's only the second bit of scripture I know.

******

Chapter 5

The smell of sweet onions and therapeutic thyme drifts through the open window, filling my mouth with drool; my stomach rumbles like a runaway freight train. I put my masterful precision skills, learned in military training, to good use. I enter the unlocked back door that leads to the kitchen—her kitchen! — Her carelessness has got me closer to my goals. I stand like a statue listening to the sound of a woman's voice humming, the melody tinged with a foreignness both quaint and unappetising to the ear. A wheezing whirring of a clock as it strikes. Then the clang of metal and the sound of a door shutting as the woman breaks off in the middle of her tune to say: 'Shoo, puss!' before continuing with more vibrato than I would have liked.

******

The Chinese woman, the one from the court a few days ago who had been bawling the place down, stares at me with glassy, vacant eyes. Wearing oven gloves too large for her, the woman's arms jerk outwards to resemble a paper angel cut-out. She drops a baking tray she'd been holding and the sizzling contents splatter across the floor like a Picasso painting. The spectacular metallic clang strikes the stone-grey flagstone making my ears buzz. The words of a song come to mind:

> *"Clang, clang clang went the trolley—*
> *Ding, ding, ding went the bell..."*

Her tune falls away like falling embers in a fire-pit; the clang peters out and the sound of a ticking wall clock, dull and mechanical, now comes into prominence. There's a long pause as I shift from one foot to the other; the woman's lips move with the speed of a reluctant schoolchild translating French exercises. Not a sound. Not a breath. Bunchee Golding closes her eyes, and her round head jerks feverishly as if she's shaking off a bad dream; she swallows several times, opens her eyes slowly as a look of astonishment spreads across her blanched face. The smell of meat juices and an English herb garden make my mouth water even more. I could have dropped on all fours to devour the scattered food straight from the floor— like a starving creature.

Next the spirits of Lost Hope and Grim Despair, a pair of ruffians, kick down her outward defences, and between them shake her by the scruff of the neck until she chokes. Traces of a moustache on her upper lip glisten with sparkling beads of sweat as if she's just stepped out of a hot shower; her pallor, now ashen-coloured, gladdens my heart.

******

'You ...you come to kill me,' she says with a quavering voice. Her cheeks are flushed and pretty—she always had a dream complexion to die for.

Her eyes dart around the room like a slippery fish floundering on the floor. She clasps each side of her fleshy face, tears shining in her eyes. The baking tray lies face down on the floor, a sea of small, bronzed potatoes, and screaming bright orange baby carrots adorn the canvas of the flagstone floor. She's left the green tops on the carrots, a habit of hers that I'd never got her to change. A puslike greyish-green liquid oozes from the holes in the pricked-all-over chicken that has come apart on impact; this liquid mess has landed in random zones across the kitchen space, forming a gleaming artistic composition.

'Tsk, tsk, tsk,' I cluck, without taking my eyes off her. 'Now what have we here?' I take in the bright kitchen space, the sparkling kitchen units, and the expansive worktops. Pans and kitchen utensils, (including a whisk, box grater, potato masher), hang evenly from the beamed ceiling, the type you see in a professional television kitchen. 'Glad to see me, Bunch?' I flash my best smile.

'I not bl**dy glad to see you! How you find me?' she says in an assertive voice that I'm convinced she's been practising for this moment.

I've never heard her curse before, and my scalp prickles just to hear it.

'The court gave me your address.' I say, which is partly true. I show her the slip of paper with her address on it that I'd shown the taxi driver. 'They wrote it down for me—look!'

Bunchee Golding shakes her head, grimacing wildly. 'Liar! The court never do that!'

'That's no way to speak to an old friend!'

Her eyes widen, her lower lip trembles like a leaf in the wind.

'You no friend of mine,' she spits, shaking her head.

'Oh, don't say that, Bunch!' I say, jerking my arms backwards to take off my rucksack, before clasping it to my chest. 'There I was, just passing by, thinking to myself, "My throat's parched. Now who can I pop in to see for a nice cup of tea? I know! Bunchee Golding lives in a nice place just up the road. I think I'll go and see her,"—

'cos if anyone can make a decent cup of tea, it would be her!'

Bunchee Golding doesn't say anything, but her gulping mouth and bright red chest lighten my mood—and after being in a dazed stupor for months on end, I need moments like this. As she surveys the kitchen floor, the wasted roast dinner with all the trimmings, her hands start to shake uncontrollably.

She looks up at me and stares into the space above my left ear, before lowering her long lashes to the floor. 'Please... Sylvie. Don't—' she murmurs, her brimming eyes make her pupils twice as large.

'Don't what?' I shrug offhandedly. 'I just want some tea.' I take off my glasses, and clean them with a green tea towel and a little spit. I take a grape from a fruit bowl, popping it in my mouth.

I nearly choke on the fruit for at that moment, a tabby cat, the size of a badger, gingerly pokes its head out from under a table. My heart skips a beat. Never taking its eyes off me, the cat attempts to make off with some of the spilt stuffing.

'No, Brutus! Hot! Hot!' hisses Bunchee Golding.

I stamp my foot sharply, making Brutus's ears flick back as he scrambles to dive under the table but misjudges and runs smack into the table leg.

'Dang! He ain't starved, is he?' I say, marvelling at the beast.

'Not your business!'

'I'm just saying...'

'I feed him what he like, how much he like—'

The shininess of the kitchen appliances, the beautiful yellow and red countertops, make my nose sting, and I'm overwhelmed by a deep sense of melancholy. She's about to lose it all but doesn't know it yet.

'Bunchee...'

She doesn't respond.

'Bunchee. How long have you been here?'

'Here?'

'Yeah—how long?'

'I am here ...over a year and a—'

I roll my eyes. 'No, dummy! I meant in the UK. How long?'
'You there when I come.'

She knows what's coming. She goes along with it because it amuses me and right now, I'm in the mood for some light relief.

'*Forty* years ago, right? You've been here...for forty years! So, Bunchee....can you tell me something?' She's squirming now, shuffling on the spot where she stands.

'If you've lived here all that time, why's your English so f**king awesomely terrible?'

'I try…I not from here...' she mumbles.

I've always been good at mimicking her. '"*Where you fine me…where you fine me?*" For Chrissakes! You've been here, like forever, and yet—'

I grow tired of looking at her pinched mouth, her small beady eyes blinking rapidly, so I drop it.

'In there!' I say, clicking my fingers, at the door that I imagine leads to the living room, suddenly grown anxious to get to the truth: to make her pay.

******

Bunchee Golding bites her lower lip, tucking strands of flyaway hair behind her ear. Her hair glistens from the remnants of grease on her left hand. Sensing my mood, she tries to avoid the inevitable. Indicating the sticky path left by the chicken mess, she makes a sweeping gesture with her right hand, still encased in an oven mitt, and which now flies from her hand.

'It's untid-ee! I clean up first, plee-ase!' She looks torn, looking first at the mess and then at me. 'Dirty,' she says.

I bring my hands together in a thunderous clap and she shudders.

'In there!'

'Brutus eat it all—he get sick,' she pleads.

Then she does something unexpected.

******

Bunchee Golding seizes a sizable chunk of chicken carcass from the floor with both hands. Lifting it above her head, she hurls it at me, with the desperation of a comeback fighter in the dying seconds of the last round. I pull up my rucksack to shield myself, and with a dull squelch the chicken drops to the floor. Then plopping down on her knees, Bunchee Golding scoops up as many potatoes and carrots as she can cram into her fist, and starts hurling them at me, one by one — the right hand working wondrously fast. I continue to ward off the attack. 'Get out! Get out, you…you gaslighter!' she screams, her face scarlet and shiny.

Gaslighter?

I can see the roof of her mouth and threads of silver as she screams. 'Get out! O-ut!'

As her ammunition comes to an end, her arms drop to her side, and she looks sheepish. She's overcome by a sudden fit of the giggles, snorting and choking, her bulky frame doubling up. She's like a drunk at a party who won't shut up, cheerful and hopeful.

'Hah! I frighten you, you w**ker! Admit it!' she chirps with glee. 'You see your dumb-a*s face!'

But I've been laughing inwardly at her antics, at the sight of her pudgy little arms picking up the vegetables, and throwing them at me, more out of heart-stopping panic than in rage. Not once did she manage to hit her target.

'Ahh, Sylvie-ee,' she bleats, wringing her hand as if in prayer. 'I sorry…sorry, sorry, very sorry. We friends…yes?' She can still conjure up that old charm when she wants. She holds up her red-scorched palms. 'Look— chicken burn me…'

'In there…and don't stop!' I snap. Her face crumples and she shudders as I push her towards the living room, making her stumble. One of her flip flops comes off, turning over in its wake, and as she steps back to slip it back on—Thwack! I land a blow between her shoulder blades, before kicking her broad backside.

She whimpers, hunching her shoulders, arms raised like a surrendering prisoner, marching rapidly now.

But Bunchee Golding's small act of rebellion with the roasted missiles had, in that split second, dulled my senses so that I was as good as defenceless, rendered useless when it had most mattered! — despite my higher level skills in strategy and tactical manoeuvres. Luck had been on my side as her puny stature meant she couldn't get her hands on the pans and other implements that hung overhead. I know she would have used them,—of that I had no doubt—had she been just that little bit taller…yes, luck had been on my side!

Bunchee Golding sure has developed a backbone!

******

I proceed to check and secure the property with the enemy under control. I secure her hands and feet with "special strength" zip-ties that I've brought for this purpose. On a small dining table, lies a tray with an empty cereal bowl and half a mug of cold coffee. I place the entire tray on her lap so that she doesn't move while I perform my clearance routine. Bunchee Golding's apple cheeks accentuate her doom - laden eyes. I take out a flashlight from my rucksack and point it downwards like a revolver, FBI style. Then in a semi-crouching posture— like Groucho Marx— I sweep through the flat to make sure there are no 'hidden surprises.' With furtive gait, I approach a half-opened door on the right, but her rasping voice erupts. 'No— that room private!'

'Oh Bunchee,' I shout back in exaggerated disappointment. 'We have no secrets from each other, remember?' I kick open the door with a flourish, and lean face-forward against the outer wall, for an obligatory few seconds, in the event that shots might ring out. I crash headlong into the room with my torch clenched in both hands, aiming the light from side to side.

******

I find myself in an Aladdin's cave of cheap tat, and impulse buys that have been scoured from car boot sales and bargain basements: carpet remnants, garden utensils, rusting scrap metal. I can make out a hat stand in the shadows, a vacuum cleaner, a crockery set sitting precariously on a disused fridge that stands in a pinkish stain that's long ago dried out. The crockery has the same design of damson plums that I'd seen in Rosemarie Whittington's flat. Shoes, and endless bags full of what appears to be dressing-up clothes.

I check the bathroom in the same manner. Sparkling and clean! This is a proper home, and a timely discovery in view of my eviction notice.

I find Bunchee Golding still sitting forlornly on the settee with the ladened tea tray across her lap; her zip-tied hands have now moved from underneath the tray to rest across her chest.

Every inch of her home is adorned with mirrors of varying shapes and sizes. An ornate gilt-framed mirror, decorated with hearts and cherubs with their dangling parts, takes up the entire south-facing wall. I make a mental note to go over the rude bits later with black paint after I move in. The furniture is new and well-polished. A narrow bed stretches out along the far side of the room, near the kitchen door. A full-length screen made of Chinese silk stands half extended across to hide the bed. I run my fingers over the pink, red and gold silk stitching that looks as if it's been woven by a dedicated team of spiders. A fifty-inch flat TV screen is mounted on the wall, a star attraction in any home. I make another mental note of the remote control that sits on a low table underneath.

On a side table, in a silver frame, stands a well-lit colour studio portrait of an elderly Chinese couple, printed on glossy paper. There's a pile of opened airmail letters written in weird signs and squiggles. A low bookcase crammed with an incomplete set of a Children's Encyclopaedia Britannica, the gaps resembling missing teeth. One of these books lies on a bedside cabinet near the bed, with a feather bookmark sticking out, its multi-coloured silken tassel cascading to the floor. A large world globe, vibrant blue, on its display stand, takes pride of place next to a fake cherry wood fireplace.

'How you find me?' Bunchee Golding asks a second time. I notice that her feet barely touch the ground from her seated position.

'I told you …the court—'

'I don't believe you.'

'Are you rude like this to all your guests?'

'You not guest. You intruder.'

******

After using the bathroom, I inspect the toiletries that line the edge of the bathtub. It's a dazzling white tub, without a single crack, stain or blemish, and I can't stop staring at the red, blue and gold taps. I'm examining a bubble-gum pink bottle of bubble bath when I feel a jolt of electricity run down my leg, crisping the body hairs in its path. The bubble bath clatters to the floor, spins on the spot before rolling away. After a second it happens again, a vibration more insistent than the first. I fish out a lilac-pink mobile phone from my trouser pocket that I'd forgotten had been there. The name 'BUNCHEE' flutters like an apparition on the screen. I nearly drop the phone.

Still buzzing, I press the phone icon, placing the phone cautiously to my ear.

A low, urgent voice like a series of hushed explosions dive into my ear. 'Hello? Rosemarie? Rosemarie? …she here...she try to kill me…help…she here in my house!….Rosemarie?...oh Gahhhd!'

******

I find Bunchee Golding on her mobile phone. We swap looks of shock and confusion. A broken zip-tie lies at her feet; the tray's now on the coffee table—but only just—teetering on the edge as if carelessly put down.

Still speaking into the pink mobile phone, I approach with a light step and an even lighter voice. 'And who is it you wish to speak to, ma'am? Who should I say is calling?' I ask using my best telephone speaking voice.

'Oh, Gaa-hd!' she groans in terror, trying to stuff the phone in her dress pocket, but drops it. 'Oh, Gaa-hd!' she says again. I squeeze a finger in my left ear as her phone clatters to the floor like pounding hooves.

'I'm afraid "Gaa-hd's" not here right now,' I say. 'Would you like to leave a message?' I throw Bunchee Golding a cold, accusing stare, and as I reach to pick up her phone she slaps my arms away. A short, sharp scream from me.

******

Bunchee Golding refuses to cooperate, and it takes all of three attempts to slip on another zip-tie on her chunky wrists.

Her face is frozen in terror. Then the muscles in her face all start working at once, and a tidal wave of hysteria washes over her.

'The phone!' she gasps, looking at the lilac-pink phone I've laid on the table next to hers. 'I think you–Rosemarie! Why you have Rosemarie's phone? Why? Why?'

Her eyes are fully open and wild; not wanting to give in to a thought that's entered her head, not wanting to believe it, her mind at war, she lets out a hiss of astonishment. 'You kill her!'

Then with strong, deft movements she prises her wrists apart so that the recently tied zip-tie falls away. 'You kill Rosemarie! Now you come to kill me!' she cries, glaring at me. Her forefinger jabs the space under my nose, and the smell of chicken grease mixed with stale vegetables hits my nose.

I avert my face, covering my face in my sleeve. 'For God's sake, your hands stink!'

She gets up, knocking over the precariously positioned tray, spilling cold coffee everywhere.

'Where the fu** are you going?' I shout in terror at my sudden loss of any control over her. A biting rage slices through me at her complete disregard for my rules, doing whatever she pleases. Her brazenness leaves me short of breath, and the strength and deftness of her actions, for a person of her clumsy size, make me feel sheepish—and second rate!

She covers her groin with her hand. 'Bathroom...,' she says quickly.

As I stand there confounded as to what to do, Bunchee Golding moves off like a hefty panther, anxious to get away. The bathroom door creaks open before clicking shut. I flop down on the settee she's vacated, pulling the broken zip tie in all directions— '"Special strength," my foot!'

'Leave the door open!' I bawl after her, letting her know who gives the orders, 'or I'll ...I'll...' I slump forward, defeated. Then a reversal of sounds: the unlocking of the door ... slowly creaking open ...taps turning on, water gushing much too fast, gurgling much too hard...the rushed patter of feet...a rustle of material, the clank-clanking of metal—a solid whoosh of air. A minute later, the water's still flowing forcefully. How long does it take to wash one's hands?

I kick open the bathroom door to see that bi**h, Bunchee Golding, hanging out of the open window, her broad backside up in the air; one slipper's upturned under the sink, the other's dangling on the end of her left foot. I swoop down on her like a bird of prey whose main meal of the day is disappearing before its eyes, and I haul her back inside by the legs. Her piercing shriek sets off a metallic ringing sound inside my head.

'Shut up!' I warn her, and afraid that someone will hear her terrified shouts, I strike her across the back of the head. She slumps to the floor like a baby seal sliding down an icy crevasse.

As she lays sprawled on the ground, her legs up against the bathtub, I give her a passing soft kick in the ribs before I turn off the taps and close the window.

'As**ole!' I shout close to her ear, sliding my arms under hers, to get her to stand, but Bunchee Golding's inert and floppy, the dead weight of a corpse.

Grabbing a bunch of her grey-white stringy hair, I twist and pull upwards until she's forced to find her feet, her contorted face unrecognisable.

'No, don't please!' she shrieks, shuffling across the floor as I drag her back to the living room.

I twist her arm, pressing her head into the settee while pinioning her down with my knee between her shoulders. She groans: 'Ah, ha, ahh...ahh-ha, ahhh...'

I whisper: 'If you do anything like that again, I *will* kill you! Get it?' She doesn't reply. I twist her arm again, and she lets out a whelp of pain.

'Yes, yes,—you hurting me!' pleads Bunchee Golding, 'Please!'

I notice a small circle of red-raw scalp on the top of her head where her hair is missing. I straighten up at the sight of it, loosening my grip.

Her left arm plummets to smack the floor, her face buried in the settee. Her right hand slowly draws up to nurse her head, shoulders heaving uncontrollably.

A few strands of grey hair curl around my fingers, and a well of disgust fills me. Wrapping them into a tight ball, I throw it at her. 'Look what you've made me do!' I say between gasps, knocking her with my foot. 'D'you think I enjoy all your—fu**ing drama?' She lies motionless, her head under her arms.

'What d'you run off for?' I wheeze, rubbing my face and wiping my hand on my trousers. 'D'you think you can escape me? Huh? After what you've done? D'you think I can ever let you go, knowing what I know?'

******

The clock on the mantel chimes brightly; a Chinese figure, no larger than a pepper pot, wielding a delicately small hammer, comes out of a red and gold door, to strike an anvil twelve times. The beauty in the artistry of this mechanical object stirs something within me, and I blink away scorching tears.

As an act of rebellion, Bunchee Golding refuses to open her eyes or sit up. I move over to the other side of the settee to get a better look– her squashed up face transformed into a silvery mask of tears and dejection. With my right arm under her left shoulder, I heave her up to a sitting position, but she flops over, quivering like a wounded bird.

******

Wringing out a flannel in warm water, I wipe her face caked with mucus, tears, loose hair and lashes. Briny tears have made her cheeks ruddy and blotchy, almost septic.

A vision of a young Bunchee Golding in former times comes to my mind; her succulent lips as pink as a rose in full bloom, her figure slim and curvaceous; ferociously coiffured hair that made her taller than her five-foot frame. The two of us blowing bubbles in the garden on a summer's day, our voices piping. I was a lanky, pony-tail wearing girl, with a taste for men's baggy shirts and trousers that had been outlawed at my own family home as being too 'laddish' and

'unladylike.'

I break out of my reverie to see her with her eyes squeezed tight as if opening them to the light might hurt them.

'You come to kill me,' she croaks.

I sit next to her on the armrest, but the smell of curdled milk assaults my nose.

'Hush now …Sarsaparilla,' I say, without tenderness, stroking her shoulder with one finger, just for something to do. 'There now.'

This makes tiny hairs on the nape of her neck bristle. She looks up at me, her eyes filled with horror as she abruptly heaves herself upright, nearly dislodging me from my seated position on the armrest— deliberately!

'Don't call me that!' she says, and the heat of aggression, that's been simmering since our paths crossed that day, comes through. I clench my fists in readiness.

'Sarsaparilla?'

'Don't!'

'It's a term of...affection…'

'—You not understand!' she says, gloomily.

'...your favourite drink.'

'*He* call me that—'

On a brown armchair, I spot Brutus sitting with his back to me; one hefty leg outstretched towards the ceiling, his head jerking downward, rhythmically, across a white mound of stomach. I throw the wet flannel at him which lands with a dull smack of fur and leather. The dust flies as he scrambles away.

'You were lucky, Bunch,' I say, taking the cat's place on the chair. 'No-one ever gave me a nice nickname! Not Ron, not my family, not school, not anyone. It's always been plain old Sylvie!' A faraway look falls like a curtain over her eyes, a blue-black vein strums across her forehead.

'Oh, but you have one,' she says, her face suddenly animated with a spiteful charm.

'I don't think so...'

'In the New Horizon! *We* make nickname for you.' I throw her a look of warning—but it's too late!

'Commandant! We call you Commandant!' and her steely glare knocks me sideways like a bowling pin.

******

Chapter 6

I seize Bunchee Golding by her neck chain, winding it around my fingers. It sinks like butter, making the fleshy part of her throat bulge like the sides of a bread roll. I pull back my fist, but she instinctively draws her arms over her head, and lets out a piercing scream that could wake the devil. 'Not my face!' she shrieks. 'Not my face...please... not today!'

I leap up, thrusting my fingers in my ears, moving my lower jaw from side to side to adjust the ringing she's set off there.

'Bl**dy hell! You've busted my fu**ing ears!'

'Stop hitting me—!'

I pause to take in what she's said.

'What the f**k does that mean?—"not today," ' I ask, each syllable brisk and marching, She scrambles lithely behind the couch, staring at me, her mouth pursed shut. She savours the fact that she knows something I don't— victory creasing her eyes and mouth. 'Well?' I demand, digging my fingernails into my palms.

Bunchee Golding's voice drops to a whisper. 'You not going to like what I say...' she says, massaging two red streaks on her neck with the tips of her fingers.

'Won't like what?'

There she goes—the slow drip-drip-drip of information; her sentences tailing off to keep me guessing! It's always been like that between us. Like pulling teeth!

'Promise not to hit me...'

'Tell me!'

She swallows hard as if chewing something bitter, her lips frantically searching for the right words to save herself.

'I ..I...go to...'

'Come on!'

'... the television studio...'

She might just as well have told me that she was going to the seaside to play on fruit machines. It doesn't register.

'Television studio?'

She indicates a royal blue and gold-edged mantel clock that displays the late afternoon time with its shimmering gilt hands.

'They come soon,' Bunchee Golding says, nodding with suppressed relief; her beady eyes, steady and unblinking, make me want to knock her down again!

She snatches up her phone, retrieves a message to show me. 'I do interview—look my messages —'

I dab my face which fizzes with pain.

'What? You're doing an interview? About New Horizons? About…us?' I say in disbelief. With lips slightly parted, she neither confirms nor denies.

I jeer at her. 'On national television? …You?'

A long pause stretches before us. 'Let me get this straight. You're going on national TV to talk about me…our private lives?' I ask.

'Not about you, Sylvie —'

'As**hole! You! Me! Us!— it's all the same!'

She shudders, wincing, biting her lip. 'I must go…what you—' She squeals as I stomp towards her.

Leaning over, I clasp her by the shoulders with moist hands. 'Are you crazy? Are you out of your fu**ing teensy-weensy mind? Do *you* think, Bunchee Golding, that I'm going to let you do *that*?'   She flinches as a few drops of my spittle lands in her hair, glistening like bits of plastic beads.

'I must…'

'Don't keep saying that!'

Her chin quivers, her eyes clenched shut for a moment before she says in a voice I can barely hear. 'Sylvie. It's all arranged—'

'D'you think that I'm going to let *you* shoot your mouth off on national TV?' I say, glaring at her.

'But they expecting me!'

'I don't fu**ing care!'

As I shake her, her head rolls loosely about her shoulders as if about to fall off. 'You're not going and that's that!'

At that moment, an ear-splitting peal of a doorbell sounds. I jump to my feet, clutching her sleeve instinctively, holding her to me as if she were a shield. An invisible weight squeezes itself to fit the space in my throat. I have no breath for speech.

******

Chapter 7

A merry jingle sounds in the lock. The creaking of rusty hinges. The stomping of feet. My legs turn to blocks of ice as terror sparks a frost fire that races through my veins. My upper lip tingles and my heart beats so fast, I fear it'll give out. A woman's voice sails in from the hallway, bright as the bells at Sunday church.

'Are you ready, Bunchee?' says the voice. The question hangs in the air like spectral heat before it reaches us.

My lumpy inaction unleashes, in contrast, a tidal wave of energy in Bunchee Golding, who springs along on the spongy balls of her bare feet. She grabs my arm and starts to shove me behind the Chinese screen that hides the narrow, unmade bed. An assortment of toys lies in a haphazard heap at the pillow end: a small yellow and white striped tiger with a piece of wire sticking out from beneath the soft material where its eye had once been; a moth-eaten black and white cat, and a nude-pink blonde doll with a missing leg.

'Shhh! Sit!' hisses Bunchee Golding, helping to manoeuvre me onto the bed as my legs have no inclination to work themselves. 'Don't show your feet!' she urges, raising my feet, and I'm surprised at the ease at which she can move them.

The living room door swings open to hit the wall. The stately clacking of business heels crosses the wooden floor.

'You didn't answer my calls,' says the voice, now accusing. 'I was so-oo worried—I must've called you a hundred times—I was going to get the police to do a welfare check!'

'No police,' says Bunchee Golding, laughing as if the woman is exaggerating. 'I have a quick sleep,' she says, yawning loudly as if she's just got up. She scrabbles around for her flip-flops and puts them on, pulling the screen across the entire length of the bed to hide me.

After a pause, a clucking sound of a flustered hen.

'You're not even ready!' exclaims the woman in a high-pitched tone that's now familiar to me.

'I am sleeping'

I imagine Bunchee Golding looking guiltily at the Chinese screen, mouthing her predicament to her visitor: "I'm in trouble!" I imagine the sly witch handing a secret note to her visitor, with the words "Help Me!" scribbled on it—I wouldn't put it past her!

Suppressing a yawn, Bunchee Golding approaches her guest. 'You look real nice,' she ventures.

'D'you know what *time* it is?'

I strain to keep still, to keep my numb, useless legs from tumbling onto the floor. The yellow-and white-striped tiger, with the missing eye, falls off the bed with a soft thud. I hold my breath.

'God, I'm dying for a pee!' says the woman, the clackety-clack of her heels heading towards the bathroom.

I peer out from behind the screen. A smell of perfume lingers in the air. I have smelled it before. Bunchee Golding is sitting on the settee, clutching her head as if it's sore, not wanting to meet my gaze.

I put up a finger. 'You tell her you're not going!' I hiss, 'Don't make me —'

Holding a finger to her lips, she mouths back: 'Shh! She will hear you!'

'Tell her you're feeling sick!'

She shakes her head. 'I ca-an't!'

'Otherwise—I swear I'll fu**ing kill you!'

On hearing the bathroom door open, I lurch back behind the screen. But I've landed on my back, further down the bed than I'd intended, and I have to keep my legs raised in the air to avoid my legs being seen.

The visitor breathes in deeply, slowly and deliberately. Her peevish voice is now replaced with one that can draw all the sugar-mad flies and bees from the gardens.

'Mmm! Do I smell chicken?'

'I get some for you,' Bunchee Golding says cheerily, and she flounces past the bed, towards the kitchen.

'Just a small plate, then, Bunchee!' calls the woman after her. A pair of internal bellows stokes up a sudden pang of hunger within me.

From where I lie on my back, legs up, it's hard to breathe. I turn my head to the left, and find myself staring through a centimetre crack in the wooden frame where the Chinese screen folds—a manufacturer's defect. The woman is sitting at the dining table. A swathe of yellow material hangs from the back of her chair.

It's Annie Lederer, Director of Unchained, from a few days ago— or is it a day or two ago? It could be three. I've never been good at keeping time— one day just rolls into the next for me.

Annie's frilly snow-white blouse bursts through from under her crisp, mauve suit, at the neck and sleeves so that she resembles a blossoming magnolia bush. Her hair's grown more luxuriant than when I last saw her; scooped high on her head, held in place with glittering pins. She wears dark eye make-up, and her lips gleam as if dipped in cherry red shoe polish.

Then the purring of a dialling tone. 'Sam?' she says in her telephone voice. 'Listen, Sam...we're running a bit late. She overslept.....would you let the studio know?...good girl. Yes...great PR...if we can pull it off!—'

She breaks off with a cheery 'toodle-oo!' and snap-shuts her phone. Bunchee Golding returns wordlessly, setting down a steaming plate of food before her hungry guest, cutlery and a glass of water. 'What have we got here?' asks Annie, her phone clattering, as if she's tossed it onto the dining table. She cracks her fingers together, running her eyes over the food. 'You need to work on your food presentation, dear,' she says between mouthfuls. 'This looks like an abstract painting!' I chuckle inwardly. She's eating the roast dinner scraped off Bunchee Golding's kitchen floor!

With lowered head and a monk-like expression, Bunchee Golding says a little too quickly, sounding a little insincere: 'I hope you like. I make it today.' The smell of chicken reaches me, and an involuntary gurgle flies from my stomach to jab the air. I hold my breath, squeezing my stomach with both hands to silence further eruptions.

'What was that—?' asks Annie, her face askew, looking in my direction as her jaws ease to a standstill.

'What?' asks Bunchee Golding, her eyes nervously following Annie's gaze.

'A growl....like a bear's'

'The radiator, I think,' says my former friend with a shrug of her shoulders, and she busies herself wiping down a table mat as if her life depended on it.

My stomach lets rip again, a much louder rumble than the first, and I hear the sound of light paws padding past me...

'It's Brutus—I forgot his lunch!' says Bunchee Golding, picking up her cat. 'No lunch, paw- boy!' She nuzzles the cat's ear and kisses it. 'Paw-boy!'

With one side of her face bulging, moving up and down as she chews, Annie peers at Bunchee Golding, pointing at her with her knife, her words strange and muffled by food. 'Your eyes...your face ...all puffy!'

'I think about my life…after Ron goes to jail—' Bunchee Golding breaks off choking back tears. 'I cry...and cry.' It's a performance worthy of an award-winning actor, in her effort to distract Annie from my stomach grumbles. And that surprises me.

******

'Do we need to go over what you're going to say?' asks Annie.
'No, I remember,' says Bunchee Golding.
Annie frowns and says: 'Try not to mumble when you speak. Your mouth.... speak...clearly'.... I can't make out the rest of what she's saying as she chomps, slurps and chews her way through her chicken meal.
'Annie'
'And *please,* listen to the questions!'
'Annie, I—'
'We'll talk in the car. Did I tell you they've sent a car?' she beams a sunny smile exposing her gapped teeth.
'A car?'
'A Cadillac with a driver!'
'Annie, I must —'
'Let's talk in the car, okay!'
'But I'm afraid! Please Annie!'
I hold my breath as a bead of sweat caterpillars down my face. I steel myself as to what she might say next.
Annie shakes her by the shoulders. 'Don't be silly! He's locked up. He'll never be able to hurt you again—'
Bunchee Golding shakes her head inconsolably, her eyes communing with the floor as if something deep and meaningful lies in its wood pattern.
'It's not that. I'm afraid… I'm afraid of the dark.'

******

Chapter 8

'Everything has a price tag,' Ron used to say to us, whether it was a piece of porcelain, working towards one's ambitions, forming relationships or just existing day-to-day. Everything can be bought and sold. I go through each room in turn, mentally cataloguing every item Bunchee Golding has bought with her thirty pieces of silver. I prise open every cupboard, every drawer and container in her flat, running my feverish fingers over them, scrutinising objects as if through touch I'm seeing them for the first time; feeling the grooves and bumps as well as the smooth and rough edges that give each one its own uniqueness. People are the same.

A pair of samurai swords, their handles encrusted with coloured fake gems, reeking of cheap fascination, hang prettily over the mantel shelf. How was I to know (much later) that they were worth five thousand pounds each! I gaze at the enormous television and imagine Bunchee Golding lying on her sofa watching countless detective and crime programmes that she and I had always enjoyed in New Horizons. The enormous tabby, Brutus, washes himself on his mistress's spot on the settee, his pink tongue flicking in and out like a tiny flame, his busy paw scraping his solid striped face. I throw a half-filled plastic bottle of water that catches the right side of his torso, whereupon a magnificent growl jump-starts his throat. Then the sound of knives abseiling down leather followed by the thud of a tightly-packed snowball falling onto the ground.

I scour the rancid-smelling kitchen for food. The remnants of roast chicken are now in the bin; greasy stains, brown bits of rubbery skin, red and green flecks daub the flagstone floor, as well as the lower half of the sparkling kitchen units.

I find and wolf down three tomatoes, two dry fish-fingers stained with tomato sauce –and a hardened stem of lettuce. All washed down with two glasses of Sarsaparilla.

Inside the bedside unit, I find a neat bundle of foreign air mail correspondence tied with red cotton thread. Letters written in Chinese, probably from her parents, look as if they've been penned with a pin dipped in cool blue blood. Squiggly, weird writing. I'm just about to read the address, the only part in English, when from the corner of my eye, I glimpse a piece of paper with a blue and red logo stamped at the top.

I snatch up the page in a half-crazed frenzy. It's a bank statement curled up with other general correspondence, and it's the same bank as the one I used to have when I lived with my parents. My eyes leap across the page to land on the most essential information at the top: a row of figures in bold print. I scan again, counting and recounting, the boastful series of noughts— fat noughts, each swollen with majestic pride, and I savour each one before swallowing them whole.

An anchor-like weight lifts from my shoulders and my ears pop, clearing my breathing system. I skip and twirl over to the mantel shelf, taking down one of the samurai swords. I leap about the room, lunging and thrusting like a swashbuckler, striking the furniture with the flat of the blade. I plunge the blade into a cushion, but it catches awkwardly making the feathers fly. Brutus has made himself scarce.

Ten thousand pounds! 'Bunchee m' little darlin'! You assiduous little saver,' I parade my admiration of her by running through our flat shouting at the top of my lungs. 'You little Ching-Chong darling!'

I start to make plans. I shall cost it all out like a proper business proposal, with proper double headings and columns; I shall create a document file labelled in bold letters—the type you see in a solicitor's office—but l have yet to decide what to call our project. 'The Break-Out Project?' 'The Great Appeal Project?' 'Ron's Appeal?'

I can't wait to see Bunchee Golding's expression when I let her know the cost of possessing a loose tongue, and a reckless nature— the consequences of which she must now pay; the consequences of which now spreads itself, like sticky fingers, across her nose and mouth—to cut off her air supply!

******

I also find a letter from a psychiatric hospital. I laugh out loud as I read it. What a bunch of clinical ass*oles! She doesn't need this! It's too late for any kind of intervention! All they have to do is ask me— I can tell them everything they want to know! I can tell them what I've known all along about her: that Bunchee Golding had long ago taken leave of her senses.

******

Chapter 9

After the disbandment of New Horizons, and Ron's arrest, my life broke up into a thousand pieces like a jigsaw puzzle, only I couldn't put them back together again. I no longer understood which piece went where. I couldn't remember much of what had happened to me at the time. I remember staring out of a window hoping for someone to return, but not knowing who it was. I had a vision of a rake thin figure bent double, a rucksack on her back, hobbling along a high street paved with gum, dog excrement, crumpled leaves, and other disease choked street debris. A girl-woman, tall and willowy, hair piled high, catching the yellow rays of the sun, was following the one staggering around like a drunkard, but doing it inconspicuously, sneakily. With a painter's easel strapped on her back, church leaflets falling from her hands, this tall girl-woman was trying to catch up with the one scrabbling on the ground on her knees.

******

When I re-learned how sentences were strung together, and I could speak again, I mentioned my memory lapses to the Glass of Water who instantly turned soggier than ever, pleased that I was reaching out to her. Her eyes moistened and she plunged her hand in her dress pocket to wizard up an electric blue business card belonging to one 'Eva Buchwald: Behavioural Psychologist'. It was as if the Glass had spent her entire life waiting for someone like me to cross her path for the explicit purpose of giving me this dog-eared, dirty-looking card, that told me to "hang in there", and that help was on its way. Smiles wreathed her watery little face, as she gave me perceptible nods of approval of what she believed to be baby steps on the road to recovery, and my re-entry into civilised society.

We were on different wavelengths. She and I.

Despite my treating her like a skivvy, keeping her up at nights with my 'rages' while she balanced cold compresses on my forehead, to douse the disordered fevers from the past. The Glass makes a magnanimous gesture by offering to pay for an introductory session with Dr Anna Buchwald, Behavioural Psychologist. I shrugged and told the GOW that she must be the only homeless person who could afford a shrink.

'I'm sure you'd do the same for me, Sylvie,' she purred stupidly, and I even let her pat my arm. Young people were always on a mission to change something. The Glass had also found God, and when she wasn't skipping to church every Sunday (and other prayer days), a bible swinging from one arm, she'd be evangelising on the streets, hoping to transform grizzled old dogs with the offer of a meaty bone called religious sustenance.

I toyed with the idea of letting her accompany me to the offices of Dr Anna Buchwald as, in truth, I felt nervous of the unknown, of going to a place that could have been ...well...anywhere.

The prospect of being face-to-face with a professional grave-digger of the mind, being probed by one of her suction-cupped tentacles of discovery, was in itself an act of madness, borne of a desperation to get 'normal' again. But on the day I walked into the offices of Anna Buchwald, without the Glass accompanying me, to sit on one of the doctor's plush pink armchairs, I surprised myself and decided that since I was in so deep anyway, I might as well go totally mad—and engage! I had planned to be a no-show.

The wall behind the psychologist's desk was decorated with framed certificates— diplomas and doctorates—each chronicling the different stages of knowledge and understanding reached by the good doctor in her studies of clinical madness.

Dr Buchwald clearly ate, breathed madness and took it to bed with her. But was she what I was looking for?

On the opposite wall hung a series of framed sheet music of songs from long ago: 'Oh, Mistress Mine', 'Bach's Minuet in G,' and 'Danny Boy,'

There was also a large vintage poster of the film, 'Frankenstein,' depicting a stony-faced creature, with hands bound in metallic chains, his eyes awash with tears, filled with terror. His mouth contorted, stark and pitiful, rendered the creature more human than the puny starched-collared bespectacled man who commandeered this hapless soul for the gratification of his own scientific ambitions.

Dr Buchwald's desk, neat and orderly, had a framed photograph of a large-boned girl and a boy posing in school uniform, showing the same crowded teeth that featured in Dr Anna Buchwald's own mouth. Could her sapling physique, her scrawny pelvis have pushed out these two hefty spuds?

The contents of a box of Kleenex, half wrenched out of its opening, formed a pretty mound of lilac-white. Dr Buchwald asked me a whole battery of questions to which I had to score myself on a scale from one to ten, questions that I found pointless and disrespectful: Can I sit still without fidgeting? Can I get out of the house? Do I have thoughts of harming myself? Am I going to act on any thoughts of harming myself?

Dr Buchwald gave me a mechanical smile. 'Let me start by saying thank you for attending to discuss specific issues that have been troubling you. Everything we say in this space is confidential.' Then she spent five minutes going over some 'ground rules:' how important it was to maintain trust between the parties, issues of consent and information sharing, her tone, all the while, veering between a treacly one and one as harsh as sandpaper. I felt that I had entered a different time zone, where all motion was suspended, and I was travelling in slow motion: the psychologist's mouth moved in exaggerated slowness, everything so-oo sl-oow— my eyelids began to droop... I felt myself sinking into a throne of soft, pink cushions...

A sharp rap on the table jerked me to my senses; the woman opposite was watching me intently.

'.... before you make up your mind whether you wish to continue... indeed if you think I can be of any use to you at this point in time…'

I nodded vigorously like one of those nodding dogs you see in a toy shop.

'Have you ever seen someone like me before?' she asked.

I stared at the wall, not used to strangers watching me, judging me, thinking up all sorts of lies about me.

I'd made a mistake. I wondered if I could cancel the session...but the Glass of Water had already paid for it.

'No, never,' I said, running my finger along the smooth-as-silk seams of the velvet chair. 'You're a luxury item.'

Doctor Buchwald immediately fell to writing on a spiral notepad.

'Let's start with an icebreaker, shall we?' she continued, clicking the tip of her pen, so that the sound burrowed into my brain like an itch. I wanted to knock the pen out of her hand.

'Tell me two things about yourself, and then I'll—'

'I'm really sorry,' I jerked to my feet. 'I know you're trying to break the ice and all that, but I'm supposed to be at the Job Centre. They expect me to be on time...find myself a job pretty soon, otherwise they'll take away my benefits.'

'Ah! There you go!' says Doctor Buchwald clapping her hands, and signalling for me to sit down. 'One— you can make appointments with professional agencies. Two— you like to be punctual! Good! Now, it's my —'

I cut her off before she could tell me anything about herself. 'You've ...got two children...' I said, looking at the glossy photograph on her desk.

Dr Buchwald nodded vigorously, smiling.

'And...um, you probably had relatives living in Nazi Germany.'

She stopped nodding. Placing her pen down, she clasped her fingers inwardly in the style of "the church, steeple and all the people. 'Okay,' she said briskly, ignoring my request to leave. 'Perhaps these ice breakers aren't for everybody. Hmm? Maybe you can tell me what's brought you here?' With her pen poised for action, she tamed some stray strands of blonde hair by squashing them behind her ear.

I wanted to tell her that I'd lived on air and ice since losing my home, but I'd only just met her. She stared at me, her mouth agape that made me want to snap it shut.

'I can't remember stuff that's happened to me,' I blurted out. 'There are gaps...' and, at this point, I tapped my forehead... 'that I can't account for.'

'How does that make you feel?'

'I dunno .... I want to know if I'll ever get back to—well, you know,—how I was before...'

'Before...?'

'Before they ...switched me off.'

'Who switched you off?'

'I can't remember...'

'Hmm. Some people can't remember past experiences for all sorts of reasons. It could be indicative of whole raft of things—'

'But I have a great memory,' I interrupted, at the same time she said: '—brain degeneration or an injury—'

I tried to keep the boastfulness out of my voice.

'I can remember every face of everyone I've ever met, every gesture, expression, every conversation, interaction, every accusation...confrontation...every punch thrown, from way back...'

A sliver of irritation hardened her voice. 'Okay!' she said, and planting her hands face down on the table, she hoisted herself suddenly to her feet which made me jump. Reaching into her desk drawer, she took out a stick of chewing gum, and popped it into her mouth; her lips puckered up as the juices started to pool.

'So what's it all about?' I asked.

There was a pause as she chewed.

'It can sometimes be to do with shock; people can be traumatised by a sudden or unexpected event—say an episode of ill health—the loss of a job... the loss of a loved one... divorce... a physical assault...' Dr Buchwald had paused after each suggestion to scrutinise my face, trying to detect a reaction. She gave me a benign smile as if to a child who had been scratching the surface of her soft furnishings with their fingernails.

'I had a Chinese friend whose pet dog went missing ...he just didn't come home. After that my friend couldn't say what day of the week it was, or what she'd done the day before ...she just stayed in bed...just through missing him. I was very sorry afterwards...I mean I felt very sorry for her...'

Dr Buchwald sipped from a glass, pausing for me to continue. 'Well...eighteen months ago...it could be less...or more, I had to leave the house where I was living. I remember that part...'

The good doctor clapped her thighs. 'There you go! An eviction!'

'Not exactly –not a proper one anyway,' I said.

'An illegal eviction can be more traumatising,' she nodded.

'I came home one afternoon and my key…my key didn't work. I thought I had the wrong door—I couldn't work it out. A voice told me not to go in. But I had to. I banged on the door, but nobody came.' I licked my chapped lips, my words sounding shrill and shrewish.

My back was drenched with sweat.

'There was police tape everywhere...' I continued. 'I thought somebody had died.... I couldn't find any of my friends...'

Dr Buchwald looked up briefly without saying anything. She was writing on her pad with the fury of one possessed, her mouth resembling the opening of a money pouch.

'Someone said...and I can't recall who...said that they were after me…' I said.

'After you?'

'I don't know...but I remember hearing voices,—'

'What kind of voices?'

'Well, one voice really—'

Dr Buchwald focussed on her notepad. 'Did you recognise the person?'

'Er, yes...it sounded like me...'

'Okay...and what did this voice say?'

'"Run, run, as fast as you can! You can't catch me I'm the Gingerbread Man!"'

******

Anna Buchwald stopped writing and looked up at me, her mouth like a slice of melon turned upside down.

After a while she asked, 'Is there anything else you remember?'

'A Glass of Water looked after me'.

'A glass of water?'

'I met her when she was giving out church leaflets...she took me to an empty building, 'cos I didn't have anywhere to stay. She gave me a phone and her spectacles...that helped...I stayed in my room in the squat for six months. I was afraid of my own shadow...and when I finally managed to go outside, people had changed into giant insects, always buzzing around my head, snapping their mandibles at me. I had to outsmart them. I had to get away!

'I see'

'I felt this...coil-shaped thing like a rope wrapping itself around my ribcage—squeezing the god**mned life outta me!'

The doctor looked at me, a smile playing on her lips. 'You like using American expressions' she observed.

'I don't reckon so'

'Hmm. Tell me, have you experienced this ...state of anxiety before?'

'You bet!'

'When?'

'My first-year law degree— I failed every module. I pretended to my parents that I was still attending University. I couldn't keep that up forever, and I knew that I had to—'

My vision started to blur over, my heart pounded in my ribcage. A high-pitched squeal as when an old-fashioned television transmitter gets blown, filled my ears, and I blocked the noise with my fingers.

'I think you might have conflated separate incidents here...'

'Oh, I don't know what's what anymore,' I let out a sigh through my mouth and nose. 'Perhaps I don't care...'

'Oh, come now!—' she said, tossing her pen down. 'You must care—otherwise you wouldn't be here!' She glared at me, and picking up her pen, started writing again.

I licked my lips, savouring the rough and salty skin.

I uncrossed my legs and sat upright, hooking a foot around the leg of the chair so that I didn't slip off.

'The one thing I've always feared is...'

The doctor's eyebrows shot up, encouraging me to carry on. '...that they would eventually collar me, lock me up... throw away the key...'

'Your parents?'

'Oh, I don't know...it could be....could be anybody. But I heard this man's voice...'

'Ah! The Gingerbread Man!' she said in wonder, her eyes softening, almost tender.

I closed my eyes, holding the table to ease myself to a standing position.

I was sure that Dr Buchwald and I would probably never meet again as doctor-patient. But how was I to know that we'd encounter each other again—in a courtroom, with me all hunched forward in the dock, and the good, capable Anna Buchwald in the witness box, giving evidence of our meeting—this very meeting—to a very one-sided and judgmental court!

And as I moved to leave, I brought down my arm to swoop up her notepad. She let out a startled squawk. It turned out to be a waste of time as I couldn't read her handwriting when I later tried to read all that stuff she had written about me.

******

The Glass of Water (Melanie) dropped her sandwich on seeing me. She watched me warily as I opened the fridge to check the expiry dates on various pots of yoghurts. I remembered my military trainer had once told me that the truth was often in front of you, and that all you had to do was follow the clues.

'How did it go?' the Glass of Water asked in that hot and bothered way of hers as if she had just completed a five-mile marathon. With a dishcloth, she started to wipe away the remnants of a sandwich scattered on the worktop; she did this while keeping me in her peripheral vision.

The smell of her sandwich—fish sandwich—rank and salty made me feel queasy, so I slurped cold water straight from the tap. The Glass rarely used the kitchen.

'I know all about it!' I said in triumph, wiping my mouth on my sleeve.

'Oh? All about what?' she asked, half-twisting her head to throw a glance at me, her voice all-a-flutter as the corners of her smile twitched.

'You and me.'

She stopped wiping and cleared her throat. 'What about, er...you and me?' Her eyebrows had vanished under her hairline.

'Thanks to the good doctor, I've figured it out—.'

'Ah. Well, I'm glad about that, Sylvie...'

'I know who you are...'

She let out a huge sigh, almost of relief, that dried, at once, the wet surfaces she had just wiped down.

She even sounded as chirpy as a songbird. 'I...I was beginning to think you might not get there...' Her mouth showed all its bonny little teeth.

'What have you got to be so da**ned well relieved about?'

'I'm just glad you've taken it so well...'

'No, I haven't taken it well!' I screamed.

'Well... and I'm talking about myself here... it was getting to...you know...to be a bit of a burden...' she said.

'Burden? What the f**k are you talking about?'

'Well, it's not in my nature to—'

I lost patience with her gobbledygook and told her that the trip to the psychologist—*her* psychologist— had triggered in me certain memories. At that, The Glass of Water's head became perfectly still, her now lugubrious eyes scanned the ground as a bird looking for a worm. She said nothing, did nothing but, instead, gulped like a fish.

'Oh, yes. I know all about you –you little liar...you meddler in other people's lives...!' I said. And she gulped again.

******

I informed The Glass that after the break-up of New Horizons, I remembered her looking down at me, like so much useless flesh, while she checked for vital signs. She had found me in the street, stinking and incoherent, ignored by passersby. She had put her arm under my arm, holding me up as we walked at a snail's pace to a house, where a noisy group of people with giant roller brushes were painting the walls magnolia white. 'Is that her, then?' I had heard a woman ask before my benefactor shushed her. 'She's our guest...'

The Glass now gave a half-shrug.

'I don't understand,' she said gloomily.

'Yet you told me that I'd met you near the church where you were giving out those stupid leaflets, and that I'd asked you for a place to stay...two different accounts of how we met. Two da**ned different accounts, Mel! Which one's the real one?'

She shook her head, unwilling to say. 'Well? How did we find each other?' I demanded.

Her chest rose as if to sigh again but she stopped herself. 'Does it really matter?' she asked weakly.

'Of course it matters!'

'It's so petty...'

'You can't ...you can't just change my history willy-nilly!'

I opened my mouth to show my tongue run around my blackened stubble of teeth and flaccid gums—pleased as punch to show it. ''See this? This is who I am! Sylvie DaSouza! Down-trodden, deprived,

denied, decayed— and d**mned well proud of it!' She nodded vigorously, anxious to please.

'Don't ever re-write my past—not even the merest detail! Don't you ever do that again!'

******

Chapter 10

I wake to a whirling constellation of sparks splashing around me. It takes me a minute to realise I'm in Bunchee Golding's flat. A cold wetness behind my ear makes my fingers sticky and I recoil at the touch. I take what's nearest my head— it's soft and cushiony to the touch, fits the span of my hand. Wiping away the rivulet of drool with it, something digs in— and I rub my cheek to find a scratch made by the toy with the missing eye that I've picked up. I hurl it aside. I watch luminous silver and blue slivers of light bounce off the walls and ceiling. Am I in a state of concussion? I bolt down the acrid mess in my mouth, smacking my lips to get rid of the taste. My gums ache and I massage my upper lip and jaws with my thumb.

The television is on without sound. I had earlier moved it to face Bunchee Golding's bed for a better view. I swing my legs over the side of the bed, knocking something that crashes forward. It's the Chinese screen.

My heart misses a beat before picking up apace to hurtle like a steam train. I let out a gasp as Bunchee Golding appears on the television screen! I fumble for the TV remote and turn up the volume. Under the glare of the television studio lights, the skin around her eyes is translucent and puffy; a fine, beaded track of red underlines the left one. I reckon she did that to herself when she tried to get out of the bathroom window. Her image washes over me, and I wonder why I had let her leave.

Her mouth is pulled down, but flickers intermittently with the briefest of smiles, in the way she does when she wants to please. Her eyes are opaque like those of an overlooked sprat at a fish stall at closing time, staring dully, reflecting the wreckage of her soul.

The late-night inquisitor, of small screen fame, Maisie Small is bending her scrawny body like a bow towards Bunchee Golding, her polo neck pulled up as far as it can go. The tip of the presenter's tongue pokes out as she hangs onto every word that the programme's star attraction is saying.

'...I have bad marriage, very bad...nowhere to go, no money, no family. Someone tell me I go to this place –New Horizons—they help women. I go there. Everything is good at first. I do the cooking,

cleaning ...helping the other women there...we look after each other...'
The more Bunchee Golding sweats, the more the dampness enlivens her fine moustache. She swallows hard like the guilty t*rd she is, pausing often to gather her thoughts, speaking slowly, sounding more like a frightened child than a pensioner.

Maisie Small is saying: 'Now, I'm not going to go into the sexual side of your relationship with your perpetrator, Ms Golding—but can you describe how you and the other women were treated within the cult— and let's be clear about this—this *was* a sex cult you lived in?'

'Yes...it is. Every month we check our weight... everyone have ...a weight chart. If we get too fat we don't get to eat....' She swallows several times, her stare fixed on a space in front of her. 'Sometimes we are hungry...I develop stomach problem. We have no doctor...or dentist ...our teeth fall out...we don't have glasses; some of us get so bad –we don't see our fingers in front of face—'

'So, he stopped the New Horizons women accessing health services?'

The pause lasts the length of a bowler bowling a ball at a cricket match.

'No. He never stop us exactly...it is...it is never like that. But we know he get upset if we say we want medical help. He say to us, "God give us two eyes to see, he...God... make sure we only see what we *need* to see, and we do not need more than that"...so no glasses...we do not get glasses.'

Maisie Small's mouth drops open, her head jerks to one side as if she has suffered a blow to the head. 'That's some twisted logic...!' she says, shaking her head, her indignation ready to pop through her bright, peach-hot skin.

Bunchee Golding continues: '"Glasses for the eye is against God's will—it make us to have more than what God give us," he tell us. It seems silly now, but at the time we believe it ...with all our hearts.'

'And did your captor keep you all under lock and key?' Bunchee shakes her head vigorously.

Maisie Small's braided head sways from side to side. 'So, *why* didn't you just run away?'

'We are scared,' says Bunchee Golding, glancing over her left shoulder, as if communing with a ghost. She looks down shyly, her eyelashes, long and black, stroke her cheeks. 'There is always shouting...' she says

'...a lot of anger...it seems...?' asks the television inquisitor.

'—burning like the sun'

'Did he use threats of violence?'

'There is... a lot of violence in that house.'

'Bunchee—help me understand this... and our viewers at home will want to understand this as well. Ron Partridge held you and the other women captive, although you've said—and this was also reported at his trial —that he allowed you all to go to the park, yes?'

'Yes'

'Local parks and shops...the library…cinema…'

'It is true… but no English class…my English…his fault…'

Maisie Small squints, her head shaking in disbelief; she presses forward in her chair so that her face almost smacks the table. 'Your perpetrator imprisoned you— in New Horizons for forty years— why didn't you just leave?'

As Bunchee Golding sips from a glass of water, deep grooves appear on her forehead as if she's considering Maisie's question for the first time… under the melting studio lights. 'I…I don't know,' she falters.

I yell at the television. 'You low-life bi*ch! You loved our home—that's why you didn't leave!' Phlegm dislodges in my throat and I fall into a coughing fit.

The presenter turns to Annie Lederer, the Director of Unchained, proud and sturdy, awaiting her turn.

'Perhaps Annie, you can shed some light on this. The idea that there were opportunities for the women to escape…that they could've left at any time…'

Annie to the rescue. Smart. Confident. A-know-it-all bi**h.

'Yes, Maisie, absolutely….viewers might find it difficult to wrap their head around this; but what we must remember is that the women in the New Horizons cult, of whom Ms Golding was one, were severely traumatised over an inordinately long period of time. We also know that the vast majority of women who lived at New Horizons did indeed summon up enough courage to leave. Many, in fact, did just that. Others simply couldn't for whatever reason. They were, if you like, imprisoned by 'invisible chains' that transcend concepts of "captor" and "captive"… "gaoler" and "gaoled." Each of the women had signed a contract with their perpetrator which bound them to him...'

I scream at the television. 'There was no real contract, you attention-seeking sh*t! We pretended to have one for a laugh!'

Annie continues. 'Our research at Unchained has established that in cases of sexual servitude, as well as in cases of domestic violence, women can be transformed—even strong, assertive women— into zombies who can't think or act for themselves; they're unable to risk individual and group safety by breaking the rules set by their perpetrator. They've been coerced—brainwashed, if you like, into thinking: "This man is more important—much stronger, more capable than I am— his needs and wants are greater than mine: He matters. I don't." Perpetrators, like Ron Partridge, crave compliant women, and if a woman fails to cooperate or is a threat to the survival of the whole group, then she must be punished by him and by the *rest* of the group...'

'Now what you've said there is very interesting. "The rest of the group?" Could you shed some light on what you mean?'

'Some women will also enforce the rules of the cult against non-compliant members so as to escape the risk of punishment from the perpetrator themselves...'

I hurl the television remote at Annie's image. Pieces of plastic break off and disperse like confetti; a large piece bounces back to hit me in the face. A brisk "poof" sound followed by a metallic "pling." The dancing kaleidoscope of colours in the room shuts down to leave me submerged in the gloom of a bottomless pit.

I was there for forty years! Why didn't they ask me?

******

Chapter 11

A jingle of keys tickles the lock before the front door creaks open just as I'm pulling up my pants in Bunchee Golding's bathroom. I'm about to find out if she's brought the authorities with her.

I switch off the bathroom light and leap into the bathtub under a futuristic-looking silver shower head, studded with rivulets. I pull the navy-blue shower curtain halfway across so as not to draw attention to it by drawing it fully across. The shower head leaks tiny droplets and I shiver as the ice cool water dribbles on me. I hold the two collar ends of my shirt together.

I remember that I've left the light on in the living room! Dread fills my chest and I hold my breath, willing my heart to stop beating so fast. The bathroom door's ajar and I can make out muffled voices in the hallway. A high-pitched voice, like that of a hysterical mother reprimanding a child, and a subdued one responding in dull monotone. The voices escalate in pitch as the living room door bursts open, hitting the wall.

'Sometimes, I just don't understand you!' It's Annie sounding incredulous, nurturing a wounded pride through her rebuke.

A contrite-sounding Bunchee Golding replies. 'I try to speak clearly…'

'Not that, you fool!'

'No?'

'All you had to do was to keep it short!'

'Sorry, Annie. I-I do better... next time.'

'There won't be a next time!'

'No?'

'Never again!'

Then the bathroom door slams against the wall, sending a whoosh of air to caress the folds of the shower curtain I'm standing behind, lifting it slightly. I squeeze my eyes shut, sinking them into oblivion. The rustle of acrylic, the tapping of shoes, the steady drizzle of liquid.

'You don't listen…' Annie barks from the toilet seat, '…in front of millions of viewers as well!'

Then the sound of gushing water, a squirt of hand soap, the retreat of snapping heels. The conversation is muffled, and I step out of the bath to find chipped paint near the door. I open the door a fraction of an inch at a time, my ears burning.

Bunchee Golding full of tears. 'I am sorry…I get so confused!'

'Sorry? You fool! Those fu**ing journalists will have a field day trying to make something of this....! Aghhh!' Annie's shriek of impatience cuts through me. 'Don't call me, okay? I mean it... I want you to think about what you've done!'

******

Bunchee Golding is lying prone on the settee, her dough-like face swallowed up by a spongy cushion. Brutus bounds up to his mistress, jumping onto her back. He nuzzles her neck, and on getting no response, follows this up with two neat jabs on the side of her head. On seeing me, his ears prick up instantly, and the overfed beast falls pell-mell to the floor. With slouching shoulders, he scampers off towards the kitchen.

'Why d'you let that sh*thead speak to you like that?' I ask. 'Acting as if she owned this place!' She turns over, her eyes shut, her mouth moving as if in prayer.

'Say something, Bunch! What the hell was she ranting on about?'

'You see interview?' Her tone resonates with a sadness that makes me pay attention. 'I say foolish thing...'

'Fifteen minutes of crummy fame...izzat why you did it?'

Bunchee Golding swallows hard. 'What I say is, on my fiftieth birthday, I have a big celebration. That it is most happy day of my life...'

'So what?'

'I say I have good time in New Horizons; it is the wrong thing to say…'

Her head drops and she lets out a sob. A sign of guilt? Remorse?

My palms are tingling, flecked with tiny crescents, wet and bloody.

'You sent a good man to prison with your f**king lies!'

'I don't know what a good man look like'

'Ron's a good—!' I interrupt to shut her up

'—No, Sylvie...he use me many, many times!'

'Use you?'

'Yes!'

'Liar!'

'Others say same as me. Why we say same thing?'

'You were the only one who gave evidence…what happened there, huh?'

'They change mind…too scared.'

******

I jeer at her. 'You think I went around with my eyes shut? Is that what you're telling me?'

'No. He stop ten years before…before police come...'

With stinging palms, giving off the smell of rusty nails, I thrust my hands under my armpits.

'Fifty is bad age for woman from Thailand like me. We do not look so good. So when I have fifty birthday —oh! Happy day! He does not look at me anymore. Always new girls…girls coming and coming. I pray to my God, Sylvie! I pray that the queue of girls never stop! Yes! I am so happy they come to our door; silly, smiling girls, with their fresh gums and teeth; always "poor me", always need this, need that! They come and they come and they come! And I love them for it! I cook special food. I do their share of work…I put flowers in their hair…make them look nice…smell nice. When Ron is angry with them, I make peace! Always! I know how to make battlefield into rose garden—! I am a... a mother who kiss her child when she fall down!'

******

I stare at her giant forehead that looks as if a garden rake's been drawn through it. Bunchee, the peacemaker! What about my peace of mind? My life's a gaping hole because of her— reduced to rubble in the wake of a tsunami.

But I'm far from done with her. It's lucky I've got the photographs— but it doesn't pay to shout at her, or frighten her. I'm nearly there! I don't want to give her an excuse to bolt down the rabbit hole, to shut out the light forever.

Wait a minute! Something she's said.... I scrutinise her face, tracing the outline of her eyes to confirm the facts.

'You just said you're from Thailand…' I say.

'Yes'

'Since when?'

'What?'

'You've always been Chinese!'

'If you say so.'

******

Chapter 12

Bunchee Golding is sitting at the dining table, staring at the piece of paper. She sucks the lid on the grip roller pen. Her eyes roll back in her head, and she rubs them with her inky thumbs, whimpering all the while. Anyone would think I'd asked her to write her last will and testament! I don't take my eyes off the shiny steel nib between her fingers.

I bring my fist down hard on the table, startling her so that she half falls off her chair. ' "...I, Bunchee Golding, of 37_____ Road will say as follows,"' I say. 'Go on! Read what you've written!'

Her crimson tongue peeps out from the corner of her mouth, her forehead gives off a metallic shine as she takes my dictation at a snail's pace. I help her with spelling and punctuation. I watch her through my fingers, rolling my tongue over the bumpy spaces in my mouth. I flex my aching fingers, flicking the dirt from under my fingernails.

'Ple-ease, Syl-viee! I'm tired!—' she wails, crumpling the paper as she leans forward.

'Your lies put him behind bars,' I say, slapping her off the paper, smoothing it between my fingers before setting it down again. 'So it's only fitting you should set him free.'

'But Annie get mad at me-ee,' she groans, her cheeks grown ripe with grumpiness. She rocks herself back and forth, tapping her feet against the table.

'She's already mad at you,'

'Not mad...'

'She's sent you to Coventry, remember?'

'Oh no, I stay here!'

'Coventry's when you ...oh, forget it!'

'She do... something!'

'Like what?'

'I don't know…' Bunchee Golding plucks back her sleeve to reveal a bruise on her forearm, the size and colour of a Christmas stamp.

'Did that bi*ch do that?' I ask, my nose burning at the sight of it.

Her lips, taut and thin. She doesn't answer.

'I'm afraid!' she cries, her arms flying upwards to indicate her cosy little home complete with fake fireplace, toy chandeliers...and two gaudy samurai swords. 'Annie...she take everything from me...my home...my life.' The quivering lament in her voice, fuelled by fear and uncertainty, sets off a stabbing pain between my ribs. I take a sip of cold coffee...then another... and another.

'Read back what you've written,' I say more kindly, smoothing over the landscape of my hand full of grooves and wrinkles.

She squints at the paper to read her child-like scrawl. Her usual sing-song voice is replaced by a cold and unyielding tone.

'"I, Bunchee Golding, of 37 _____ Road, will say as follows:

I wish to withdraw my former statement against my former landlord, Ronald Ewing Partridge. I made it out of malice and spite—"'

I almost spill my coffee as the sly witch starts stabbing holes through the paper with the grip roller pen. She tears it up, hurling the pieces like confetti. With eyes ablaze, a smirk swinging from the left side of her face, she revels in her act of rebellion.

Then flinging herself down on the settee, she raises her legs like a cockroach on its back, kicking outwards. I push my glasses up and watch half laughing and crying at this miserable display of stupidity. But my body aches, my arms twice their weight, as I've only had a snatch of sleep in the last two days. For all I know, it could be a night of torrential rain outside or a world awash with pale sunshine.

Oh! Inconsequential, foolish, former runaway housewife and illegal alien— Bunchee Golding!

I have plan B. And knowing her as well as I do, I know I can bend her to my will.

******

I tie Bunchee Golding's legs together with a piece of flex I've cut off from the old vacuum cleaner in her bedroom-cum-storeroom. I take out two photographs from my rucksack, and hold them up to her eyes. One shows a slender, beautiful East Asian woman in a silken bathrobe that's fallen open to expose her naked front as she poses with hands on hips. She's wearing dainty white ankle socks. The other shows the same woman naked, slightly crouching with feet apart, arms stretched to one side, showing off the well-delineated muscles of her porcelain white back, brimming with a celestial life force. The figure looks across her shoulder directly into the lens of the camera, her expression jubilant.

Bunchee Golding knocks the photographs out of my hand. 'You enjoy looking at these, Sylvie? Really? –' she says, breaking off; the photographs lie face down on the floor, and on the back of each one, scrawled in blue copperplate writing is the word, "Sarsaparilla". She picks up one of the photographs, tracing the word several times with her fleshy finger, her mouth hanging open. 'Where you find these?' Bunchee Golding murmurs and, much later, looking back on this scene, I believe this was the exact point she started to shut down; her eyes seeing but not seeing, any remnant of hope forever extinguished. I snatch the photograph from her trembling fingers, and scoop up the other one before she can destroy them. I recall many years ago, Ron had caught this sly woman in possession of a secret love letter from a male neighbour, and on being discovered, the reprobate—this very same Bunchee Golding— had stuffed a portion of it into her dainty mouth, chewing like a donkey. But it was me Ron didn't speak to for almost three months.

I wave the photos under her nose, as if they're tantalising sweetmeats. 'Like your parents to see these?' I ask in a bird-like trill, pleased with myself.

She stares at me with pleading eyes, full of apology.

'A journalist friend of mine would *love* to get his hands on these!' I tell her gleefully.

Shutting her eyes, she starts to rock herself, chanting strange words in a guttural voice.

I shake her by the shoulders. 'Snap out of it! You're going to finish this retraction if it's the last thing you do!'

Too tired to argue, she gestures feebly: "You write, I sign," and tosses the pen in my direction, but I miss, and it rolls away under the radiator. By the time I've written the short retraction, the plastic beads on the chandelier are quivering from her tumultuous snores.

She can sign tomorrow.

I clamber into Bunchee Golding's bed, surrounding my head with pillows and her childish toys. I haul the duvet over my head to enjoy the soft embrace of feathered sleep.

******

'The bank will be open now,' I say cheerfully, writing the address of the Appeal Court on a pre-used envelope.

'Bank?'

'Cut it out! We need the money!'

'What money?'

I thrust my face near hers, stabbing her chest with my finger with each syllable. 'Don't ruin my good mood, Bunch!'

'I wish I have money, Sylvie'

With an exaggerated flourish, I hold up one of her bank statements, letting it drop—then another, and another, and another, before throwing the rest of the bundle at her head. 'No money, hah?—so, what's this?' I ask, pointing to the figure of ten thousand pounds. Her eyes flash in temper, her complexion darkens.

'That's private—' she says, trying to snatch the statement from me.

My finger's poised to dial for a taxi. 'What's the address of your bank?'

I have six missed calls from the Glass of Water.

She covers her mouth with a handkerchief, gazing at the blank television screen. 'There's no money,' she whispers hoarsely.

'Cut it out, Bunch!'

'Sylvie—'

'I'm warning you'

'I spend it…'

'You …spend it?' I echo, without realising the full import of her words. She refuses to meet my gaze.

'I spend it…'

'Are you kidding me?'

She reddens, tugging at a loose thread on her sleeve. 'I meet my on-line fiancée….,' she says.

Then unwrapping the flex around her legs, she jumps up to fetch a whole heap of papers kept in a hidden compartment of a writing bureau, as I watch, speechlessly. The bundle, as thick as 'War & Peace,' consists of printed emails.

'You have a computer?' I scream at her. 'Why didn't you—?'

'No more. I throw it away…after this happen, I throw away computer…' I skim through the emails. The one on the top tells me everything I need to know.

It turns out that Bunchee Golding is a victim of an on-line scam. In exchange for a promise of marriage, she has handed over to a perfect stranger, the princely sum of ten thousand pounds.

'I think it is love. But Victor trick me,' she blinks glumly.
'Who the f**k is Victor?'
'My fiancée'

I insert a knuckle in my mouth. 'You gave him...? ...all of it?' She nods sheepishly, avoiding my gaze.

'It funny, you know... I think about him— a man I never meet— But I feel ...real good in here—' she says, thumping her chest with a faraway look in her eyes but stops abruptly when she meets my glare.

'Ah...he's no good. Victor is very bad man, a very bad man...!' I know she doesn't mean it.

I run to the bathroom to throw up.

******

Chapter 13

I can no longer hold a sensible thought in my head. I breathe through my mouth, trying to suppress the flames of desperation that burn through me; being preoccupied with what my voice will sound like, I end up forgetting what I'm going to say. But as soon as I hear his voice, I'm fine again.

'Listen, Nathan' I say. 'How much…?'
'I'd like my bl**dy phone book back...'
'No problem, I've got it right here'
'You've probably—'
'It's here I tell you'
'How much for what, you snake?'
'What?'
'You said "how much…"'
'Ah, yes …how much for my story?
'This is a sudden change of heart,' he scoffs.

He gives me a three-figure sum. It's not enough.

'And Bunchee Golding's …her story?' I ask.

I hear the tapping of a pen against his teeth. 'Let me speak to her...' he says.

'I can vouch for –'

'I have to speak to *her first*,' he insists.

I cover the receiver with my hand, glancing at the snoring woman on the settee; her upper torso hanging down an inch above the floor.

She could be a corpse.

I wait a few seconds.

Do I dare? Should I? It's not as if I'm breaking the law. I've done it before—I've done it so dam*ed well in fact, that people couldn't tell us apart. Not on the phone, anyway.

I speak into the receiver.

'Bunchee Golding on phone. Who you?' I say, imitating the sing-song tone of Bunchee's telephone voice.

A raucous laugh belches out at the other end.

'Are you serious, Sylvie?' Nathan chuckles. 'Did you honestly think—?' and he's laughing so hard, he can't finish his sentence. I put the phone down on the little sh*t!

******

There she goes again. Breathing heavily through her nose.

'Sylvie, I don't have that kind of money,' The Glass says, her voice quivering like a reed in the wind.

'Five thousand then...'

'I don't have money like that...'

'But you...you're always buying stuff!'

'I borrow....from friends; and Sylvie—'

'What?'

'Are you coming to take your stuff?'

'What stuff?'

'The landlord's changing the locks—'

'Scr*w 'em!...make 'em wait!. Kick 'em in the boll**ks! Can you do that for me, Mel? Can you at least do that for me?'

******

'She's still in bed?' Nathan says in surprise when he gets to ours. 'She's had a bad night...' I say, slipping on my rucksack. 'And *don't* give her any money; she's as trustworthy as a snake in the grass—'

His mouth flies open. 'You're not leaving, are you?'

'I'll be five minutes tops—'

He puts up a hand. 'I'd rather you were here!'

'They're chucking me out, Nathan. I'm fu**ed!'

He rolls his eyes, his jaw juts forward making his face appear thin. 'Oh, great!' he says, and his flattened nose spreads even more with the heat of annoyance. He rubs his knuckles together, and surveys the slumbering 'corpse' 'But I'm a stranger —' he says, his face contorting with irritation. 'A stranger in her home!'

'I'll be back in two shakes of a lamb's tail.'

'I'm not...comfortable with this…'

'Don't be such a big girl's blouse, Nathan!'

'Does she even know why I'm here?'

I glare at him until he shifts from one foot to another.

'D'you really think I'd just throw her into something like this without talking to her first? Knowing the fragile state of mind she's in—?

'Fragile state?'

86

'Her car-crash television interview… exposed her to be the liar she is in front of millions of people. Can you imagine what that can do to a person?' I say, heading towards the door.

'That's more reason for you to stay!'

'It's your chance to find out the truth, Nathan. Isn't that what you wanted? Her story?'

And I leave him frowning at the sleeping woman, tugging at his tangled locks, deep in thought.

******

Chapter 14

I'm standing outside the gates of Skylarks behind a mature plane tree; the home I'd grown up in; the front of the house, of moody redbrick, has tall windows where people can look out at the view while nursing cocktails, indulging in talk of cruise holidays, shares and profit margins under the lights of elaborate glass-drop chandeliers. The green tiled roof shimmers like water. The house is surrounded by medium-sized shrubs, and acacia trees while fruit trees edge the skyline; a well-maintained lime green lawn measuring a half an acre runs from the house to the gate; the effect is ruined by an exaggerated, almost comical, curvaceous tarred path, running down its centre, darkly threatening like the snaky tail of the devil. The heavy perfume of tea roses carries through the air. Dribbles of morning dew heat under the warm sun, maddening the bees that glide like tiny parachutes across the erect flower beds.

It's a pouch of comfort and easy living from where I'd made good my escape. Reporters are milling around outside the main gate, chirping like carefree birds, angling their cameras to take photographs of Skylarks.

Then I spot Nathan and, in my alarm, I clutch the plane tree I'm hiding behind! He's chatting to a tall woman with voluminous goth-like hair, with ribbons of green, purple and orange streaming through it. She takes a photograph of the house.

I could scream! I'd only just left him at Bunchee Golding's!

There'll be no interview now…no payment…no High Court Appeal for Ron!

I take myself off around to the back of Skylarks, where a path leads to a bronze gate covered with tangled ivy. I have the key to the gate that I've held onto for over forty years because of its beautiful ornate antiquity. I had hoped to sell it after I'd swiped it, but then couldn't bear to part with its rusty charm.

******

A woman with a neat bun, in a prim collared dress greets me at the gloss-red painted front door. She stares at me when I tell her who I am, dropping her gaze, and widening the door with a curtsied bob. Her mouth is that of a wilful child.

There's a flurry of activity at the main gates, camera shutters clicking away as the journalists see me go inside.

The woman leads me to a sun-drenched room decorated in warm pastel colours; the sun's rays dapple playfully on the floor. The paintings, probably scoured from the prim art galleries in _____ Square, don't have a common design or colour scheme— just random pictures. So very different from how I last remembered the place when my mother was alive. Back then, her paintings had adorned the walls: delicate country scenes, pictures of children with glossy mouths and lollipops, donkey rides along the beach; the glamorous interiors of Lyons tea houses that I remember visiting as a child. And bridges. A bunch of bridges of different shapes and sizes, as if she'd been biding her time, waiting for escape, as if designing the perfect bridge she would one day cross.

I sit on an elegant chaise longue waiting for my father, my rucksack at my feet. The smell of floor polish and disinfectant permeate the air. After fifteen minutes, the door opens and a shaven man, small and stooping, in a blinding white shirt stops momentarily before entering. 'Some lassi, please, Rachel—the way I like it!' His voice is light and spry, as welcoming as a bell. Rachel, the woman who has let me in, stands behind never taking her eyes off him.

'It'll spoil your appetite,' she tells him, as she re-positions her unravelling bun, but he dismisses her with a flick of his hand.

With arms stretched out to each side, my father totters towards me like a toddler taking their first steps. His cumbersome gait surprises me. He stops a foot away, regarding me for what seems like a whole minute, but I remain seated. Rachel closes the door behind her, her mouth pursed tightly.

My father stoops to lightly brush his rough lips against my forehead, and I can feel a little heat in them. I breathe in a mixture of cologne, cigarette ash and curdled milk.

He turns away brusquely as if he's heard a noise from the far side of the room, dabbing his mouth with a handkerchief. He looks around before sitting in an armchair which draws him into the copious folds of fabric; he appears even more shrivelled than ever. The light around his ghost-like form is heightened by his white shirt, and a flurry of snow-white hair; the sight of his skin stretched over his face, like a cadaver, makes me wince.

My stomach tightens, as I recall the long hours of practising piano scales, reading books from fusty old shelves, and listening to tinny music on a Bakelite radio set. All under this roof.

My father tilts his throat and swallows hard as if something is lodged there. 'We thought you were dead, Sylvie,' he rasps. 'We thought he'd buried you out in the countryside in the fashion of American serial killers!' He chuckles amiably, but without any real warmth. I try to recall the sound of his laughter in my youth—but I can't. The sound of a low motorised rumble comes from an adjoining room, a comforting giant bee.

Just then, a child ambles in, curious about the visitor who has come to call. She stops to pull up a wilting sock with one hand. Her crushed velvet crimson dress matches her crimson trainers, and a crimson bow, like a squashed flower, is pasted to the side of her head; tight marmalade curls shake like a cluster of catkins in the wind. She drags behind her what seems to be a dead seagull, but it turns out to be a large piece of drawing paper, the stuff you buy in art shops.

'Say "hello" to your Aunty, Gracie,' my father says, flicking the child lightly on her arm. 'You're a big girl now…going to Mr Bubbles soon...aren't you?'

The child pulls down her chin, sulking. She buries her face in my father's lap, before looking askance at me.

'Let's see what you've drawn, child,' he says encouragingly, ready to take hold of the drawing to get a proper view.

But her curls bounce and sway in defiance. She hums a shapeless tune as she walks away, her picture trailing behind like a rag.

******

'You were a wispy thing with coltish legs when I last saw you, Sylvie,' my father laughs. 'We used to call you "foal"'

'I don't remember,' I say, examining my fingernails.

'You hated it,' he says with a low laugh that sounds stuck between his ribs. 'You said it sounded like "fool",' he laughs more brightly now, and I join in half-heartedly. 'How long has it been?' he asks.

He knows how long it's been.

'Speak up! My hearing isn't what it used to be!'

'I can't recall,' I mutter, gazing down at my hands.

My father sighs and turns on the TV with a remote, turning down the volume, as he'd always done when I was growing up; feeding his compulsion to keep abreast of the ever-changing news. It was as if each news item touched him personally. 'That man of yours has brought those news-vultures to our door...pecking at the same carcass... they've picked it clean...nothing left.' He flicks through the television channels in quick succession.

I feel my chafing face redden. 'His name's Ron—and he's not *my* man.' My father's ghostly gaze nuzzles my features as if he is copying what's there, to later refurbish his own facial marks and lines obliterated over the years.

'He can still make you blush,' says my father, shaking his head in wonder.

I rub my palms along the thighs of my battered camouflage trousers. 'It's good of you... to see me,' I say, shuddering inwardly at my stilted words; to my horror, the hesitation and unevenness in my voice— to my ears at least— resembles the Glass of Water's! I manage to rustle up a smile—with much effort.

'I could hardly turn you away with that rabble outside,' he says. 'They'd tear you to shreds.'

My father's wraith-like head seems to float un-detached above his open shirt collar. He reminds me of a lizard waiting for its prey, his eyes darting from wall to wall but never landing on me.

As we watch the news in silence, a serene smile paddles at each corner of his mouth. 'Well, speak of the devil!' he says, turning up the volume. 'What's he done now?'

A still picture of a scowling man in steel framed glasses and unkempt hair appears on the screen. The red and white banner underneath reads:

"BREAKING NEWS: CONVICTED
CULT LEADER ATTACKED IN PRISON!"

It doesn't sink in, at first, that the man is Ron as I've never seen him wearing glasses before.

A knot forms in my stomach at the same time a high-pitched noise detonates my ears. I crane forward to listen.

The silver-haired news reporter, Jonathan Pickles, is speaking to camera outside an ominous looking building with turrets and a heavy castle-like door. The reporter's feverish speech, like the quick-fire of artillery, at that moment, spills over into every living room up and down the country.

'... it's thought that Partridge suffered a suspected heart attack after being treated for a hand injury inflicted by another inmate— and this only after three days into his jail term for operating this country's longest surviving sex cult by an individual. And most people will remember ...Her Ladyship Judge Hollerton...the sentencing judge, in that case, who has courted much controversy by her remarks when she said, amongst other things, that she would very much like to have been a fly on the wall for each and every day that Ron Partridge serves his prison term. We understand that she has since apologised for her remarks, but has been ordered to appear before the Judicial...'

My father stirs in his chair, now alert. 'We've had enough of that scoundrel, haven't we?' He 'wands' the remote at the television that turns black at once. 'And that's just the judge! Ha! Ha!' He slaps his thigh and straightens up. 'How the mighty have fallen...he's not aged very well, has he?'

The remote slips from my father's hand and clatters onto a side table. 'Ah! The old grip's not what it used to be!' He looks at his lap, at each crease and every fold, as if the answer to a larger unasked question, solid and impregnable, lies there.

After a long pause, we talk about a whole jumble of things as you would when waiting on the station platform with a stranger: the cost of living, road traffic conditions, and the weather. He asks if I still read the Romantics, keep up with my piano playing, and I say, 'When I can,' to both. A woman in a white apron, and squeaky shoes, brings in a jug of creamy liquid and two tall glasses. She pours and carefully places one in my father's hand, leaving the other near my elbow. I take a sip of the cool, salty liquid. Its pungent, acidic taste, and a hint of spice kicks the back of my throat.

My father measures six spoonfuls of sugar, and stirs it slowly into his drink. 'It's a drink you had when you were here—remember? Your mother's recipe.' He beams proudly as if mother's there with us.

* * * * * *

"'I've never been able to work out why some people prefer to swap their palace for a ditch,' says my father. His eyes are moist, and I can't decide whether this is due to a medical condition or he's experiencing a pang of emotion.

'Please Dad.'
'Got a roof over your head?'
'I'm with a... friend.'
'Good friend, is she?'

'I suppose…'

'Where d'you meet her?'

'On the high street…she's with… the church'

'And what were you doing?'

'I was…um… shopping…'

He has a trace of a milk moustache. 'You've never made friends easily…'

I rub my upper lip. 'I prefer my own company…'

He grins. 'So you end up joining a cult…?'

'It wasn't like that…'

His eyes narrow as he mops his brow with the handkerchief. As he takes a long sip from his glass, his Adam's apple bobs up and down until the last drop.

'So what's brought you to our door, Sylvie?' he asks, 'after all this time?' I sense the wound he still carries, a deep chasm that's never healed since I first broke from him. 'No bull**itting, now!' His fingers drum lightly on the armrest of his chair.

'We're in trouble, Dad,' I croak, and I feel two spots of heat warming each cheek. Da**nit! My voice is *so* feeble!

'We?'

'No... actually… just me. I need some money, you see…'

I run my finger round the rim of my lassi glass until it squeaks. I root around for a plausible reason, but my mind goes blank, and I run my tongue over my teeth. 'My teeth, Dad, um…they're not in good shape—'

'Ah! All rotten are they?'

'They need attention'

'Rotten to the core!' As he raises his glass suddenly, silver sparks of saliva fly from his mouth, forcing me to lean to one side. His skeletal head pushes forward as if he's a jockey in the final straight of a race.

I can't think of anything to say. 'Is this a ruse?' he asks.

'Ruse?'

'The two of you in it together?'

'No, Dad—'

'I've been sending you money for years— I used to receive your dental plans... he sent me bills for your eye- check-ups.'

'I …didn't always go…I've a phobia of the dentist,' I say, baffled, at his saying he's done stuff when he hasn't. Or maybe he's confused—perhaps he meant to send money but never did.

'He did tell you I sent it?'

'Sure he did.'

'And my letters?'

'Uh-huh' I say, completely perplexed.

'Look, why don't you bill your fella at His Majesty's Pleasure? He's sure to have a secret fund stashed away with all that money I've sent him…'

******

My father slaps his bony thighs, and crows like a defiant rooster, before he's overcome by a fit of coughing that threatens to turn his lungs inside out.

'Uh-wagh-wagh-wagh!'

I jump up in alarm, and at the same time Rachel comes flying through the door, nearly falling over herself, but he 'shoos' her away. 'Can't you see I'm in conference with my daughter?' With a heaving chest, recovering between coughs, he points for me to sit down.

Rachel throws me an apologetic look before promptly leaving the room. It dawns on me that she's been sitting outside the whole time!

'How much will it cost?'

'It all depends on what needs fixing,' I say. Perhaps there's a glimmer of a chance of getting something, otherwise he wouldn't be asking.

'What does the expert say?'

'Expert?'

'You've got to have your teeth assessed properly,' my father says in a raised voice, leaning forward. 'Otherwise, it could run into thousands!'

I shrug my shoulders.

With hands resting on each armrest, my father thrusts his right forefinger at me in an accusatory manner.

'There's an awful lot of rot in there, my girl!' he says. 'All rotten!'

Then this p*xy little man with a mean little mouth, his haunches pared to the bone, nestles back into his chair, his eyes drooping as he rocks himself to sleep.

Rachel comes in, a knot stamped between her brows. She thumps the light switch with her fist. 'You've been overdoing it again, Dad,' she admonishes; his face under the strong glare of the lights takes on a different complexion: a murky olive brown.

'Nurse!' he mumbles. 'Where's nurse? I need nurse!' demands my father in a peevish voice, without opening his eyes. Rachel stoops to half-wrestle, half-heave him up from his seat; and during these arduous manoeuvres, she swivels her head from side to side to look at me. I don't know if she wants me to help her or not, so I stay as I am.

'I'm sorry…it's time for his nap,' she says, gasping, irritated.

The door closes behind them and she's gone. With my father–not hers!

******

A woman, in her late-fifties, with a strong streak of white hair in a thicket of grey-black hair, is dusting in the next room as if her life depends on it. She's oblivious to my presence as she sprays, scrubs and polishes; a cleaning trolley in the middle of the room is filled with an army of household cleaning products. A hoover is plugged into a socket near the far wall…waiting. As she straightens several cushions, her eyes widen on seeing me.

'I hope he pays you well,' I say, covering my nose from the pungent smell of furniture polish.

'Ha, that's what my daughter says,' she says with uncertainty at the joke against her employer. I can't place her accent. Swedish? Italian?

We have an in-depth discussion about the skills required for polishing silver, how they shine best after a good soak in washing powder. She tells me her name's Iñez and that she's been cleaning for my father for thirty years, supporting her only child at college, all the while polishing as if her arm is set in perpetual motion after years of habitual rubbing.

'Did you know…my mother?' I ask.

She looks away and shakes her duster from where the dust flies everywhere. 'Your mother?'

'Alice DaSouza…from Sussex…'

'Alice….' she says, savouring the name as if this helps her to remember. 'Ah! Miss Alice! She was very good to me...very kind...' She stares at me, her smile evaporating.

'Do you know where her paintings are?' I ask.

'Paintings?'

'My mother was a painter...'

'Ah, yes. They're in the gallery.'

'I thought perhaps my father had sold them,' I say.

The housekeeper shakes her head vehemently. 'Oh, no, he would never do that, Miss Sylvie!' she says, thumping a cushion into shape, placing it down and stepping back to judge the effect.

I wouldn't put it past the old miser, the tight-fisted s*d. No wonder people turn to crime! Just then, a jaunty little song pops into my head.

"In this life, one thing counts
In the bank, large amounts,
I'm afraid these don't grow on trees,
You've got to pick-a-pocket or two!"

******

Gracie ambles in, clutching a felt tip pen. Still trailing a sheet of art paper behind her, but now reduced to half its original size. On noticing me, the child's fat ringlets quake about her face, and she gazes wistfully at my father's empty chair. Her lips move to speak but nothing comes out; it looks as if she's nibbling an invisible biscuit. The bow in her hair from earlier has vanished, and her ringlets are bunched up on the left side of her head.

'Hello, little boy!' I say as a joke.

Gracie looks up, grinning, revealing dainty teeth in piping-pink gums. 'I'm not a boy, I'm a girl, silly!' she gurgles sweetly.

'Can I see your drawing?'

The child stands on one foot, craning forward as if she means to reach the floor. 'It's for Grandfather.' She pulls up her sagging sock.

'Oh, he won't mind.'

'But you're a stranger,' she lisps.

I spend the next few minutes trying to coax the little sh*t to let me see what she's drawn, leaning across several times to rumple her shi**y little ringlets with a friendly flick of my fingers.

But Gracie holds her artwork firmly behind her, her tongue rolling around in her mouth like a piece of strawberry. She enjoys the hold she has over me. The veins in my temple start to throb. I look across to the far side of the room to where Iñez is wiping down the furniture with a cloth duster. Then I remember the bauble from Unchained, and take it out of my trouser pocket with a flourish.

'Look what I've got,' I whisper, and her eyes widen instantly.

'Ooh!' she breathes, her eyes glued to the sparkling object. 'What is it?' she says with a trace of a lisp.

'It's a badge—made of pirate's gold!'

'Ooh!'

I dangle the badge over her nose that makes her look cross-eyed. 'How about you have this, yeah... for a peek at your picture?' Gracie turns to the house cleaner who has entered pushing a purring hoover.

A cold drop of sweat runs down my back, and I can't for the life of me understand my strange compulsion to see her darned picture! 'Here's a woman's face — look!' I say, holding out the badge.

The child's curiosity gets the better of her, and she inches her way towards my extended hand as if she's a hostage being released to safety.

'Unh-unh!' I warn her. 'First... the picture!' But the child doesn't understand the concept of the transaction—and her tongue pokes out as she continues to shuffle closer to the badge. As soon as she's within reach, a surge of electricity passes between us in a brief skirmish of knuckles. Her hand draws back as if bitten, her lower lip protruding as if she doesn't know whether to laugh or cry.

I hungrily unfold the picture on the coffee table. It shows a crude stick figure of a woman drawn in brown crayon, with two large black dots for breasts that are out of proportion with the rest of the small body. The woman's face is long and thin. Red and purple-brown flecks adorn her face, resembling blotches. She has a campfire of pink hair and a gaping hole for a mouth filled with black crayon, giving the expression of perpetual surprise.

'Who's this supposed to be?' I ask in an abrupt tone. Gracie shakes her head slowly and sucks the top of her felt tip pen. I seize the pen from her which accidentally catches her teeth, eliciting a puny cry. 'Oww!' The child rubs her mouth, glaring at me.

'Shall we write her name, here?' I point with the pen. 'Say... over here? Near her head?'

'I can't spell.'

'Well, you tell me the name, and I'll figure it out.'

After thinking about this, she produces a harsh, guttural sound. 'A –haw,' she says with uncertainty.

'A what?'

'A –hawwr'

'...a horse? Say it again—slowly!'

'A—hawwr,' she presses forward, one foot over the other.

A man's voice thunders above our heads. 'Gracie!' The child stumbles forward, and I jump up from my seat to face the man who is glaring at us.

'Please, don't,' he says curtly, scooping up the picture, which he crumples up into a tight ball and throws into a wastepaper bin.

The man, fiftyish and on the verge of fatness, appears as flustered and tetchy as when I'd last seen him. The man in a serge suit from whom I'd stolen Ron's sentencing report when we were both in the public gallery at the Very Important Court— although I hadn't recognised him at the time.

My brother—Richard DaSouza! He's ten years younger than me. Dickie. Tricky Dickie.

'Buzz off, go play with Iñez,' says Dickie, twisting Gracie's shoulders in the direction of Iñez who holds her arms out towards the child. 'Ay! Come here, niña Your Uncle's busy,' calls Iñez.

'My badge!' cries Gracie, her mouth pouting like a pink bloom.

'No badge,' I put up my hands, turning them over. 'See?'

'It's in her pocket!' the child whines. She looks at her uncle as if he should retrieve it at once.

'I said I'd buy her a badge...*buy* her one,' I explain.

'Her mother won't let her wear anything that's sharp' says Dickie.

'You can't mollycoddle her forever,' I say brusquely, remembering an unhappy childhood when I had been stymied at every turn: where the world was fraught with danger, where 'nasty people' lurked in shadows waiting to make off with me.

Tricky Dickie scoffs. 'She's not yet four.'

His jawline hardens; there's not a single crease or furrow on him, and I wonder if he's had Botox. With hands on hips, his long, well-built torso bending over the child, he says: 'If you're good, I'll read you a story later. Alright?' He tousles her hair, slapping her lightly across the back of her legs. He chants playfully: 'Five...four...three..' and on cue, as if they've done this many times before, Gracie outstretches her arms like a plane, screeching—'Three, two, one!'

A droning spitfire, she catapults herself into the adjacent room.

'Nee-yawwwwwwwww!'

My brother paces up and down like a burly bear in a cage as he makes brisk conversation. Dickie tells me that he's followed our father into the law, but in Wills and Probate.

I try to suppress a yawn. 'That's nice,' I say.

He hasn't met the right woman to settle down with and feels that he's left it a bit late. The years of separation between us makes it difficult to sympathise with him. Who cares about settling down? I want to tell him: 'Travel the world, have an adventure— get a disease! Help people without charging them—better still—be a volunteer!' But I don't.

He 'fills me in' with the drone of a man giving dictation. Gracie is the housekeeper's, Rachel's daughter. Rachel is separated from Gracie's father, and has a live-in job looking after our father. 'Rachel's an angel—an absolute treasure. She calls him "Dad." Dad dotes on them.' He looks up at me as if I might mind. But I'm too engrossed by the resplendent grandfather clock in the far corner of the room, its shiny face encased in bright rosy wood that gleams with Pledge.

'What are your plans?' my nosy brother asks. 'Now that he's...no more with us.'

'Who?'

'That Partridge fellow'

'He has a name and he's not dead.'

He smirks boldly, wiping his hands with a handkerchief. 'I saw that toe rag just the other day, protesting his innocence—causing the most unsavoury uproar in court with his antics.'

My chest tightens and I glare at him. The right side of my forehead starts to throb again, and I soothe the pain with my fingers. My skin starts to itch.

'He was set up by a bunch of women'

'You would say that—he's your boyfriend.'

'Did you see the alleged "victim's" interview the other night?...enjoying her birthday celebrations, having fun? That said it all, wouldn't you say?...'

Richard scratches his nose, swallowing hard. 'I did see it,' he says 'It was the most appalling thing I'd ever listened to...'

'It's all a matter of what you want to see,' I say, starting to feel bored. I wasn't going to change his opinion. I take out my phone and check for messages.

'It's so...awkward. With you here...the press outside,' says Dickie, loosening his tie from his squat neck.

'It'll be more awkward when I give them my story,' I say. His piggy eyes scrutinise my face to see if I'm bluffing.

'Do I have to spell it out, Sylvie? It's embarrassing having a sister who's lived in a sex cult all her—'

'You don't know anything about it,'

'You can't just show up—'

'I'm here, aren't I?'

'Do you honestly know what you've—?'

'I'm sure you're going to tell me!'

'My mother died of a broken heart because of you! But at least you did the decent thing and didn't come to the funeral!'

'*Our* mother,' I correct him, 'died of cancer. And I didn't come to the funeral because nobody bl**dy well bothered to tell me.'

Dickie's face turns a crimson shade. The crunch of gritted teeth.

'Liar! We sent letters...but there was... there was nothing from you...not even a wreath!'

'My ar*e, you did!' I say, looking at him squarely in the face, preparing to wrestle with him if necessary. 'You didn't want me there!'

My phone vibrates. Nathan's text message reads: 'When are you coming out?'

He had seen me go into the house!

'And *he* doesn't want you here either,' says my brother.

'Who doesn't?'

'My father'

'*Our* father,' I say, 'was pretty welcoming just now.'

Two white dots of foam boil at each corner of his mouth, as he warms to his theme. 'He could never rise above a circuit judge because of you!'

I circle a hand over my head to indicate the walls, floor and ceiling. 'He seems to have done alright for himself,' I say.

'Wherever he went he was mocked...ridiculed...'

'Have you ever tried getting counselling, Dickie?' I screw up my eyes and force a smile. 'You might find it helpful!'

'It's money, isn't it?'

'What?'

'You're after a share… in all this!'

'I don't want anything from you,' I say, flustered.

His voice is stern, but pleading. 'Just leave him alone, Sylvie! Leave *us* alone!'

A frosty chill descends and at that moment, Gracie comes running in pursued by Iñez, but Dickie motions them away. Grabbing my rucksack, I make my way to a flight of stairs, placing my hand on the bannister, ready to mount. He calls after me, his voice trembling, coated with hysteria. 'Where are you going?'

'I'm going to see my old room...'

He flounders, rooted to the spot. 'Your old room?'

I swivel my head in his direction, 'I'll be ten minutes. Then you'll never hear from me again.'

The muscles in his face relax, and the tight knot between his brows, making him appear fierce, unknots itself; his flinty eyes soften, his shallow breathing evens out.

'You promise?' My brother sounds like a small boy holding you to a promise of a sweet or a toy. I ignore him and with wide, staunch steps, I make my way up the stairs. I hear Gracie—the child-artist of nudes—making an earth-shattering roar of a plane:

'Nee- yawwwww!'—eventually tailing off at the same time as the clatter of her tiny heels comes to a halt.

'Uncle? Has the naughty lady gone?'

'Not now, Gracie.'

'What's a cereal killer?'

[intentional?]

******

As I race through a series of rooms and connecting doors, I sense a supernatural presence guiding me, propelling me forward through space and time. It's as if I'm a ghost on autopilot: I know where I am. As I enter a door leading to a long corridor, everything unfamiliar becomes familiar—just the same as it was forty years ago: a dent on the silver doorknob as small as the tip of your finger, a missing screw in the keyhole, a piece of wood that's been gouged out near the bottom half. It's all as I remembered it despite the change of colour schemes.

Skylarks is a beautiful snowball of soft, plush carpets, ornate furnishings and rich drapes that you find in television dramas. I make my way to my former bedroom. The walls are light pink, reminiscent of an indigestion tonic I used to drink as a child. My former bedroom has been turned into a simple office space, with a self-assembled desk and chair. Filing cabinets line one wall while the other walls are crammed from wall to ceiling with my mother's artwork – beach scenes, scenes from the country, the Lyons tea shop— and some one hundred or so bridges—of every conceivable shape and size. In the centre of the farthest wall, a picture labelled "Sylvie," the size of a cornflakes packet, depicts the outline of a woman's face with hair; her complexion is of varying shades of pink and red-brown. There are no features—her future's still burgeoning, still incomplete. 'Sylvie,' has no nose—no mouth— so she isn't breathing.

******

The door that used to be my parents' bedroom stands ajar like an unclosed matchbook. I peer into the room and can make out a white chair, luxurious tapestries, and a fairy-tale four poster-bed draped in pink satin sashes and large purple bows.

'Let's get the pillows up a bit more, Nurse', says Rachel fussing around a woman in her forties who is lying propped up against a cloud of pillows, enclosing her on all sides; her nightshirt is pulled down to expose her magnificent strong throat, as white as a summer swan's. She's clutching what appears to be an untidy bundle of rags to her bosom. On closer inspection I discover she's holding a child swaddled in a blanket, making sucking noises! I surmise that it must be Gracie's younger brother or sister, but why is 'Nurse' suckling the child, and not Rachel? But this 'child' has the same girth and bulk as a commercial sack of potatoes—and is much larger than a child requiring this type of nourishment.

'Nurse,' flicks dirt from underneath her fingernails on one hand, and with the other, she strokes a small, delicate head topped with a mountain of hair resembling unruly white feathers. I recognise the woman as the one who had earlier served the drinks of lassi. 'Three minutes,' announces Nurse, as if timing an egg. I tiptoe further into the room, pulled in by an irresistible curiosity to learn why such a bulky child, clearly at an advanced stage of development—perhaps aged ten or twelve— should still be feeding at its nurse's breast.

Then I realise what I'm looking at! I cover my mouth, stumbling back, chewing my knuckle to stop myself crying out. My head nearly strikes the floor as my body flops forward, dry-retching until my sides hurt.

'Is it coming through, sweetie pie? Goob-boy!' says 'Nurse.' Her mouth puckers up tenderly as with two fingers she draws back the nipple to increase suction for the tight-fitting mouth that gorges on it, sucking mechanically, pulling furiously.

'Not too much, Bev,' says Rachel. 'All that lassi never agrees with him!'

With shaky legs, I flutter further forward; the taste of creamy-vomit floats to the top of my throat, and I'm on the verge of heaving my stomach contents onto the plush, emerald-green patterned carpet.

I pounce on a startled Rachel, taking hold of her arm. She swipes me with a pillow, yanking her arm away, before rubbing at the red patch that's shaped like fingers on her arm. 'What the fu*k is this?' I demand. 'What the f**k are you doing to my father?'

On realising it's me, her hand flies up in front of her face as if she expects me to strike her. 'Sylvie...Sylvie,' says Rachel soothingly, while "Nurse" tries to cover up, tugging at the bedclothes, and tucking them around and over my father's head as if he were a secret treasure. I roar at them. 'He's a grown man—you pair of bas**rds!'

'Please ....you're getting worked up...' says Rachel, smoothing her hair that's come undone, pulling at the collar of her dress.

'If I hadn't seen this—perversion with my own eyes, I'd never have believed it—'

'There's nothing perverse about it, Sylvie,' Rachel says gently,

'I'm sorry you've had to —'

'What can explain this...this?' I break off to dry-retch again, leaning against a dressing table full of spray canisters and bottles with beautiful ornate tops.

Rachel's eyes, wide and beseeching, swivel between me and my father, her pretty mouth askew. Her tone is serious and matter-of-fact.

'We...we do this twice a week....it's nutritious...he's rarely ill ...'

It's like I've been coshed on the back of the head.

'We? Who's we? No! No! Don't tell me *you*—ohhh...oohh!' I clutch my head as a strong drizzle escapes my throat and splashes onto the floor.

'Get her out! She's curdling the milk,' barks 'Nurse' before switching to baby talk: 'Is Papa getting all upset? Is that naughty woman disturbing Papa?' My father's mouth works even harder, pulling on the prominent nipple, his concave cheeks, drawing in and out like a suction pump...in blissful oblivion.

'Has he got a choice in this?' I bawl at them. 'Or are you satisfying your own twisted needs? I've known perverted women like you!'

I graze my arm against the bannister before flying out the front door, my knees weak and wobbly, my rucksack dragging behind me, catching my feet...

******

Chapter 15

The lawns and gardens appear less verdant and picturesque than when I'd first arrived. My rapid breathing clouds over my spectacles, blinding me, so I have to take them off. With palms pressing down on each collapsing knee, bent double, a mess of bubbly saffron-infused liquid shoots from my nostrils and mouth, sprinkling the ground. I will my trembling legs to stand, dragging myself to the back gate, veering into the path of small trees and bushes as tears stream down my face. I locate the Glass of Water's number in my phone to tell her to pick me up as I don't have sufficient sensible language to phone for a taxi; they wouldn't understand my garbled words. I realise I don't have sufficient sensible language for the Glass either, so I'm forced to hang up when she says, "Hello." I try sending a text, but my hands are too numb to hold the god**mned phone!

******

Nathan's flattened nose—the fleshy bits that still have a bit of life in them— screws up when he sees me.

'You look as if you need a stiff drink,' he says. I'm glad to see a familiar face even if it's his. He keeps peering at me which annoys me, as I have to look at that nose of his, askew on his face. I imagine his home to be a cold, lonely bedsitter. One kettle, a mug and a cooking pot. One knife, one fork.

Then I remember Bunchee Golding. 'Why are you even here? You said you'd—' I break off in exasperation.

'I'll explain in a minute,' he says, not meeting my gaze.

As I trail behind him, visions of a woman's firm, plump teat jiggling on a pillow, the cheeks of my father—sucking gleefully— churn through my mind, tightening my stomach. I send Bunchee Golding a text message: "Phone you later, shan't be long."

Looking back, I wish I hadn't swiped Rosemarie Whittington's mobile phone. Bunchee Golding's only friend. She might have had a sporting chance. But hindsight is a gift we don't have until we are in full possession of the facts. My excuse—and it's one I repeat for the rest of my life— to keep my mind from being dislodged into the realms of snakes and insanity—is that I DID NOT KNOW! I am filled with embarrassment, shame and regret in the moment I learned that I had let her down. Who would ever trust me again? I wouldn't. But that comes later.

******

The Tawny Owl pub is a sound construction of oak beams and joists, with deep recesses where people can sit opposite each other, without being seen by hateful husbands and nagging wives.

I refuse Nathan's offer of a drink and watch him order a couple of drinks for himself at the bar. I notice two fine scratches under his left eye. 'Sure you don't want anything?' he asks.

I shake my head, and wonder what people do in a pub when they come in: stand near the bar? Go upstairs for privacy, or head outside to let off steam in the sun-filled gardens.

'We can sit over there, if you like,' says Nathan motioning with his drinks. He leads me to a table for four, three tables from where a couple sits with their drinks. A woman with glossy tangerine lips, lowers her voice as we ease ourselves into our seats, giggling at us from behind a roguish hand. Her male companion offers her a menu which she dismisses with her hand. The man wears a black leather jacket, the collar at the nape dampened with sweat. My back is against the couple which unnerves me as Nathan continues to observe them over my shoulder. His eyes light up whenever the pair does something to amuse him; at one point he brings up his glass to salute them, a big grin on his face.

'D'you know them?' I ask coldly. Nathan shakes his head.

My phone vibrates up my leg. Bunchee Golding has sent me a text: 'When you back?'

Nathan passes me a packet of crisps which I tear open and devour like a starved wolf. I sense his eyes crawling over me in wonder, so I slow down.

Nathan indicates the two drinks with his head. 'Want one?'

I tap the crisp packet on the table, and with the crumbs gathered in one corner, I slide them into my mouth. 'I don't drink,' I say with my mouth full.

'Tell me what you think of this,' and with inky fingers, he pushes the coaster with his drink on it towards the centre of the table. When I screw up my face and shake my head, he pushes the glass more vigorously under my nose. I can't take my eyes off the mass of froth, floating like scum. The gassy bubbles sprinkle my glasses, dance up my nose, crisp and cleansing, to provoke a sneeze which amuses him. The acrid taste makes my lips swell on touch. I don't enjoy it, but I continue to sip because it's high time that I opened myself up to different kinds of experiences. But the absence of any lower front teeth makes the liquid seep out, and I dab my mouth with my fingers. 'I need a go**amn straw,' I say, irritably. Nathan doesn't hear as his eyes are too busy communing with the couple to respond; his lips crack open to reveal strong white teeth, and he throws his head back once or twice as if he's enjoying himself.

'Sip it slowly, not all at once,' he says to me.

The barman, now joined by other bar staff, is taking a steady stream of orders. That side of the bar is busier as it leads to a garden at the back of the pub.

Nathan points to the scratches under his eyes, his good mood gone.

'See that?' he announces simply. 'Your friend did that.'

'What friend?'

'Bunchee Golding.'

'She did what?'

'Would you want to wake up to find a strange man in your home?' He continues gloomily, scowling into his hand. 'No sooner than you'd left, she wakes up and starts squawking like I'm about to scalp her. S**t, man! And when I tell her I'm a journalist, and what I'm there for— she goes apes*it – just lunges at me like a tigress—see, here?' He shows me the underside of his left wrist where a purple abrasion surrounded by scuffed up skin shows through. 'You didn't tell her I was coming, did you?'

I shrug my shoulders, blowing the froth on my beer, enjoying the way the velvety sheen rises like a scrap of creamy material.

'...going on and on about some photographs or what-not, wanting to know where they'd got to. Jeez! And every time I…I tried to calm her down, she kept taking a swing at me!'

'Photographs?'

'...and she said to tell you: "Tell the bi*ch I'm not signing anything." And by this time, I'd had enough…so I left.'

'Liar!' I said. 'She probably said, "Tell bi*ch, I no sign nothing!" Not the way *you* said it!' I wet my fingers with beer and flick them at him. 'You promised to wait until I—'

'And you said—' he says accusingly, 'you'd only be a few minutes...' He wipes the beer off. We sip our dinks slowly, simmering like a couple of boiling pans. After a long pause he asks, 'So what did your father say?'

'I don't know why you bother with them,' I say, rapping the table sharply. 'They'll never talk. His mind's turned all...mushy.'

'That's sad,' he says gazing up at the ancient beams. 'You were unsteady on your feet ...I thought you'd been shot—'

I carry on drinking.

'Hey...' says Nathan with excitement as if he's remembered something. He pulls out a creased piece of paper from his wallet and lays it on the table. 'See the date?'

What he says doesn't interest me in the least, so I turn to look at the vintage black and white framed pictures on the pub walls, that show men in top hats and frock coats, women in hooped dresses carrying parasols; in another, carriage-drawn horses are lined up outside a railway station.

'It's a report about your father...he was brought up before the Bar Council for urinating in a lay-by and lying about it. There's a line about you—: "...his daughter, Sylvie DaSouza, aged nineteen, disappeared while attending university, launching a police hunt involving more than a two hundred police officers and volunteers'

Swabbing the crisp crumbs on the table with my forefinger, I pop them into my mouth. Nathan draws his long, inky fingers through his mass of curly hair before returning the newspaper clipping inside his wallet, a casualty of my indifference.

'What made you leave home...without telling anyone?' he asks.

He sighs in exasperation when I remain silent.

'Is a family reunion in the offing?' he ventures again.

'My brother and I butt heads too much,' I say, surprised at myself for sharing this with him. 'He's sh*t-scared about his inheritance...'

'So, in time ...you could be rich.'

'I don't need my father's money,' I say, trying to keep the sourness out of my voice. 'I've always managed without him.'

Nathan shrugs his shoulders, and throws a sly look in the direction of the couple behind me, his tongue resting on his upper lip, his nose with no life in it at all. I look behind me, to see Tangerine Lips still chatting s**t, cackling hard, as she flicks strands of hair from her face, exposing her smooth white neck. I push my glasses up my nose.

A group of people enter the pub, peering at their mobiles, carefree and laughing; they look at each other squarely in the face, interested and engaged; or they gaze into their partner's eyes; stroking hands, clutching wrists, pushing and prodding as if everything's a game, getting up close... and enjoying the company of the group. It comes so naturally.

I rap the table to get Nathan's attention.

He jerks back in his chair.

'You left Bunchee Golding to follow me, to spy on me.'

'You used me to babysit her...!'

'I can see you for what you are...you lowlife'

'You can't see jacks**t!' he scoffs.

I glare at him, brushing off the crumbs on my chest with fingertips stained with red chilli.

After a pause, he says with impatience. 'Oh, come off it, Sylvie! Forty years of living together, breathing, eating, sleeping... and you never saw anything—?'

'Oh, here we go again!' I want to take a swipe at him, but my legs are like a pair of logs that have fallen across each other. I take a swig of beer, instead.

My eyes begin to droop, and I stifle a yawn. My legs, sprawled under the table, brush against his feet to which he says "sorry." With eyes shut, I see sperm-like tails encased in a pink-jellied haze, swimming in all directions. I feel pleasant and warm inside.

'Are you alright?' he asks but I don't answer. Picking up his mobile he shoves it into his pocket and gets up muttering something I don't catch. 'Don't get into mischief,' he says as he walks away.

******

A shooting pain stabs my eyes that are awash with tears. I wipe them away and look at my phone. Several messages from Melanie

MELANIE: Are you okay?
MELANIE: Where are you?
ME: Have we got anywhere to move to?
MELANIE: I'm going to my parents
ME: Can I tag along?
MELANIE: They say 'no'—sorry.
ME: I might stay at a friend's

MELANIE: Great news!

I look around to see if I can spot Nathan. Tangerine Lips isn't there either, and her leathered-up boyfriend's swiping his mobile screen with a little finger that's distinctly curved. His hair is curly but not as abundant as Nathan's. Next to the man's elbow is a near-full abandoned glass of beer which makes my heart flutter, my mouth water. I approach him nonchalantly in the fashion of one stretching their legs...a leisurely little saunter…

'Want that?' I ask but he doesn't hear me as it's grown far noisier now than when we first came in. I carry off the glass of beer to my own table and down it as if I've been doing it all my life. I press the empty glass into the hands of a passing bar staff. Wiping my mouth with my sleeve, I ask the youngster to fetch me another. He's on the point of refusing when I hold out my taxi fare for the journey home. 'Keep the change', I say, sounding clear and confident as they do in American films.

'Yessum,' says the boy.

'Bring it in ten minutes.'

'Yessum'

I squint at the pub clock which I can't see as my glasses have stopped working.

I'm finding my way in the world. Me. In here. By myself. Who'd have thought?

******

'....How about a "hello?" at least....huh? What's your problem? Okay, I get that you don't want to talk. But a conversation's supposed to be a two–way thing—but it's okay— I'll do the talking.' No response.

'Can you guess where I am?... Hear that?... music…clinking of glasses? I'm out carousing!'

A low mutter from her end.

'I'm checking in on you...because I care! I care! I care! I care! As you're all alone, and so one of us must...care. Listen up! Here's the deal...I'm getting evicted... so I'm gonna come live with you, Bunch... yeah? Wodge yer think?' Not a murmur.

'It'll be just like in the good old days! Just you and me! That's alright— you don't have to sing it from the rooftops!' The sound of sniffing and blubbering now.

'Oh, Gah-add! Wodge-yer crying for? Wait a minute—is there someone with you?

...I know you, you bi*ch! You've called the police ...you or that Annie Boll**ks fellah!...but let me tell you something...you owe me big time...it's all your bl**dy fault that I've got no place to stay! All them lies...wodge yer go do that for? You what? What's that supposed—? Are you threatening me, Bunchee Golding? Don't go putting your evil eye on me! Die bi*ch! Die!'

The phone cuts out. Bubbles are percolating in my head, and the resulting burp clears my ears.

Some of the patrons are peering at me over their drinks, some smirking at their neighbour while others shake their heads with looks of pity. A bearded man raises his glass in my direction. 'You tell 'em, love!' he says.

******

The pub clock says it's later than it was the last time.

I slam the table when Nathan gets back. I place my phone next to my empty beer glass.

'Nathan! That was *the* long-gest s*it ever! Were you kidnapped by aliens or something—?' He avoids my glare, rubbing his glistening face with a tissue; his shirt's hanging out, his curly locks flattened on one side, a burr bush on the other.

I'm in a pretty good mood. He looks exhausted from showing me how to have a good time.

'Guess what?'

'What?'

'She's willing to give you her story'

'Cut it out,' he says with irritation, smoothing his hair with both hands. 'No...not after what happened....'

'I've just spoken to her, Nate... it took a lot of convincing, but I managed to turn it around. She's sorry she bashed you....'

He snorts in disbelief. 'She's done enough interviews for now,' he says tucking in his shirt, smoothing out the creases. He 'brushes' his front teeth with his forefinger and makes strange shapes with his mouth like the ghostly figure in Munch's painting. I can't help looking at his squashed nose.

As I hold up an old text from Bunchee Golding, his forehead furrows in thought as he reads it.

"BUNCHEE: I want to tell my story please, Sylvie," reads the text.

'That could be days old—'

'Don't be a jerk, Nathan! Don't punish Bunch because you put the fear of God into her when you crept up on her'

'I did what?'

'She lashed out at you…you scared her.'

'Shut up!'

'She might tell you …who shopped Ron to the police…just ask her.'

Nathan rolls his eyes, buttoning his shirt sleeves. 'If I decide to interview her—and it's a very big "if," I'll prepare my own questions, thank you!'

High five! If we play my cards right, I won't need my father's help…the stingy old pervert…

I follow Nathan's gaze to see what he's staring at.

But it's only Tangerine Lips bounding back to her leather-bound beau, like a long-legged gazelle; her tousled hair, a sign of her independent spirit and untameable free will. A freshly applied layer of tangerine lipstick beams like a gleam from a lighthouse. 'Let's go, Pete!' she says, and an untidy concerto strikes up: a chair scraping back, a gentle thud against wood, accompanied by the shuffling of feet. A stony silence from Pete who scowls at his sweetheart, and then at me—or in our direction at any rate. He shoves his hands in his leather pockets with a defiance I don't understand.

'What?' asks Tangerine Lips, her tone querulous, her chest puffing out; they argue all the way to the exit, and I'm glad to see them leave.

'Need a lift?' Nathan asks, tugging on his jacket. My drink hasn't arrived, so I refuse. 'Don't drink anymore,' he warns. I'm just about to tell him it's up to me how much I drink when I notice a lustrous sheen in his eyes, a glassiness that provokes a memory within me—that I can't quite put my finger on! A faint smear of orange sparkles in the tissue he's just discarded in the ashtray. But for that nose, hammered into oblivion by an act of madness, our Nathan might still be in with a chance of finding a 'mate'.

******

Chapter 16

"Ah-kerching-Ah-kerching,"

The sound of my own snoring jerks me awake. The smell of waste products that fills the air turns my innards inside out; I'm choking in a dark, unknown place.

Reaching out with my right hand, I brush against an ice-cold pile of slush that gives off an electric shock. I yank my hand away and hold it up to my eyes: a daub of yellow paste-like substance, the consistency of curry and the unmistakable smell of—ughh! I turn my head sideways, taking in small breaths with my mouth, trying not to vomit. I wipe my hand against a cardboard box with a picture of a pizza stamped on the lid with the logo: "Potty 4 Pizza." My other hand is trapped under my back—I think I must have landed awkwardly. I have two hands. I have two. I'm surrounded by bulging black bin bags, and I can't remember what I was doing before I ended up here. My glasses are half-dislodged, and I can see through only one lens.

My head is split open. I need to find a new head. A sharp chillness trickles through me that makes me wonder if I'm lying in a puddle. A faint scuffle rustles past my ear, making me instinctively hunch my shoulders. The slippery sound of something slithering—and then it's gone! A grey cobweb of smoke rises above my face, half-clears, then clouds again. The dampness in the air grazes my skin and blots my eyes as I strain to keep them open.

I'm lying under a blood-purple sky full of blinking stars that stab my sight. My head's cracked open like an egg, and the turmeric-yellow yolk has blemished my hand.

Oh, no! Oh, Gaah-d! Help me! No!

My vision's split in two – and I'm neither here nor there. A spider's leg lays sprawled across my eyeball: my world's disjointed...out of kilter. I can't rub my eye or give it a soft gouging with my 'good' hand... as it's bunched up underneath me. I'd give anything to make my vision whole again!

******

A couple is standing in an archway under a Victorian-styled streetlamp. They are bathed in a glow of liquid gold –unlike me with those vicious stabbing stars up above! The woman is in a tangled embrace with a man whose shoulders are like a plough-pulling ox. He stoops over her, his cape, black and brooding as the night, wraps around her from head to toe. A man of indeterminate age. I can't tell his eye colour nor the texture of his hair or skin, even though I'm sprawled on the ground, just a stone's throw behind them. I change my mind about calling out to them. I was going to ask for a lift home, but they don't look the obliging kind. I could have put out my hand— so easily to have joined in their hopeless tangle—I am that close! I quieten the fury of my breath, not wishing to draw attention to myself, but feeling like an interloper in a slow-unfurling drama.

This is a story about a kiss— and I, a mere bystander, am compelled to see how it turns out; and whether, like a good drama, there will be copious twists and turns to heat the soul before it lands.

Oh! A vision of Bunchee Golding appears above me—Ah! there she is! I recognise her by the shape of her beak; she has a massive chicken's head affixed to her shoulders instead of her own; she's strutting and twerking to a tune birthed out of wind and raging ice-storms, expressed musically through a high-spirited Chinese bow.

I must get to her! Something she had said last night after I told her that I was moving in with her…but what? Yes! "God help us," she had said.

Bunch-eeee! I'm coming to rescue you! My love!

But I can't extricate myself—I'm in too deep! I can't stand up and I'm in no way presentable. Although I'm a spare part in these proceedings, I am yet necessary, as I'm the spirit of the imagination, the dark water that springs from rusty pipes, the flamboyant earth that puts flesh on scavenged bones. The vision of Bunchee Golding, unremarkable and unloved, disperses like strands of agitated egg white; she evaporates, and is no more!

******

The man's fine-veined hand cups her alabaster face which gives off a creamy texture of light, a translucence that eclipses at once the jittery stars. His other arm wraps around her shoulders— two figures melded into one so that you can't tell where one begins and the other ends, their bones fossilised on touch.

Hey! Am I pis*ed out of my head? – or are they swaying ever-so-slightly? Yes—I think they are, and they're bouncing lightly on their toes, their heads bobbing to the sound of faraway music only they can hear. No, my mistake! It's the breeze lifting his cape giving an impression of movement, or it could be my cracked eye that makes my vision jump about like a pencil in a glass of water. They're statues alright. Stone dead statues! You can't always believe what you see. And if you see something and you swear it's true, and it turns out not to be, you're the one who ends up with egg on your face. It's sometimes best to look the other way.

******

Leaning in, face upturned, eyes closed. The tilt of her head, an expectant mouth, slightly opened; but hah!—startle me not! One corner's flecked with a bruise like a summer berry that's burst with the heat. Did she arrive with this blemish? ...or did he have something to do with it?

******

But wait! Questions pierce my brain like needles. When does the kisser become the kissed? The kissed— the kisser? Or is it the same thing? A dual identity, confirmed in togetherness and separateness.

******

And when does a kiss begin? Does it begin with the clink of the garden gate? Or just before? Or as it races up the path with the stealthy legs of one much-missed, now returned? Is a kiss capable of signalling itself to the intended recipient within? How long does it linger before it disperses? A week? A summer? An eternity? Has a kiss got any lift? Can you get a lift out of one? Can a kiss get me a lift home? Can it soar to touch the soft-pillowed skies or swoop helter-skelter down a mountainside in the anticipation of a thrill?

I look up at the archway. The couple has melted into a graveyard darkness that hurts my eyes. Ah, no! I've missed how the kiss played out; I've missed the ending to the scene!

If you ask me, there was something not right about that embrace. For a start, you couldn't tell whether the man was holding the woman in a headlock or in a life-affirming embrace; was he using a controlling force? Or a guiding one? I'm not the right person to answer these questions. One person's grunge is another's sweet potato. In some cultures, kisses are seen as one person sucking the true essence out of another—horrible!—in this way, a kisser becomes a killer, who can suck the life force out of you; or a kiss can turn a prince into a frog. So much for the kiss!

And it could have landed badly or been pushed away. But really? I'd chew off my arm to have seen their grand finale…a bit of action!

The night breeze beats the embers of my cheeks to coolness, and I lie there wondering how I'm going to get home, my arm ensconced behind me.

******

Chapter 17

I enter the back door at Number 37. An eerie silence submerges the whole place, and the smell of rotting flesh hangs in the air. That's it. She's run away and is now probably sipping cocoa with a blanket over her shoulders, making a formal police statement. Complaining of course— telling them lies about me! I wish Nathan were here. What could I tell him? How could I explain?

I reach for the light switch.

I kick aside the silk screen drawn across Bunchee Golding's bed to reveal a shapeless trench under the haphazard clump of bedclothes. Her flip flops are in the middle of the room as if she'd not long been standing there when a celestial force blasted her out of them.

Just then Brutus pads in with an easy gait, tail erect. His head swings low past his chest as he passes me, his throat full of growls. Surely, she wouldn't leave him to starve.

The door of the cupboard in the hallway stands open a few inches. It's bugging me and as I go to shut it, layers of clothing hanging inside make it impossible to shut. I snatch up a scarf from an elegant hall table, and wrap it around the lower half of my face. I open the front door and walk to the gate, looking up and down both sides of the street. A woman from next door comes out and, on seeing me, she throws up her brittle, spidery fingers to her throat; her liver spots on her hands begin to quiver under the warm glare of the sun as if they might fly off.

'Have you seen the lady in number 37?' I ask.

She screws up her eyes heavenwards, scratching her furry chin.

'You mean Bunchee?'

'Yes,'

'She rarely goes out unless a car comes for her,'

'A car?'

'No car today though. But a car did come for her a few nights ago, only it wasn't her usual one.'

'Oh?'

'A white Cadillac… in the evening, but it left not long afterwards with a woman and they came back pretty late.'

'What's the other car...the "usual car" for?'

'For her agoraphobia,' explains the woman, seeing my baffled expression. Then her eyes narrow, running them feverishly over me in case she needs to report me to the appropriate authorities. Her voice is stern and grating. 'You don't seem to know much about her...do you?'

'I believe you're right,' I say blithely, and pulling up my scarf towards my eyebrows, I scurry back inside.

******

Brutus is scratching furiously at the hallway cupboard from where the coats peep out. I bring my foot under his belly to ease him away, but the son-of-a-b*tch lands a hefty tap on my leg. The cat hisses, sprinkling silver droplets of saliva on the top of my boot. I crush and squeeze the coats back inside, trying to shut the door at the same time. My hand brushes up against a firm yet soft mound, and I receive a charge of static electricity. Not what you get with your usual bundle of coats. I open the door wide to investigate, and find myself staring into the chalk-white face of Bunchee Golding!—nose to nose! A brown belt, pulled around her neck, suspends her from a massive water pipe above the door. Her face, frozen as if in a spasmodic bubble, marks the last unnatural expression in her natural life; her eyes bulge like fruit bobbing in sugar syrup, a ghastly vacant stare. Her lopsided mouth, borne of an act of abject terror stops my heart, and everything turns dark.

******

I don't want her to see me—not even in death— so I close her eyes. Her bare feet, once supple, lean and smooth, now thick-ankled and purple-veined, are a clear two feet off the ground—perfectly still.

A bundle of Yellow Pages telephone directories, numbering five or six, lie askew at her feet—the steps to her gallows. Water pools on the floor under the directories, giving off an acrid stench. Covering my nose with my sleeve, I touch her bulbous wrist with a trembling finger.

Still warm!

I should cut her down and try to resuscitate her. 'That good–for–nothing ar*e-hole— Nathan! I told him not to leave you!' I say out loud, hoping she'll understand. Perhaps it's not too late—perhaps she's still alive, and in a giddiness of hope, I clutch and pull at the leather belt sunk deep around her bloated neck, but my fingers are repelled by its tightness; it's not a belt but a dog's lead with the name "Crazy Horse" printed several times in gilt lettering along its entire underside.

I drop the lead, still attached to her, my whitened knuckles halfway down my throat.

******

Chapter 18

Although it hadn't begun that way, Crazy Horse had belonged to Bunchee Golding when she was a resident at New Horizons. There were only seven or eight of us during the early days. After a spate of local robberies, Ron called a TurnTable meeting to come up with ideas of protecting ourselves from these unscrupulous thugs. By a landslide majority, we voted to get a guard dog. And so it was that Crazy Horse, a frisky Golden Retriever puppy came to live with us, personally attaching himself to Bunchee, becoming at once her admirer, friend and bodyguard. No-one minded. The dog would lick her face, her hair and hands and, in return, Bunchee would run a brush through his coat until it burnished like golden sand that hurt your eyes when you looked at it. She counted out chocolate treats and fed them to Crazy Horse from her mouth. She tied ribbons in his hair and cuddled him like a baby. She cleaned up after him with perfumed wipes, shared a toothbrush with him, and took him for walks in the woods nearby. When conversing with Crazy Horse, she used a mixture of baby talk and Chinese that made her sound a bit daft. I was amazed when the dog could understand Chinese when asked to 'come,' 'sit,' 'lie down' or 'fetch the ball' in that language. Ron, a man indifferent to the charms of Crazy Horse, enjoyed accompanying Bunchee when she took her golden-spun bundle for walks in the woods behind our house. While there Ron and Bunchee Golding would practise English conversation. In those early days, her smile, in Ron's words, was like "a fresh summer's bloom", and she could only say short phrases in English like "hello," "goodbye," and "I don't know." Ron found her company agreeable, and praised her for being the only house resident who never gossiped, never contradicted anyone or complained. I set up board games in the lounge for the residents while the two of them went for their walks practising phrases, like: 'How much is the cauliflower, please?' and 'The bread's past its sell-by date. Can I have a refund, please?'

It was as if an invisible umbilical cord ran between the pair, — Bunchee and Crazy Horse that is— a strength of attachment that was difficult to find between humans let alone with a dog, whose only raison d'etre was to capture his mistress's reflection in his eyes.

We marvelled at how the dog grew three times its size within three months, developing a healthy zest for life at our expense by snatching food off our table. We had long stopped laughing whenever Crazy Horse cocked his soppy head to one side in the hope of cadging scraps. We had to get a lock for the fridge on discovering he could open it standing on his hind legs; and sometimes we'd kick him mercilessly until he howled while his mistress was taking a shower.

One day Crazy Horse ran amok, and peed all over Ron's information leaflets about the services offered by New Horizons. Ron kicked open every door in the house shouting the dog's name; hot in the face, his blond tresses pressed down across one side of his face. 'Where's that god**mned Veronica Lake?' he cussed. 'That son of a bi*ch! I must've been out of my mind to allow a pooch in here!'

Had an ordinary bystander been looking on at the antics between dog and mistress, he (or she) would have thought that the latter herself, had gone down on her haunches and given birth to that canine lump.

One morning, the mutt failed to jump up on Bunchee's bed, failed to lick her face in preparation for the routine doggy frolics that the rest of us had grown to find tiresome. Ron launched an inquiry to find out when we had last seen the Golden Retriever, while Bunchee murmured his name, sobbing inconsolably:

'Cras-eee Haaw-ss. Where you go, Cras-eee?'

She rubbed her pet's brown leather lead between her fingers as if she derived comfort from it, breaking off to produce swooning sighs that made anyone in their path shiver and stutter with cold.

'This is a big deal for Sarsaparilla,' said Ron, his lips thin and grim.

'And I want to get to the bottom of this.'

'Well, I found the back door unlocked,' someone ventured as if that explained everything.

'A burglar took him,' suggested Blow-Torch.

'Crazy Horse was a useless guard dog,' said Fish-Tank.

'Now, if we'd gotten a parrot, like I'd wanted, the bird would have squawked the house down.'

Four-Wheels added, 'The dog was always wanting to please.'

'The Chinese restaurant up in town...?' suggested Earthy Ma'am prompting Ron to point to the door. 'Just saying,' she muttered on her way out.

Trish and Angie and one other offered up no submissions.

'Crazy Horse will turn up, Bunchee,' said the normally surly Killjoy (Rosemarie), making sympathetic clucking noises, 'and if he doesn't, Ron can always get you another one. Won't you Ron?' Then she looked across at me and held me in her gaze until I shifted in my chair. 'Sylvie might know,' continued Rosemary, nodding at me, all the while forcing a lot of teeth to erupt in her mouth as if displaying them made the point she wished to make.

Bunchee glanced at me tearfully, a perceptible crease embedded in her usually smooth brow, as she tried to understand what was being said.

With forefinger and thumb, Rosemarie 'cocked a gun' at Ron. 'You crock of sh*t, Ron! Did the dog get too expensive to look after? Did you feel left out of all the attention it got?' She kicked back her chair, and stomped out of the room, pleased to have put a bullet in him.

But used to Rosemarie's frequent outbursts, the bullet had merely grazed him; Ron scratched the bridge of his nose. 'Wodja say, Sylvie?' he asked, avoiding my gaze, fidgeting with his nails. 'We've gotta help Sarsaparilla—she's going ape-sh*t over this.'

My evidence to the Inquiry was that I, too, had found the back door open. That I had, in the past, seen the dog twist the door handle with his mouth. He had, in all probability, gone out and got lost.

'And should we get a replacement dog?' Ron asked looking at the group, but I could tell that he was focussing on me more in his peripheral vision than anyone else. He was nodding encouragingly as if he, personally, would not object to getting another dog.

I sat bolt upright, grinning like a lunatic, stroking my cheeks. It was as clear as day. I knew from which branch of the cherry tree Ron wanted me to pick. I patted Bunchee's arm, but she flinched as if I'd pinched her. But Rosemarie's accusation, however slight Bunchee's understanding of it, had stained her view of me— as blackberries do on fingers.

I steepled my fingers together, and after a long silence, pronounced my decision like an overly concerned judge. 'Perhaps it's best not to get another dog, eh, Bunch? You'll feel worse…a substitute dog wouldn't be half as smart or as lovable or, um, ….as eccentric as your Crazy Horse was, and that would make you very, very unhappy. You might end up hating any replacement—spurning it even— through no fault of its own.' I turned to Bunchee, wagging my finger from side to side, speaking slowly to assist understanding. 'No dog, understand? No more dog!'

'Sylvie's right, you know,' said Ron, nodding sympathetically.

I don't know how much Bunchee had understood but she never spoke of the dog again. And that day I discovered that I could use my abilities 'to read' a situation, to offer up the right answers and get the right outcomes.

From this time onwards, I was to hold all future TurnTable meetings in Ron's absence, have control of the agenda and the casting vote in all matters. I cherished the authority and trust Ron had placed in me and declared New Horizons a pet-free zone. I exerted my newfound powers to ban The Killjoy (Rosemarie) from all future meetings. After a few slanging matches with Ron, she left New Horizons, without so much as a word to the rest of us.

******

Chapter 19

The solicitor's office is situated in a three-storey building above an undertaker's office. Wreaths, the size of rubber dinghies, decorate an oak coffin with a plush purple lined interior that's displayed in the shop window. On the first floor, a series of elongated arched windows stretches across the front; the lower half of each pane of glass is decorated in giant gold copperplate script that glints against the sunlight: Cotters & Co Solicitors. A throbbing pain inflames my temples at the prospect of seeing her again. Irene Cotter. Sole trader.

From across the road, near the crossing that leads to Irene Cotters' door, a bright, pink-faced woman in a brown trouser suit and striped blouse, is standing at the entrance of Cotters' Solicitors. She uses her foot, encased in fashionable leopard print footwear, to prop open the door. It's Irene Cotter. She looks the same as her legal profile on the internet, the same squirrel-like cheeks used for stashing nuts for a rainy day. Cotter is showing out a woman in a camel coat whose back is towards me. She is head-to-head with the woman, who nods every two seconds, wiping her nose with a pink handkerchief. Cotter starts to shut the door, but a sharp yelp makes her throw it open again, her face full of concern as she stares down at her leopard spotted feet. The solicitor says something to the nose-blowing woman who is tugging at a dog's lead at the end of which is ….Sinbad! The pit-bull looks as if he could easily do a hundred push-ups, his eyes protruding madly, his tongue dangling like a curly bacon slice, his beloved owner in tow: Rosemarie Whittington. I track them as they head towards the shops on the high street. Rosemarie slows down to dab her nose every sixth step while Sinbad's whip-like tail lashes his own smooth, fleshy behind. A passing pedestrian bumps into a price board outside a tea shop as he tries to give the pair as wide a berth as possible.

I wonder how Cotter will react when she sees me.

There's a new entry system that wasn't there the last time. I press the buzzer and speak into the speaker phone.

'I'd like to make an appointment to see a solicitor,' I say brightly. 'The office is closed now, I'm afraid', says a woman at the other end. 'Can you come back tomorrow?' she yawns.

'I'm being evicted...can I at least make an appointment...now that I'm here?' I plead.

The door buzzes and after a skirmish with the greasy doorknob, the door locks before I can open it, and I have to be buzzed in again.

A girl with a feathered haircut that frames her neck like a feather boa, is on the phone in reception. As I climb the stairs, the receptionist cries out after me, 'One minute, madam!' Navy blue files, crisply labelled, and crammed with documents, line one half of the stairs like soldiers on parade, leading the way to her office.

I nudge open a door with my foot. A babbling group of people are getting ready to leave, putting on their coats, zipping up their bags. I find Irene Cotter on the telephone in the next room, standing behind a desk that's ladened with the same navy-blue files on the stairs. A sharp intake of breath as she breaks off her conversation, the receiver resting against her ear. Her hand goes up to her cheek and her eyes resemble those of a pilchard in the chilled compartment of a supermarket. 'That's okay, Pat' she says, holding my gaze. 'Hold my calls, will you?' Cotter flashes me one of her 'burial' smiles— fake smiles that people give you when they wish to 'bury' their true feelings about you— in the same way you'd use a pretty tablecloth to cover a gnarled table that you didn't want on show.

Her smile unnerves me given our last encounter eighteen months earlier –in these same offices—when I was forced to pin her to the floor, tugging her hair while she punched me mercilessly in the ribs. At the time, she had refused to convey a message to Ron or to tell me where he was.

'Miss Da Souza, this is a surprise!' she says with a bubbling warmth that raises my scalp and prickles my eyes. The only armchair in the room is stacked with piles of documents tied with pink ribbon. Royal blue folders lie in collapsed heaps, their contents slithering across the floor, and along the tops of several filing cabinets, where they gather dust. The bin near her table is crammed with paper scrunched up into the size of cricket balls. A half-eaten sandwich, in its packaging balances precariously on top of the pile. A legal certificate with Cotter's name emblazoned on it in blue-gold ink, lies detached from its splintered frame in the middle of her crowded table.

Cotter removes the files from the armchair, and places them on her file-infested desk.

'I'd rather stand,' I say peevishly.

She shrugs her shoulders and with fumbling fingers locates a letter opener. She starts to open a pile of letters, but the opener drops from her grasp. She soon gets into her stride and slices open envelopes with a dexterity usually reserved for succulent Sunday roasts.

'How's your father, Sylvie? He's retired now, isn't he?' Her tone is unctuous, slippery. Before I can answer, she falls into one of those fire-side monologues that people gather around to listen to on windswept evenings. She chuckles, trying to appear friendly, as she recalls how as a young solicitor, she had observed a trial where a triple chinned gentleman in his fifties faced a judge in the criminal assizes, mounds of pink flesh spilling around him as he sat in the dock with not a stitch on. He declared his right to be naked in any public or private setting. My father, then a much younger man, was defending him on a charge of outraging public decency, amongst other things.

Cotter describes how the defendant, a gardener wearing only gardening gloves and a mother-of-pearl necklace for his court appearance, cheered every time my father opened his mouth. 'Go on, my boy! Give it some welly!'

Cotter tells me, 'Your father didn't manage to get his client off, but the judge, known for his prudishness and lack of humour, leaned forward to ask your father, "And Mr DaSouza, how does the defendant manage to prune his rose bushes in his state of undress?" To which your father said, "With pruning gloves and a bl**dy good pair of secateurs!"

I wonder why Cotter is bringing up stories about my father. She pauses to gaze at a coffee mug on her desk that reads, "Legal Beagle of The Year." Her head cocks to one side. 'Back in the day, your father was a cause celebre amongst his peers! He was known for accepting cases other lawyers would turn their noses up at—'

'Piffling, inconsequential little cases, you mean?' I ask.

Cotter stops opening her letters. 'Some-one's got to do them... Sylvie. Sometimes we've got to do the jobs other people don't want to do. Your father did just fine.'

She's happy as a lark, chirpy and cheerful, accepting and welcoming of me. 'Bernard –your father – came here in the fifties to work as a railway driver. Folk over here didn't want to work in that sector in those days. Long hours, you see.'

My nostrils start to burn. This woman, who is a stranger to me, appears well informed about my family baggage and lineage.

My brother's words come to mind like a bone rattling in an empty dinner pail: *'Everywhere he went he was mocked...ridiculed.'* My legs wobble underneath me.

At that moment, a woman wearing a hair protector and rubber gloves shuffles into the room. "Sorry," she says without looking up, and after stuffing the contents of the wastepaper bin into a black bin bag, she shuffles out again.

I wonder how Ron came to choose Irene Cotter as his lawyer.

A painful twinge runs down the back of my legs, and as I go to sit opposite her, Cotter's shoulders jerk back at my sudden movement.

'I haven't come to talk about my father,' I snap. 'I want a legal visit. I want to see him.'

'Oh?' she says, about to gouge open another letter. I lunge across the table and snatch the letter opener from her hand, tossing it into the newly emptied bin. The wild jangle of metal reverberates interminably, but before it stops, a skinny young man, with hedgehog-like hair, pops his head round the door, eyebrows skyward. 'Is everything okay, Irene?' he asks, his face flushed and shiny. Cotter shoos him away with a gesture of her lily-white hand, a hand that in all probability has never cleaned a pot or pan.

Cotter picks out a yellow leaflet from the flotsam and jetsam of jumble on her desk and holds it out to me, and when I refuse to take it, she shrugs and picks up a pencil instead. She starts tapping the desk with it, and I stare at her until she stops.

'I want *you* to arrange a legal visit for me,' I say.

'Members of the public...don't get legal visits. There's a telephone number on that leaflet.'

'I said I want you to fix it,' I say. 'Here's my passport,' and I throw it on her desk. Irene examines it with an impatient, 'Hrr-umph,' before throwing up her wrinkly hands in the air. 'What am I? A miracle worker?'

'I need to see him as soon as possible!'

'But it takes time to—'

I eyeball her until she becomes attentive.

'How many live files have you got, Irene...? It's the first time I've called her Irene, and I tail off as I don't know what I'm going to say next.

Her eyes widen when she hears me use her name, and she shoots me a look of concern.

'It sure looks like hundreds to me...I hope you're insured...I hope and pray you're insured.'

'Insured?'

I indicate the office with my hand, taking my time to consider all four walls, the tall windows and her musty old files. 'Old creaky buildings - anything can happen to old creaky buildings!'

The pencil falls from her hand, and she disappears under her desk to retrieve it. When she's back in her seat, her chest is bright red.

'I can't work miracles!–' she protests. 'Your passport's expired...' Then after considering the matter and chewing the end of her pencil, she offers me a notepad and a pen. 'Leave me your contact number.'

'The last time I gave it you, you never contacted me— I missed Ron's god**mned trial because of you!'

Cotter fishes out the letter opener from the bin.

'You *didn't* leave a contact number,' she says through gritted teeth, 'and your family didn't know where you were.' Then without looking up, she adds, 'Besides, I was following instructions'

'What instructions?'

'Ron thought it best not to have you there.'

I dig my fists deep into my pockets until the stitching along the seams starts to creak. 'Bull***t!'

'He thought—' she breaks off, her face fearful.

'But I could've straightened things out...I ...I could've helped him!' Her face turns dark and brooding as she fixes me with a grey stare. A hollow laugh escapes her chewed-up, murderous lips.

'You really are the most ridiculous person I've ever met...' she says, stroking her chin.

And with two deft movements of the wrist she slices open another letter.

******

Chapter 20

I jump as my phone strikes up a cheerful chime. I look at his response to my text.

> SYLVIE: Is the time ok 4 u?
> NATHAN: You going 2 b there?
> SYLVIE: YES!
> NATHAN: And you'll stay?

I wind down the window to let in a light breeze that shaves past my ears, lifting my hair.

'Oh, my God! You don't like incense?' The taxi driver sounds anxious

'Too exotic for me'

His head pivots to look at me. 'I thought ... you'd be used to it, no?' I decide not to answer him.

A white marble statue of an Indian deity, blue in the face with multiple arms sits on the dashboard. The driver wears two thin silver bracelets that travel down to his elbow, and as he steers, they jangle in symphony. He tells me how his brother-in-law got him a taxi-driving job to support his studies in Accountancy. 'I was an accountant back home,' he explains, 'but my overseas qualifications weren't recognised over here.'

'Ah, shame,' I yawn.

'How long have you been here?' he asks. I close my eyes and pretend to be asleep; the breeze caresses my face, sending my hair flying in all directions.

The scene with Cotter plays over my mind. The way she had been pleasant, almost civil, but then had shown her former obnoxious side. Something was off. It had all been too…easy.

The taxi-driver is describing the packed lunch his wife had made that day, all sorts of exotic-sounding treats, impossible to pronounce.

What kind of life was it for a woman to mark out her love for a man with a lifetime's supply of packed lunches? What would happen if she'd said, 'You know what? I don't want to do this anymore—make your own bl*sted lunch, you cockroach!'

As we approach the road where Bunchee Golding lives... used to live... a heavy weight tugs my heart. I look around to see if anyone's been following us before we stop. I spot Nathan parked outside the house in his blue Volvo. I wipe my nose with the sleeve of my coat.

'Give your wife a rest and make your own godda*n lunch, okay?' I say to the taxi-driver, slamming the car door as I leave, slipping the fare back into my pocket.

******

'There's a note on the fridge door' says Nathan. '"Gone out. Be back soon,"' he reads.

'Silly girl—she knew we were coming,' I say, removing cups from the countertop and placing them in the sink.

Nathan covers his nose with his hand. 'What *is* that smell?'

'A roast chicken in the bin...I think'

'... like a sheep's head left out in the sun.'

'It'll help set the tone for your article,' I say

'I feel ...like an intruder...it all feels a bit...'

I stare at him in disgust, pointing at Bunchee Golding's note.

'She'll be back...'

'We don't know when it was written though,' he says.

I should have put today's date on it when I'd written the da**ned thing.

'How ever did you become a journalist, Nathan? Don't you have *any* curiosity at all?'

I make my way to the living room.

'Let's see the text she sent you,—'

'I showed you in the pub!'

'You didn't let me see it properly,' he says, his eyes full of mistrust.

'For s**t's sake!'

He holds out his hand. 'Let me see!'

I wave my phone at him, wincing. 'Sorry. I've deleted it.'

'Oh yeah,' he scoffs, showing bright teeth. 'Pull the other—'

I put up a warning finger. 'Shhh! What was that?' I say in a hushed voice.

'What?' he whispers back. He bows his head, sucking in his cheeks.

I point in the direction of the hallway. 'I can hear someone... moaning!' We stand in silence for a few seconds, looking at each other. I shake my head and shrug my shoulders nonchalantly. 'It's probably that cat of hers.' His interest piqued, he tiptoes to the hallway.

I stride across to the bathroom, locking myself in. He will do the rest.

******

I find Nathan sitting on the living room floor, with his legs akimbo, his back against the wall. His moist eyes, searching for familiar things to connect with as he tries to make sense of the world, his cheeks streaked with tears. I can't understand his strange mutterings. His hand points in the direction where I know she's hanging stone dead. I go out to the hall to 'discover' her as if for the first time. Brutus, sprawled out on the mat near the front door, is washing his smudged face; he growls as I approach and scarpers. Bunchee Golding's swollen blue-black fingers peek out from behind the cupboard door, just as I'd posed them in readiness during my last visit. I open and shut my jaws several times to release the ache that is there. Fluting a low whistle and making appropriate noises of surprise for Nathan's benefit, I stomp back to where he sits, his shoulders jerking like a broken marionette.

******

I heave him over to sit on Bunchee Golding's settee, the spot where she had last sat. His body spasms like high-powered machinery, uncontrolled and uncontrollable.

His face twitches, the whites of his eyes gleaming like greasy cooked egg whites. 'Is she...? Is she...?' he stammers,

'Dead?' I snap, showering him with saliva. 'Yes, Nathan! As dead as a doornail!'

A low groan from him, as he clutches a cushion against his stomach, rocking himself.

'Do you see what's happened here, Nathan? I'm not blaming anyone, but *this* is exactly what I was afraid of,' I say, emphasising my words carefully. '*This* is what I wanted to avoid. *This* is why I pleaded with you to stay with her that day.' More wailing from him.

'You must've known that her television interview unsettled the balance of her mind. Oh, Nathan! It was the worst possible time to leave her! Do you understand what a serious lapse of judgement you had? ...I left her in *your* care.'

The upper half of his body topples to one side, and his Tarzan-like head comes to rest on the armrest: typhoon-like currents of breath flow from his mouth. He puts a hand over his face and shakes his head. 'No-ooo!' he snuffles loudly.

'In your search for a good story—you've as good as killed her!' I say. We sit in silence before I remember other considerations to be taken care of. I shake him. 'Nathan? Have you sorted out the payment for my story?'

With eyes shut tight, his lips move softly.

I shake him again, and his eyes flutter like butterfly wings.

'Nathan! My story? Yeah?'

He stares at me as if I'm a ghost.

'As Bunchee Golding can't give you her story, I can give you mine. That's the least I can do for you.' Then after a pause: 'I can give you *her* story as well...hers *and* mine. So perhaps I can be...paid for both?' His eyes now scour the room as if he's remembered something. He leaps to his feet, pointing at the dining table.

'Where is it, Sylvie?' he croaks, bowling an accusatory stare at me, his mouth, ugly and snarling 'Where is it?'

I step away from him, picking up a solid, pear-shaped paperweight from a side table without him noticing.

'Where's the f**king letter?'

My arms plummet to their side. 'What letter?'

The sharpness of his tone startles me. 'The letter she was writing when I was with her that day. She left it on *this* table!'

'You know what, Nathan?' I say, wagging my finger at him. 'I'd be more concerned about what you did to that ...that little old lady out there— in that closet out there— than freak out over a letter which *I've* never seen and, if truth be told, I very much doubt exists!' My throat feels as if it's tearing apart, and I realise I'm screaming at him.

'I've been so fu**ing gullible!' he groans, his gestures growing more erratic as he paces frantically.

Holding the paperweight behind my back, I'm ready to strike.

His eyes narrow, as they bore into me. '*You* killed her, and you're trying to pin the blame on me!'

'I killed her?'

'You either killed her out of revenge for sending old lover-boy to prison or something went horribly wrong after that television interview...I don't know… and then you used her 'story' as a ruse to get me here!'

'It'll be your DNA under her fingernails,' I say. 'She scratched you, remember?'

He edges closer to me. I clasp the paperweight so hard that the blood vessels pop in my ears.

'You won't get away with it, Nathan. I have a text from you saying you'd "kill for her story." How're you going to explain that?'

He backs out of the room, his gaze never once leaving me.

******

Chapter 21

The security man in the glass booth looks askance at me, and then at the paperwork in front of him. He does this several times, so I do up the top button of my blouse. He has my passport, the one I'd picked up from Irene Cotter's offices earlier that day. He mutters something that sounds like "s**t" but I'm too busy looking over the things on the other side of the counter: several bunches of keys, a pile of sweets in individually wrapped gold, red and green foil paper, a half-eaten pork pie still in its plastic wrapping, and a pile of papers stapled together, like the one he's now scrutinising.

'Bernice Schmidt?' he asks, and judging by his raised tone, I think this is the second time he's said it. 'Bernice Schmidt?' Third time.

I look behind me but there's no-one there.

'Er, what?' I say, confused because he keeps getting my name wrong!

'You were miles away, Ms Schmidt,' he says as his pen hovers above a document.

'Legal Visit?'

My tongue turns to stone. My inner voice tells me to go with the flow.

I shift from one foot to another. 'Er... sorry?'

'Bernice Schmidt? I've got you down for a legal?' he says.

'Um...Cotters Solicitors booked me a visit...?' I offer tentatively, hoping this will sort out the confusion. I press my forehead against the cool glass of the booth to get a better view of the documents that he's examining. 'Can I just ...see that?' I ask.

The security man holds up my passport photo briefly.

'Oh, sorry! Yes, that's me', I say, meaning that the image is mine. 'Date of birth?' I give this to him.

'Got your letter of introduction?'

'Ah ...guess they forgot to give me one   '

He smiles. 'No, you're alright —it's here!'

And, for the first time, I notice a folded piece of paper attached to the inside cover of my passport. I remember the receptionist at Cotters Solicitors insisting that I wait to speak to Irene Cotter first before going to my visit.

'Ah, Miss Cotter's firm!' The corners of his eyes crease as he nods with approval and returns my passport. He continues, 'She's probably still in there…you might just catch her yet.'

As I check my new passport, a feeling of dread comes over me. A whimper flies from my dry mouth, and I must hold onto the counter for support. Cotter's put the wrong name on my passport!

The prison guard continues his bird-like chatter. 'She's married to this god-forsaken place! Been coming here for years, that Cotter!' He picks up a giant set of brass keys that look as if they date back from the days of punishment by ducking stools and trial by fire.

My stomach tightens at the cheery way he says, 'This way, Ms Schmidt.' He thinks I'm a solicitor! On unsteady feet, I follow him through a series of locked gates, across a vast concrete concourse surrounded by walls built with stone slabs, each the size of a Volkswagen.

I hope to run into Irene Cotter. It will be her last legal visit!

******

I wait in the "Waiting Area" with a gaggle of smartly dressed "legals," all talking at once, catching up with each other as if at a tea dance. I listen to a man with a large head describing how mad his client is, the maddest things his client has said; the maddest thing his client has done that far outweighs the madness of all the other mad clients he's ever had.

A familiar looking man wearing an ostentatious blue signet ring, recounts how his client had allegedly tricked a whole bunch of women to work as "comforter-givers" in specially built underground chambers under the basement of his house. His client was insisting that these women were bona fide "tenants" over whom he exerted no control.

The man speaking is Mr Pemberton, the barrister who had represented Ron at trial and sentencing hearing and had made a pig's ear of both. Mr Love-Bird himself, without his gown and wig. I'm tempted to cut him down to size, but given that I'm in possession of a dodgy passport, I can't afford to draw attention to myself.

While the other lawyers continue to talk as a pack, I slide my passport through a drain cover near a secluded patch of grass.

******

Chapter 22

A peck on the cheek? A handshake? How about a high-five? Perhaps not. Ron had always been embarrassed by any sort of physical contact. But he, himself, had been tactile with the residents in New Horizons, as a way of giving them support and encouragement.

I go through a whole heap of questions I have for him. Do you have a prison cell to yourself? Are you allowed a vegan diet? An afternoon nap? Will they let you order stuff from the States? Can you play cards when you like? But I'm annoyed with myself for thinking up such childish questions that may all too well bring back memories of happier times for him—memories he'd rather not think about right now.

As I wait, corralled in a concrete pen with the chatty lawyers, taking in the smell of aftershave mingled with grass, my mind turns to the past.

******

In his quest to help residents reach their potential, Ron had called upon the local community college to form what he called 'a partnership arrangement'. A red-haired man with a fisherman's beard, much older than Ron, called Patrick Murphy turned up one morning to teach at New Horizons. Ron had expressly asked for a female tutor. Patrick's glasses would slide down his nose as he spoke, so he ended up peering over them, and as he did so, he waved comically with the tips of his fingers to whoever happened to be in his eye-line. He wore a shapeless, field-green jumper with arms of uneven length. When we pointed this out to him, his cheeks instantly daubed with the colour of a robin's red-rust chest. Patrick waved his arms in the air, and plucked the neckline of the green garment. 'Ah, ladies! What can I tell ye? T'were designed with love in mind—that it were!' he said beaming. As a large man, we expected him to have a booming voice, but it was tinny and as scratchy as his jumper. 'And t'were stitched together with a woman's love! But sometimes love, in its haste, cannot measure well; it goes askew—a little off course...and we end up with this,' he rasped, pulling the uneven sleeves of his jumper in merriment, tears glistening in his eyes. 'At least there's a hole for the head,' he chuckled, 'and it fits in all the other places!'

The residents looked at each other with teeth flashing, absorbing everything he said like sponges. We could have listened to him all day; he spoke in a quaint fashion we'd not heard before, and we put this down to his Irish roots. When a resident asked why he wore a 'crooked' jumper, he paused for a long time as if considering the matter with a great deal of thought and was about to say something momentous. 'I wear de da*n t'ing so that my bal*s don't freeze and fall off!' And we all bayed like a pack of wolves, hoping he'd never leave us. The women raced to make the tea, and the kitchen was filled with nervous chatter and laughter. Patrick Murphy noisily opened numerous cupboards and drawers, pretending to be helpful, but didn't know where anything was kept. The residents' hearts were a-flutter and they moved with the grace and softness of quivering butterfly wings; the shyer ones huddled together, furtively eyeing the man with marmalade hair, and his sloppily knitted uneven sleeves. Two bolder ones, the youngest in our group, asked for his telephone number, and Bunchee and I gave them admonishing looks to quash their forwardness, but not too forcefully. Patrick Murphy dug his hands in his pockets as if they were cold and, when everyone had quietened down, he said, 'Ah, dem da*ned College regulations dictate that I can't be giving ye any personal stuff about me!' When he saw the wave of disappointment rise from us, he promised he would take us to a pub at the end of the teaching term and buy us all a drink. 'Be that a firm date then, ladies?' he asked, raising his teacup in salute. We shifted uneasily in our chairs, playing with our pencils, our mouths downturned, and by the end of his three hours with us, we began to feel a twinge of hatred towards him.

We never saw Patrick Murphy again after that day. In fact, we never had a tutor again. After we learned that our teacher was not returning, a few of us took a risk and, on the pretext of taking our twice weekly walks, we went up to the grounds of the community college, hoping to bump into the man wearing an ill-fitting, field-green jumper. But we never did. We went back to our former rules, and did not stray further than the children's park.

Ron had decided that the tutors from the community college were too laid-back, and probably didn't have any teaching credentials. 'Gaa-hd! That man they sent us...the one in that unwashed jumper – he was one fox who'd dived headfirst into the chicken coop! With his ho-ho-ho-s and his rat-a-tat-tats!' said Ron, his shoulders heaving fitfully as he laughed. He was met with a stony silence. It was one of the rare occasions that I felt part of the whole group, resolved as we were in our cause to have Patrick Murphy with us again.

'But t'were made of love!' said Doh-Ray-Mee, imitating our recently departed teacher. 'But sometimes love cannot measure well—it goes askew—a little off course.' Then she turned to face a grim, red-faced looking Ron. 'We could all do with a jumper like Mr Murphy's to keep us warm in this very, very cold house!' Doh-Ray-Mee scurried out of the room, struck down with the broom of melancholia that sometimes attacked each one of us at one time or another; and with every glancing blow, as imperceptible as the soft thud of snow, dislodged within us something fragile and irreplaceable

'And besides, we can do in-house courses ourselves,' Ron said as if he'd just hit on the idea. He told us how special we all were, how smart and clever and organised.

'Fishtank!' he cried out to a skinny girl who jumped bolt upright on hearing her name called out in this way. 'Fishtank—you can teach English poetry. Okay? Is that alright with you? Sarsaparilla, you can teach rustic cookery from your region. ...' In this way, like a drill sergeant, he allocated a subject for each resident to teach to the rest of the group, all within the scope of their knowledge, skills and life experiences. I noticed some of the others glancing at me, chewing their lips, their knuckles white as the bone that floated underneath.

'What about Syl-bee?' demanded Spanish Conchita pointing at me. 'What is she to do?' Conchita had the appetite of a sparrow, and her shoulder blades stuck out like a pair of knitting needles. I cringed inwardly whenever she opened her big, fat incomprehensible mouth. Spanish Conchita continued. 'Syl-bee can teach 'ow to put the chokehold on pee-ple!' She grinned as a collective snigger erupted from the others. Ron trained his finger on her like a gun. 'Cut that out!' he said.

With fingers pressing together, Ron spoke like a priest, soft and reverential. 'Sylvie can teach us about Jurisprudence and Land Law...' The women's brows creased; their noses flared like grumpy horses as if a vile smell had contaminated the air. 'After all she's the only one who's been to University—and that there's some da*n fine achievement!' said Ron. The admiration in his voice extended like a warm blanket about my shoulders, and my cheeks grew hot as if each had been given a transfusion of freshly squeezed blood. Then to my surprise, Ron stood up and drew me to him, my back towards him, his arms around my neck. He nuzzled his face in my long hair, burrowing deeply, jerking his head from side to side all about my head, until I giggled. A stony silence descended, and through the waterfall of my hair, I noticed the residents and even Bunchee, my closest ally—my only ally— looking flushed and confounded; one or two of them left the room scowling and muttering to themselves.

******

That same night, as we were doing laundry, Bunchee told me a story about a man from her village known as "Two-Plaits," who had set fire to a prestigious holy building in the middle of the night. He had sat on his haunches, watching the hungry flames transform everything in its path to bleached ashes. Just before the police arrived to arrest the fire starter, he had run away to a spot that the villagers later testified as being his favourite: a communal courtyard full of tiny statues of the chubby, serene-looking Buddha. He then poured gasoline over himself, setting alight his two plaits.

'I go out with a bucket of water—but can do nothing,' said Bunchee, her breathing hot and shallow, her eyes like limpid pools as she relived the awful sight forever seared in her memory.

'Sylvie! When Ron hugged you today—I remember the fire-lover's eyes from my village—his red-hot eyes of yesterday are like your eyes I see today!'

******

'Excuse me! How much longer do I have to wait?' I ask a passing prison officer outside the waiting room. He gives off a strong garlicky odour; his shirt is buttoned all the way up to the top, and two dark patches mark out the stretch of his armpits.

'It's unusual for an inmate to have two legals in one day,' the guard says, stifling a yawn with the back of his hand. 'You should really be in there with them now.'

'It's way past my appointment time...' I say indicating the clock on the wall, hoping to get him to see what the holdup is. He pulls out a tangerine from his pocket, peels it in one continuous movement, before tilting his head back to down the whole fruit.

He starts to splutter, blinking rapidly as tears flood his eyes. 'Your Mr Partridge—'

'He's not *my* Mr Partridge—'

'—likes playing games'

'Games?'

'Games are popular here, and can go on for days. Cards. Dominoes. Chess—mostly cards, though.' The guard wraps up the tangerine peel in a tissue and discards it in a used coffee cup. 'Your Mr Partridge wins the lot. Poker, I think, is his specialty.'

I look down to survey my navy-blue court shoes, bought by Melanie.

'Ah, here we are! Follow me,' he says and leads me to the visiting area. A knot forms in my stomach as we pass Ron leaning forward in his chair, chatting earnestly with Irene Cotter opposite him. With eyes downcast, her expression tinged with forlorn hopelessness, she looks quite different to the woman I'd last seen scalping letters in her office, stern and unyielding. She daubs her eyes with a handkerchief. A blue notebook lies unopened on the table, a silver pen on top.

Hiding behind the security officer a few metres from them, I rub the lens of my steamed-up glasses with my fingers. I can make out Ron's voice, his tone light and jocular: 'I know what I'm doing— it's no big deal (I can't make out the next few words above the hubbub of prison visiting noise)… we've got to make do with what we've got,' he says before they both stand up. Their fingers lock and unlock momentarily before Cotter walks away, glancing wistfully behind to gaze at him, her yellowing face stamped with a streak of impending doom. I'd dearly love to run after her—to pound her head against the ground for doctoring my passport, for criminalising me! But I decide against it, as I'm sure to come off worse—after all, who'd believe something you only ever see on television?

******

Not knowing how to respond to Ron's request, I survey the rows of tables with inmates and lawyers in the visiting hall that's bristling with genial conversation.

With his elbows on the table, Ron leans in, his head lower than his shoulders, trying to look me in the eye. His right hand is bandaged inexpertly, and his lobster-red blistered skin peeks underneath it.

'Are you in, Sylvie?' he whispers hoarsely, like a furtive stranger. Gone is the jovial, sympathetic tone, the twinkle in his eye that he had used with Cotter. As he clenches his slack jaws, deep grooves darken his sweaty brow. The crisscross of veins on the surface of his 'good' hand, form a complex weave like a map, all over his blotchy skin. His even teeth radiate whiteness that makes me run my tongue over the bombsite of missing teeth and charred surfaces in my own mouth.

His tone grows more insistent, full of tired fury. 'Well? Are you?' I puff out my cheeks as if I'm making a big effort to remember.

'I don't know Ron,' I complain. 'I mean, I don't even know what this Linda-wot-ser-name looks like.'

Ron's chair clatters as he jerks backwards. 'Oh, Gah-dd!' His tone can cut down bullets. 'Come off it, Sylvie! Sure you remember! She was a black girl, and we didn't get many of those—!' he breaks off to see if this has jogged my memory, his blue eyes burrowing into me. I breathe in his haunted look of desperation as I have done many, many times, usually before a call to action.

Ron's pinched expression makes me wonder if he's on medication. I have watched documentaries where the prison authorities cram their inmates with all sorts of drugs as a way of dulling them from boredom and pain. And, in some cases, to make them dopier and more compliant.

I shake my head. 'I can't say I do, Ron...' I stare into my lap. 'Nope, can't remember her, I'm afraid.'

'Linda Cleverly was a real reserved type...real nice...'

'This may seem perverse, Ron, but I can never remember the real nice ones—' I chuckle. 'Only the real nasty ones—and we had more of –'

I break off as a flash of temper floods his face.

But he takes up a conciliatory tone, giving a dismissive wave. 'Pfff! Forget what she looks like. All I want you to do is to pass on a message...at her place of business.'

The heat of blood gushes down my neck and across my chest. My tongue turns into a lump of lead, and I take in quick breaths through my mouth. Have I come all this way to be his messenger girl? Does he know I've come to see him on a fake passport forged by *his* own solicitor? What's that all about?

As Ron looks around, pulling up his shirt collar, he launches into a speech I've heard many, many times before, so many times that I recite it word for word, silently...inwardly.

'When I signed up for the army in Lexington,—aged twenty-one—I had to be prepared to get my hands a little dirty—for the defence of all I held to be true. I didn't particularly want to, but there you are—' he breaks off to see the effect of his words.

'—I had to be true to the cause,' I say, finishing his speech for him. Ron tilts his head to one side, addressing me as if I'm a child. 'Do you think you could do this one little thing for me… hun?' He chews his lower lip, his brows arching so that the choppy white hairs stand erect.

I lean back in my chair: 'I don't know where she god**mm lives!'

'Oh, I've got that information, sweetheart. Linda's got some kind of–heck—what's it called now? A beauty salon—?' His eyes narrow and he clicks his fingers like a flamenco dancer trying to remember. 'All I know is, it's behind a train station...where is it now?' And he names a well-known road that even I've heard of.

I would like to roll my eyes and say— 'That's one heck of a long road, Ron! A little more specificity would go a long way!' But I say nothing.

He winces as he pulls down his sleeve to cover his injured hand, looking me squarely in the face. The hairs on the back of my neck rise as he recites the whole address— to the last letter of the postcode. The tips of Ron's ears turn bright pink as if he's read my thoughts.

'Linda left a forwarding address for her mail when she left—' I'd like to ask, 'What's this all about, Ron? I mean what's this *really* about?' But I don't.

******

It's a well-trodden path we've walked down before; placating and soothing, persuading and cajoling.

'What about that Cotter woman?' I suggest tentatively. 'Can't she find this Linda?'

His face jerks to one side as if he's been hit on the head. His face turns ashen—almost ugly! He drags his chair back slowly, perching a baseball cap on his head.

'It's okay. Forget it. We're done, here!' he says coldly. I tug his sleeve in desperation, but he yanks his arm away as if I've stuck a pin in him, making me slide off my chair.

'I'm sorry!' I call after him. 'I'll do whatever you want…please! Ron, please don't leave me like this!' The bustling noise in the visiting room subsides as every pair of eyes stops to stare at us. 'Don't leave me, plee-ase!' I can see a whole bunch of people – strangers – smirking and rolling their eyes, making me an object of their amusement!

Ron turns towards me, his lips pursed and business-like. As he shuffles closer, the muscles in his face relax and he whispers in my ear; his hot, moist breath blooms over me. 'Give her this number—43812BY.' He repeats it twice more, and I store the figures mechanically in my mind. 'Got that?' he asks.

An unsmiling, silver-haired security officer slopes over to us, concerned at my earlier outburst. 'We're done—she's leaving,' Ron tells the guard who stops a few inches away from him. A metallic jingle rings out like pennies dropping into a jar as the guard puts a pair of handcuffs on him.

As Ron marches quickly away, guard in tow, I call after him: 'If you tell me what you want doing, maybe I can do it myself!' But each decisive step seems to pump up the two slack orbs of his backside to the size of firm oranges that now bob away from my sight. I hope he'll wave to me. But he doesn't. He hasn't even said "goodbye."

'Are you alright ma'am?' asks the officer peering at me as he sees me out the gates.

'43812BY,' I say.

******

Chapter 23

'Do we know who brought it in?' Detective Sergeant Dan Hubble asks Sam, the Desk Sergeant. Dan's face screws up as he drains the remaining dregs in his coffee cup, a challenge he sets himself each time he has coffee. His eyes narrow as he considers an A5 size paper that's been handed to him in a protective see-through evidence bag; his six-year-old, Gregory, draws like this. The picture shows a row of houses, three in total, with the name of the road written underneath; all are drawn with pointed roofs and uneven square windows. An arrow points to one of the doors marked "37" with the word "korpse" next to it.

'The artist's even drawn a little corpse in the house,' says Hubble. 'A practical joke, perhaps?'

'Mmmn?' says DS Hubble, not taking in what the desk sergeant's just said. He mouths the word "korpse." Gregory wouldn't be able to spell it correctly either.

'You must have seen who left it?' asks the detective, holding the drawing up to the light.

'Nope. I'd gone to get my date stamp from 'Charlie, the Magpie,' and when I'd got back the envelope was there... on my desk.'

'"To the Police",' reads the detective, tracing the letters of the envelope under the plastic folder with his forefinger as if the act of tracing it hard enough would reveal a further clue. 'It's either someone with dyslexia...' he suggests tentatively. 'Or... someone who's trying to put us off the scent.'

'You mean pretending he can't spell'

'Perhaps…we need to pull the CCTV'

'We're checking that as we speak, –Ah, there we go!' Sam says as a "ping" registers on Hubble's computer. A flurry of fingers locates the correct file for viewing and Hubble opens it, his curiosity piqued. Together they watch a hooded-up figure moving like a furtive crab through the police station's reception area, and towards the glassed-up front desk.

The figure looks around several times, their head bowed.

'Nah...can't see his face!' clucks the detective with impatience.

'It's a woman, Guv!'

'How can you tell?'

'Play it again....look... the way she stands and that. Curvy like,' says Sam. 'Look up here...' and he thumps his chest with both hands.
'With a penchant for army fatigues?' asks Hubble.
'A lot of women go for that look.'
'Yeah'
'Dykes and such'
'Now, now!' the detective says wincing, his eyes still glued to the screen, as Sam chuckles. 'His hoodie's down to his chin!'
'It's a woman I tell you,' insists Sam.
'Let's stop it there...there's the envelope in his hand....Wait a minute!—' Hubble breaks off.
'What?'
'I've seen this person before?'
'Who?'
'Who d'you think?' he says, annoyed at Sam's slowness.
'Where?'
'CCTV footage from that came in a few days ago.'
'Oh?'
'The court clerk from the Crown Court ...the one who was shoved down the stairs—wait there!' Hubble lowers his head, waiting for the second file on his computer to download. 'I'm sure it's the same perp as the one in ours...!'
'You've lost me,' says Sam scratching his greying head as the young detective taps the computer keys with brisk fingers.
'Here we go!' With eyes pinned to the computer screen, Hubble watches CCTV footage of a bearded man falling over himself as he exits the court turnstile. 'Definitely the same person...same camouflage trousers—but it's definitely a bloke! He's got a beard.'
They both watch the CCTV footage in silence. 'I still say that's a woman,' says Sam,
'Ten quid says it's not,'
'Twenty,' says Sam.
'You're on!' Hubble prints the downloaded image of the person who left the "korpse" drawing. 'I'll take PC Hollis with me,' he says, snatching up the picture and slipping on his jacket. 'Let's see what this "korpse" is about!'
'"She took him by the left leg and threw him down the stairs!" Just like a woman!' cackles Sam as he watches the retreating figure of the broad-shouldered detective.

******

Chapter 24

'The Hair Gallery' is situated on the corner of a side street just off the main road. It's the only hair and beauty business there so it must be the one. Spots of rain splashes my glasses, and the clouds block out any patch of blue sky. Three teenage boys, in expensive leisure wear, are playing football on a patch of grassy enclosure, more straw-coloured than green. The tallest boy, of mixed-race heritage, tries to defend a ball that ends up striking him on the side of his handsome face, knocking off his baseball hat. His companions snort with laughter. The boy looks up on hearing me gasp when he'd been hit. I wave to him in sympathy. He smiles sheepishly, pulls the fallen cap back on before kicking the ball to a shorter, stouter boy who heads it expertly to a third boy with shaved back and sides, a waterfall of hair falling over his eyes. This last boy heads the ball into the air, flops forwards with arms outstretched, so that it lands in the crook of his back. They cackle and screech as they tousle for the ball like a group of excitable girls.

******

The salon doorbell sounds its tinny giggle as I enter. A spotty girl with bulging eyes, the lenses in her glasses as thick as Perspex, greets me by cocking her head to one side and sizing me up. Her upper lip is swollen, and metal sparks flash from her mouth. She garbles something that sounds like, "What the hell?" but common sense tells me it's probably more like, "Can I help?"

The room looks as if tins of pink paint has been thrown everywhere to splash the chairs, reception desk, hooded hair dryers, curtains and framed mirrors.

'I've an appointment with Linda,' I say, sitting down on a soft-cushioned pink chair before being asked.

The girl doesn't respond, as at that moment the shop doorbell tinkles again and a woman, with one foot over the threshold, facing outwards, shakes a see-through plastic umbrella like a fencer parrying a sword in the face of an opponent. The receptionist helps the woman with her coat and goes to hang it up. The woman drops the soaking wet umbrella in a golden umbrella stand, patting her hair with thin, elegant fingers.

She wears a white woollen dress that went out with the sixties, a matching white plastic belt as broad as the span of my hand. As she stands swaying on the balls of a pair of high heels, she resembles a crouching cat lining up to pounce on its prey. There is not a trace of makeup on her face. Not that she needs it. Her coral lips are in full bloom, and her skin glows a burnished copper brown; her skull-cropped hair looks as if it's been blasted a gloss-raven colour with a blow torch. Her eyes glitter like the diamonds in a high-end jewellers' display tray.

It's her – Linda Cleverly. I remember her alright. I remembered her the minute Ron mentioned her name during my prison visit.

Bunchee Golding had once called this woman 'a rare revelation and a curse,' but as her English vocabulary did not, at the time, extend that far, I reckon she must've heard it from another resident in New Horizons.

Not having conducted a military 'sweep' of the establishment, as is my custom, I feel an uneasy heaving in the pit of my stomach, an acrid taste in my mouth.

'Linda!' calls the receptionist, shooting an accusing look in my direction, with mouth agape. 'She's not in the diary,' she bawls, tapping her pen on the page of the appointment book.

I pretend to read a magazine on hearing Linda's soft clicking footsteps approach.

'No!' she gasps, covering her mouth as recognition dawns on her.

I look up to see a pair of wide eyes that give her a startled expression.

On bent knees, as if rudderless, Linda shuffles two paces forth and two back, then a brisk full circle before she approaches with outstretched arms, and a warm smile to melt hardened hearts.

'Sylvie! So good to see ya, girl!' she says, placing her shapely arms around me. I crouch instinctively to hug her slim, firm shape. It's a messy embrace. A mixture of chemical lavender and honeysuckle clambers up my nostrils as they press up against her earlobe; a perfume probably concocted in giant commercial vats in Paris or Rome—that sets off a queasiness in me. In an effort not to throw up, I cling onto her a hairsbreadth longer than I should. Her brown eyes light up with surprise. 'Hold the fort for me, will you, Janet?' she says to the bespectacled receptionist who gurgles a response that I can't make out.

******

Linda ushers me through a narrow corridor to a gleaming, functional kitchen decorated in the same pink colours as the main salon. The cerise colour of the cooker, fridge and washing machine lifts my spirits to the skies.

I decide to test her.

'One night we heard you being sick. Then the next thing—' I blow on my curled fingers and unclench them. '—Poof! You were gone!' I stroke the outline of my phone.

'It was a touch of food poisoning—if I remember correctly,' she says as penny-dimples stamp her pretty cheeks.

Linda continues: 'I was only there for three months...what was the name of the place? New Haven?'

'New Horizons.'

'They were good people. *Really* good people.'

'But you didn't stay,' I say, trying to keep out the nervous strain in my voice. She's failed my little test.

'I guess... I felt it was time to move on,' she giggles nervously, looking down at the patterned linoleum.

Yep! Definitely failed.

'That wasn't the case though, was it?' I ask, looking her squarely in the eyes.

She pauses, her expression anxious, teeth gritted. 'No...?'

'You left because you were fifteen...' I say, looking into her murky pupils that can't keep still. 'Ron told us.'

She folds her arms across her chest. 'He...he told you that?'

'You were underage for us,' I smile, pleased as punch for catching her out.

She licks her lips, swallowing hard. 'Ron said that?'

'No, a woman called Bunchee Golding,' I say, about to play my trump card. 'They were ...as thick as thieves...Ron used to tell her everything...'

'I see...'

'New Horizons was a charity –a retreat if you like—for women aged eighteen and over...and that's why Ron asked you to leave—you were a child pretending to be older.'

Linda turns to watch the rain streaming down the windows; the faint rumble of a thunderstorm pulsates overhead like a disgruntled ogre.

It's as clear as day. Ron had sent her packing as she had lied about her age.

******

'Everyone has a story?' I say sipping a Ribena drink out of a straw.

What's yours?'

'Story?'

'What did you do next after you left us?'

'Oh, I went to New York...tried acting school for a bit, and ended up staying for thirteen years.' She takes a gentle sip from her mug, savouring the warm liquid. 'I met Louis out there so that was the added attraction,'

'I expect it was hard for your son to adjust to life over here?'

She turns to look me fully in the face. Her chest rises, giving her a more solid bust. 'How do you know I have a son?'

'I saw him playing outside.'

A long pause follows, and I wonder if I've upset her. 'His father's out of the picture. It's just me and him...and we do just fine.'

'Didn't he mind leaving all his friends behind in the States?'

'Kids can adapt to most things,' she laughs with uncertainty.

'Oh, I don't know,' I say, giving her the benefit of my experience. 'I think we expect children to step in line with what the grown-ups want to do. Without really giving them a choice.'

'Ah, you have children—' she says.

'Parents! They organise your life, tell you what tee-shirt you can wear...what biscuits you can eat, how you should stand and sit, when you can s*it ...and then before you know it—you end up in a place called New Horizons!' She doesn't join in with my laughter, but looks deep in thought.

There's a knock on the door, and a pair of owl-like spectacles peers in on us.

'Mrs Knight's here for her.... (she mumbles something incoherently),' says Janet. 'Wosalie ain't come in yet.'

'Get her a coffee, will you? Rosalie's just a bit late...' says Linda. 'I shan't be long, love,' she adds, but Janet's already disappeared.

'Are you happy with your receptionist?' I ask, picking up a hairdryer with a missing pressure head. I test the on-off switch, enjoying the clicking sound it makes.

'What— Janet?'

'Customers need to understand what she's saying,' I say.

Linda picks up an empty Ribena carton lying on its side and tosses it in a bin under the sink. 'Janet's got a mild form of Down's Syndrome' she says.

'Ah! I thought it was all that wire stuck in her teeth.'

'The Job Centre sent her. She's been a godsend.'

My attention is drawn to a bunch of plump black grapes, huddling together in a pink heart-shaped bowl.

'Tell me,' she says. 'How did you know where to find me?' The raised pitch in her voice replaces the warm solicitude of ten minutes ago.

Plucking a grape from its stalk, I wipe it on my sleeve before popping it in my mouth. 'Ron told me.'

'You could have knocked me down with a feather when I saw you, Sylvie. I never thought I'd see anyone from New Haven—'

'New Horizons,' I correct her.

'…from my past— my way back past!'

Just then, the gangly, mixed-race youth, whom I'd seen playing outside, appears; his looming stature fills the door frame, and he bends slightly before entering.

Linda drops a spoon and mutters under her breath. 'Can't you see, I'm in a meeting, honey?' she chides the youth, trying to sweep him out of the kitchen with her eyes. But he doesn't notice, traipsing around the kitchen like an awakened junior lion looking for its next kill. He turns his baseball cap back-to-front to see me better, his eyes as green as the lapping oceans edging paradise beaches that are depicted in holiday brochures.

The boy's drawl is playful and respectful. His accent, unlike hers, is a strong American one. 'Sorry mom, I didn't know,—' he breaks off and shoots a look at me, bringing two fingers to land a salute on his forehead.

'Love the hat!' I say.

'My mum got it in El Paso…' says the boy who strides over to the fridge. He swings the door open, stooping to survey its contents. 'When are we going to see Dad?' he asks.

'Alex!' Linda pulls him brusquely aside, slamming shut the fridge door which catches his foot.

Hopping on one foot, his mouth a little circle, he stares at his pint-sized mother. He brings down his jaws together in quick succession, clacking his teeth like a small child. 'Aww, Mom, I'm starving!' With feverish fingers, she reaches for a cracked teapot on a high shelf and hands him a twenty-pound note. 'Get some lunch for your friends as well, okay?' Alex brightens, snatches the note and darts away, as his mother calls after him: 'Don't buy any junk food!'

Linda surveys the kitchen before placing the teapot in a new spot, in a box under the sink with an army of shampoo bottles. She sinks down in a chair, closing her eyes for a few seconds, before staring up at the ceiling, arms across her chest. If I had a camera on my phone, I would have taken a photograph of her head, to memorialise the delicate, intricate contours of her tight little skull.

Alex's departure tugs at my heart. His long, broad torso and easy gait, his lion-king features—even his clothes hung attractively on him. I had admired his exuberance and easy-going nature that only young people possess… the way he had tilted his head back, the way he had groaned at his mother's meanness over food, unafraid to show his feelings. And I can't help smiling.

'How old is —?'

'—Thirteen' she interjects before I've even finished my question; her cheeks are twitching, and her arms are still pinned across her chest. She rubs her upper arms as if she's cold. She's like a jittery moth near a light. 'Alex...' she pauses to slow down, 'is...let me see...thirteen. Thirteen, yes thirteen…' she says as if she's doing a mental calculation.

My mouth falls open. 'Wow! What d'you feed him on?' I chortle. 'He's a Jolly Green Giant, ain't he? I expect he takes after his father.' The world of children, growth, DNA and inherited traits are new to me. My eyes rove over her scrawny loins as she stares vacantly at the fridge.

Sitting bolt upright, Linda plucks back her sleeve to reveal a white watch that matches the rest of her outfit. She lights a cigarette.

'I take it you didn't come to get your hair—?' Linda breaks off taking two puffs in quick succession. Without aim, she flicks the cigarette in the direction of an ashtray, making the ash bounce back over her. She slaps away the miniscule, orange-red globules, cigarette between her fingers. Her lips are taut like a piece of stretched wire, the muscles in her face pulled down.

The bloom has gone.

******

'Tell me. What's your connection with Ron...?' I ask. 'Ron Partridge.'

Linda Cleverly. I recall the time she had left New Horizons, like a thief in the dead of night. A teenager who was always throwing up, who knew bu*ger all about life, and was as interesting as beeswax. We had wondered if she had lupus. We wondered if we would catch it too.

'Ron from New...Horizons?' Her eyebrows bounce off the dark hairline of her scalp. 'I haven't seen him since—'

'Did you go to his trial?'

'No…why would I?'

'To help him...to help clear his name.'

She shrugs her shoulders, rubbing her knuckles, avoiding my gaze.

'Why d'you think they fed the court a pack of lies?' I ask, and feeling hot, I start to pace the room.

'I ...I really couldn't say. I was only there—'

'Why didn't you come to his trial and say that?' I ask. 'Why the f**k didn't you come to help him?'

'I was abroad at the time.'

'There's something's going on, Linda! I don't know what it is, but I sure as hell aim to find out!'

'There's nothing going on, Sylvie,' she murmurs gently, and I imagine her using the same tone with Alex when consoling her giant easy-going son after a childish tantrum or setback.

'Your son's just asked about his father! You told me ten minutes ago that the guy's been out of the picture. Now which is it?'

'It's true. Louis...my ex-partner has recently been trying to see our son.'

'Then you say you lived in New York one minute.... then it's El Paso - whatever, the next. You need to get your story straight!'

My eyes burn into her, searching for the merest hint of a clue— a guilty look, an involuntary gesture, a misplaced sigh— anything that might give Linda Cleverly away.

She stands as if someone's run a pole through the top of her head, pinning her to the ground.

'I don't know any more than you.'

I take out a piece of paper with Ron's numbers on it, and set it down next to her. 'I suppose you don't know what this is about, either?'

Linda takes up the paper gingerly, and stares at it. Then shrugging her shoulders, she tosses her hands, palm upwards, into the air. 'Beats me!'

'Is it some sort of code?' I ask

'I have no idea'

'It must mean something!'

'I've told you—I don't know!'

'He wouldn't go through all this trouble... for you not to know'

Her voice wobbles. 'How many times must ...I tell you?'

Grabbing a notepad and pen from a shelf, she writes down the numbers on pink business headed notepaper. She writes them again, rotating the numbers in different rows each time, forming new sets of numbers.

'What the f**k does it mean?'

'Shh! I'm trying to think!' she hisses, continuing to write the numbers in different sequences, and after a while, she hurls the notepad aside.

'Is this to do with some plan he –?'

'I don't know Sylvie. I swear I don't.'

Linda studies the door, scampers up to it before pulling it open. The boy, Alex, half-stumbles through the door. His face flushes a crimson red before he rights himself, a crooked smirk on his face.

'Mom, Mrs What's-er-name says her appointment's with you, and not with Rosalie—'

'Were you snooping?' Linda snaps at him, and before he can reply, she puts her thin arms about his bear-like frame and starts pushing him through the door with a fierce desperation.

'I won't be long,' she murmurs, without looking at me, closing the door behind them.

I can hear them from behind the door. 'Can I have some money for a movie, then?'

'For God's sake, Alex!'

'Plee-ase, Mom!'

'Alright! Ask Janet to take it from the till. But don't take it all, mind!'

'Who's the old crinkly?'

'Shut the f**k up, Alex!'

'Ooh, temper, temper!' I hear his gruff laugh receding as he darts away.

'I know how much there is!' she shouts after him.

She comes back in, shutting the door firmly behind her. 'Listen, Sylvie. I've got clients threatening to walk out—'

'I can sit here …I'll be quiet'

'Let me call you—'

'—You're never gonna call me!' I scoff, holding her stare as she scratches her ear.

'I'll have to ask around, find out what this s**t means!' She waves the scrap of paper as if it were a flag.

'Like hell you will!'

'I don't have answers for you! So, please— can you come back tomorrow?—no! Actually...make it the day after tomorrow…and hopefully I'd have figured it out.'

I take out my phone and ring the number on the salon's headed notepaper that's on the table. The mobile in her dress pocket buzzes to play a tune called the 'Macarena.'

'You call me first thing tomorrow,' I say, poking her in her bony chest after each word.

'Please...Wednesday,'

'Alright! Wednesday! See that you do!'

Beads of sweat glisten on her upper lip, and with my face a few inches from hers, I dab them off with a serviette taken from a pile on the microwave. 'Or I swear, Linda, I'll tear this place apart with my bare hands!'

She nods, gulping hard. 'Wednesday,' she promises. And with that, she's gone.

I take some cheese and ham from the fridge and place it in my rucksack. I take the money out of the teapot under the sink and squirrel that away too.

And my mind turns to Alex, and I'm already looking forward to seeing him again on Wednesday.

******

Chapter 25

Annie Lederer sits with her eyes shut, pummelling with plump fingers, a bulbous foot that's propped up on her enormous executive desk. Sighs of deep and unfathomable pleasure dribble from her mean-thin burgundy lips. She wears a loose-fitting emerald-green dress, with purple sequins, and a laced high collar worn by opera divas on television who are about to burst into a baroque aria. On a hanger, on the back of the door, is the same canary yellow hunting jacket she had worn when I first met her a few weeks ago.

I've been holding my breath wondering whether any second now she'll strip away my cloak of deception. I imagine her saying: 'You're that scruffy woman disguised as a bloke at The Very Important Court, who missed the entire Partridge trial.' But there isn't the remotest flicker of recognition, and I'm not surprised as I look very different today: a Lorena Lee jungle print dress (I never wear dresses) with a little cleavage, a cropped denim jacket and white canvas shoes. At first, I had gone over my lips and cheeks with a cherry-red 'Baby Driver,' but it gave me a healthy glow instead of the drab appearance I'm trying to convey. I wipe away all traces of 'Baby Driver,' and try out several hairstyles before deciding to wear my hair down. My hair–turned grey through stress and not eating properly.

With an eye-shadow kit and brush that I've managed to sneak out of a chemist superstore, I've created some spectacular moss-green, autumnal-yellow and belly-purple 'bruises' on the underside of my neck. I've darkened the layers of folded skin around my eyes, and the contours of my cheeks to give a careworn and haggard appearance. When I inspect the overall effect in a hand mirror: a pair of racoon eyes stares back at me. I let out a sigh of exasperation. I've no time to clean it off and start again.

Annie Lederer – the saviour of survivors of domestic abuse and sexual servitude, the solid-looking CEO—Head Beast of the charity organisation, Unchained.

'I'm Annie,' she says without getting up, offering me a bright pink hand. I make a show of scratching the back of my hands. 'Eczema,' I say, refusing her stinking hand, and I thank her for seeing me. I spend the next half hour narrating my life with 'Peter,' a self-medicating alcoholic, a deadbeat creep with possessive tendencies! I show her the inside of my mouth as if to a dentist. 'Look—he's knocked out my teeth ...and I have to wear turtlenecks in the summer.' I try to sound stoic, without feeling too sorry for myself.

Annie leans forward, making whooshing noises and wincing at the same time, but I don't know if this is due to her self-administered foot massage or in response to my predicament.

'What a lowlife!' she wheezes.

'Peter doesn't give me any money for food,' I complain, tugging at my loose waistband.

Annie drops her crusty heel, and rocks the upper half of her body, her mouth lathering venom over an enemy she has never seen. 'I'd like to make him *my* punch bag!' she puffs.

'And when I didn't pass him his cigarettes the other day, he threw the TV remote at me square between the eyes!' I lift my grey curtained fringe to display a scarlet bruise the size of an old five pence piece that I've drawn on with 'Baby Driver.'

'How long's this been going on?' she asks, the tips of her cheeks and nose flushed red.

I screw up my eyes towards the ceiling, trying to remember my research on the internet at the library, about how survivors of domestic violence take many blows to the head, how they injure themselves 'slipping' or 'tripping,' or losing consciousness from being choked by their partners that affects their ability to tell a logical narrative.

'A few years...my memory's....a bit hazy. I'm just grateful we didn't have children.' I massage my temples with two fingers. 'I get mixed up all the time and I even miss my medical appointments!'

'No children. Well, that's a mercy! But we'll show the coward!' Annie's carbon-copy niece, who I had met outside The Very Important Court after Ron's sentencing hearing, and who had given me a pretty charity badge, now enters with a tray of tea and biscuits, placing them down on a side table. The sight of her sends my heart galloping, and I cover my face with my hands, peering through a crack in my fingers.

'Ah, tea! Thank you, dear!' says Annie, clapping her hands and wiping them on her thighs. Dead skin showers the floor, white and powdery.

Before turning to leave, the younger woman shoots me a glance, and there's a momentary flicker of recognition in her ever-narrowing eyes; but she doesn't say anything. Annie's squeaky chair grates on my ear as she gets up; shoeless, she scuttles over to inspect the tray, her fingers setting off a startling tune of china and spoons.

'We'll get the little s**t!—See if we don't!' She pours from a teapot. 'Help yourself.' she says, mechanically, her attention no longer on me.

The noise of munching biscuits, two or more at once, drowns out the ticking of the wall-mounted clock.

'I came to ask if I could have a place to stay where...he can't find me,' I say.

'Did you file a police report?' Annie asks between loud chomps.

I decide it might be to my advantage to say that I had.

'Sure I did! They always have a new form ready for me whenever I go in to make a complaint.'

A look of consternation sweeps her face, and she stops chewing.

'I'm sorry. I don't mean to be flippant. It's just that I've got to keep things light otherwise I'll –I'll–' I say, choking on imaginary tears, my head on my knees, as I put on a display of dry heaving.

She returns to stuff more biscuits into her mouth, crunching and speaking at the same time.

'We need copies of those police reports to help decide what to do next,'

'Copies?'

'To lodge an ex-parte application against that brute so that he'll leave you alone. Then we'll put him where he belongs—'

'—You mean prison?'

'The man's a monster! We must bring him to his knees!'

'All I want is never to have to see him again!'

'And you won't! He must be punished to the fullest extent of the law!'

'But he'll come looking for me.'

'Don't you have family or friends—?' Annie ventures.

'In times of trouble people turn their backs on you. My own family …don't want to know.' I swab my eyes with a tissue, dabbing them every now and again.

'...most unfortunate ...'

'Perhaps I could get a flat?' I ask, tentatively

Annie drums her fingers on her desk. 'We're getting a wee bit ahead of ourselves...'

'...a bedsit...I'm not fussed,'

'There's a waiting list. We prioritise women who've been referred to us from all over—housing, social services, the criminal justice system.' She downs her tea and sighs. 'A refuge would be the best place for you, but they're pretty full at the moment— but let's see what happens.'

With shoulders heaving, my face wracked with pain, I sob quietly.

'The last thing he said was that he'd put my body where nobody would find me-eee!' I cry.

The stress of listening to me has her reaching for another biscuit, but the plate is empty.

Drawing her fingers through her hair, Annie puts on a pair of crystal earrings. 'Prepare for a long and bloody battle!'

'I just want to get away—'

'We might be able to sort you out in one of our partner organisations. But in the meantime, we need to gather evidence of your partner's abuse.'

'Evidence?' I stare at her stupidly

'Police reports, your doctor's medical reports, people who've witnessed violence between the two of you—'

'I've never disclosed anything to my doctor'

She turns to face me, taken aback. 'Why ever not?'

'My doctor would never have believed me! Peter…um is a respectable financial adviser!'

The sound of a drawer opening, the rustle of a plastic bag.

'We'll get him! We shall hunt him down—if it's the last thing we do!'

'I need to take pictures of your bruises,' says Annie. I look at her through the cracks between my fingers. She's pointing a camera at me.

'Then we'll get an independent medic to look at your injuries…and perhaps a referral to a psychologist.'

Just then the phone on her desk phone buzzes and we both jump.

'Excuse me,' she says, her chair squeaking as she swivels round to turn her back on me. 'That's a reminder for me to check my messages …it'll only take a second.'

I notice that my fingers are green and mouldy-looking, and I pull away in disgust. I survey my face in my compact mirror to find it awash with streaks of green and yellow. 'B**ger!' I say under my breath, sensing her looking over her curvy shoulder at me.

Then a beeping sound of a telephone message fills the room:

Woman's voice: 'Annie your photos are ready...you look amazing girl...you can collect anytime! Bye!'

'S**t! ... the wrong button!' says Annie, feverishly tapping the buttons on her phone, but the next voice message comes on...

Woman's voice: *'Please, Annie, I need to speak- (incoherent) not feeling well.'*

'Oh, no, not you! Go away! Go away!' She thumps several telephone buttons with her ham-like fist, attempting to block the message with her fat, clumsy fingers.

My stomach churns, my chest tightens.

Woman's Voice: *'Ple—ase, I sorry...forgive me, Annie—I need your help—'*

It's Bunchee Golding!—her foreign-sounding voice—thin and spectral pierces my mind like a spear. Resurrected from the dead! I try to block out the sound of her voice with my fingers in my ears. Like excess baggage, too large to fit anywhere, I throw them off. I can't allow the weight of the past to slow me down.

With her back still turned, Annie continues to thump the phone; I slip out of the second-floor office. Blinking away tears, my heart pounds against my ribcage, my back drenched with sweat.

******

Chapter 26

It's late Wednesday afternoon by the time I get to 'The Hair Gallery', panting and clutching my sides. A glint of steely light dazzles me, forcing me to look away. An expanse of steel shutters that seals up the shop front, like a can of sardines, signals no sign of life. I rap on the front shutters until my knuckles ache. Two passersby give me a wide berth, and after putting some distance between us, they turn to scrutinise me as if memorising details to produce a future photo-fit.

'What are you fu**ing staring at?' I shout after them, and they scamper off, each dragging the other along. A hand-written sign in block letters, stuck to the front of the beauty salon, reads:

'CLOSED UNTIL FURTHER NOTICE.'

'No! No!' I cry, and pound even harder with my fists. 'You can't be fu**ing closed!' I scream, noticing red streaks on the metal sheet from where my knuckles have split.

As I lick the bruised and open skin, a bitter, metallic taste fills my mouth. The two boys I'd seen two days ago with Alex, are passing a football between them; they scoop up the ball when it dribbles further out from the borders of the grass verge they play on. The shorter of the two, his shirt hanging out, his mouth full of sharp teeth, eyes me and eases off playing. He tries to catch the attention of his friend whose hair flops over his eyes with each jerk of his head. This boy— Flopsy— noticing that the ball's no longer in play, follows the direction of his friend's gaze, and on seeing me, he also winds down like a mechanical toy.

'Do you know,' I ask, indicating the shuttered-up salon, 'where they've got to?'

'Nah, miss. We're as puzzled as you are,' says Shorty, sounding very much softer and more feminine today. I peer more closely at the 'boys' –who are in fact girls! Shorty's face breaks into a grin as she realises my mistake.

Flopsy turns to find a space, and bouncing the football on the spot, she throws it aloft, using both left and right foot in turn to keep the ball in the air.

'Alex... he's your friend, right?' I ask

'That depends,' says Shorty, giving a quick fake smile, and without taking her eyes off me.

'Depends...?'

'On how much it's worth, of course!'

I peer at this strange street urchin, not knowing what she means.

'How much? Cuanto cuesta?' says Shorty with irritation.

'She wants money,' Flopsy says, pretending to be helpful.

'What about you?'

'I'm not bothered.'

'Otherwise our lips are sealed—so hand over the dough!' says Shorty imitating the accent of an American hoodlum from a gangster movie.

I upturn my palms. 'I don't have any....'

Shorty spits on the pavement in disgust. 'What kind of person doesn't have any money on them?'

'She's homeless,' Flopsy pipes up. 'She looks homeless, don't she?'

'A-dirty-down-and-outer!'

'I need to get hold of Alex's mother...it's urgent,' I say.

Shorty stands her ground, holding out her chubby little hand, her mouth a firm, thin line. She rubs her fingers together, grinning like an idiot.

I make a show of turning out my pockets before pretending to find a five-pound note in my breast pocket. 'This is all I've got,' and I turn to sit on a pile of cardboard boxes, stamped with pictures of curly wigs and hair dryers, that are piled up outside the premises. I lean forward, facing them, waving the note playfully under the gazes of this pair of snotty-nosed vultures.

'I knew she was lying!' says a jubilant Shorty, turning to her friend who marvels at her cleverness.

'What d'you wanna know?' asks Flopsy.

'No-oo, Trace! The money first!' hisses Shorty.

'Answer my questions—' I bark, '—or the deal's off!' Their heads jerk back, their faces crestfallen. The intoxication of money roots them to the spot like zombies, their shiny eyes never wavering from the five-pound note.

'Where's Alex and his mother?'

'They had to go somewhere' says Flopsy. 'An emergency or something—'

'—Back to the States?' I interrupt.

They nod, anxious to please. 'How d'you know?' I ask.

'Alex texted me yesterday—' says Flopsy, showing me a text that reads: 'Got 2 go, 2 meet my dad...keep in touch. Alex xx'

I say in a hollow voice, swallowing hard to keep up. 'His dad? Where...?'

'In prison!' they chant in unison.

This information is too much to absorb, and a question that's been playing on my mind asserts itself.

'How old is ...Alex?' I ask.

'He's two years above us... in Year—'

'I don't know what all this Year s**t rubbish means!' I say, taking a deep breath. 'Just tell me his age!'

The girls pull faces at each other.

'Fifteen,' they announce with the conviction of a sober judge.

'Don't fu**ing guess!'

Shorty's eyes widen at my cursing. 'No, he *is* fifteen' she insists.

'Honest...'

'Alex had his birthday in March,' says Flopsy

'His mum had his party up at the leisure centre...the swimming pool in fact, because—'

I finish Flopsy's sentence, '—because he's a champion swimmer!'

'He is an' all! How did you know?' she asks, impressed.

And with that, Shorty snatches the five-pound note from my drop-dying hand, and what sounds like a cacophony of hens being chased breaks out as they run from me.

Not thirteen like Linda had claimed! Fifteen!

The Jolly Green Giant! Of course, he's fifteen!

My head starts to throb, and I can't find my feet. It takes longer than usual to work out this simple piece of mental arithmetic. I don't want to make a mistake. I must be sure.

*Let's see: That b**ch ...left New Horizons in September ****.....Alex born March ****...plus fifteen years to now: that takes us to May ****.... fifteen years...15 years...he looks fifteen, not thirteen...he definitely doesn't look thirteen, he looks fifteen, The Jolly Green Giant is fifteen. Of course, he's fifteen!*

This means that Linda must have conceived Alex when she was still living— No-ooo! Surely not! That doesn't make sense, it doesn't add up! My brain's saying, "Don't be ridiculous! The answer's staring you in the face!"

Nope! Can't be. My calculation's way off! Maybe the boy is thirteen...and the girls are lying ...pretending to know something they don't. Maybe he's just ...big for his age! Boys eat a ton of food these days!

I stare at the football abandoned in the grass. I spend the next few minutes letting out the air in it with my penknife.

******

Chapter 27

I recognise the shiny Bentley parked in the square. I don't know what I'm doing here, having followed the inclination of my feet with the help of a map on my upgraded phone—a gift from Melanie.

I place a call to request that my message is passed on. 'Much obliged. Goodbye,' I say cheerily.

Mr Bubbles' pre-school is an inviting place for curious-minded children. The smart, tall building that overlooks the square is set over three floors. The large square windows are decorated with the imprints of child-sized hands all around the edges. Large, pink and smaller white bubbles, painted on the facing wall, float upwards as they escape from a gleaming brown pipe balanced jauntily in the smiling mouth of a clown: a mouth that's a shade too blood-red, a tad too open, a smile too friendly.

The warm greetings from parents, caregivers and hired help are met with a mixture of weariness, disregard, and indifference from their pint-sized charges, waiting to be picked up at the end of the school day. The children root around in their individual treat bags that have been specially packed for them.

Rachel, my father's housekeeper, is there, wearing fur trimmed boots and dark sunglasses; she has just ended a call on her mobile phone. She signals to a teacher standing in the middle of the departing crowd to keep an eye on Gracie, mouthing 'for a minute…they're calling me back in.' The teacher nods, smiling.

******

Before I know it, I've scooped up the child standing near the Bentley; I cradle her to my chest, pulling her deeply under my coat—Melanie's coat that I've borrowed without her permission. The child weighs no more than a few bags of flour plus, perhaps, an additional bag of beans. I cover her mouth before she can scream.

My first instinct is to scarper like a crazed animal. But instead, I walk nonchalantly towards a gate leading to a stony alleyway. The teacher, busy saying "goodbye," hasn't noticed a thing.

******

My luck's in! I hop on a newly arrived bus through the middle doors where people are getting off. A man groans, 'Oh, for God's sake!' as I push past him carrying my wriggling load. I don't know where we're heading, but I want to put as much distance between me and Mr Bubbles' pre-school whatever... I'm just about to head to the back of the bus with the child when the driver asks to see my bus pass.

Gracie tosses and squirms, giving me little kicks in the stomach. Resisting to the end, she arches her back like a cat, her head diving towards the floor, shrieking. 'Ow!' I cry, feeling a prick on my finger when I go to stop her mouth. 'You little bu**er!'

The driver stops the bus, demanding we get off, as I don't have a bus pass. I've never had one.

******

'You're not going to scream, are you?'

With my hand over her nose and mouth, I place her sitting up on a park bench. The word 'sourpuss' is etched unevenly on the back rest— a fresh yellow-white wound embedded in wooden flesh. In the distance, where the land leaves the ground, kites fly in a blue sea of sky, as a strong wind holds them aloft.

'Not a peep from you,' I warn Gracie, giving her cheek a fierce little wrench. 'Promise?' I release my grip, inching my hand away from her face, ready to shut her up again if necessary. Beads of sweat roll down my face, and I rip off my hood and face coverings. The child appears a little blue around the gills, her shiny eyes rolling around like marbles in a bag. Her eyelids start to droop.

'Gracie!' I yell, shaking her but her head flops forward. I try to get her to stand before noticing her left shoe is missing. Lifting her up in the air with both hands, I swing her around, as if at that height, I might manage to get some oxygen into her lungs.

'Mum-eee,' she bleats, plaintively. 'I want Mummy!' I give her a sip of bottled water from my rucksack, but the water dribbles down the front of her coat.

Waves of mutiny contort her little face, and her nearly-four-year-old lungs let out a high-pitched scream that startles the birds in the trees, so that they fly off squawking. I tug at my ears to stop them ringing. Some women further away, busy swiping their phone screens and talking at the same time, peer in our direction, their faces full of consternation.

I slap the child's plump cheek that reddens instantly. Her fat creamy fingers fly to her face, and she whimpers like a wounded soul.

'Shut up! Okay?' I shout.

Gracie nods through her tears, and with chin pulled down towards her chest, her copper-coiled ringlets tremble about her shoulders as she quietly sobs.

Further down the path, dog walkers stop to mingle with other owners while their dogs give chase or try to sniff the tails of other dogs.

'Look at me,' I say more gently, directing her face towards me with one finger. She blinks under the warm sun, burbling with more restraint, her upper body twitching intermittently.

'Muu-mee!' Her lips resemble a wriggling worm. Her glittering eyes bore into me as if she's planning a pint-sized revenge.

'You should learn to do as you're told,' I upbraid her, straightening her hair with my fingers and tugging at her ruffled clothes so that she can feel pretty and normal again. A bright pink imprint of a finger buzzes on her left cheek.

'I'm going to take you to —'

'I want my shoe'

'Forget the shoe!'

'But I want it'

'We'll never find it now.'

'Plee—ase!'

'It's gone!' I pull up her sock on the foot with no shoe.

'Mummy will tell me off.'

'Stuff mummy!'

She leans forward to peer at me. 'I know where it is!'

'Where?'

'It fell off   '

'We know that!'

'... in the big house on wheels…'   '

'The big house—?'

She nods. A thought occurs to me

'Was that your first bus ride?' I ask her.

She looks confused. 'What?'

'The bus! Don't you know what a bl**dy bus is?'

'The big wheely house?'

I start to sing. 'The wheels on the bus go round and round, round and round!' I know she knows the words, but she purses her lips.

'Was that your first ride on a bus?' I ask, taking a swig of water. 'Well, don't worry… I didn't get to do basic stuff until I left home.'

A gloomy silence engulfs us. I phone for a taxi. The sun dips behind the clouds, and a sudden gust ruffles Gracie's curls. We watch the kite flyers battling with their kites, trying to gain control. The child's nose wrinkles up, and she suddenly resembles an old woman.

'How much do you think you're worth?' I ask.

She considers this for a while. 'What's "worth"?' she pouts.

'How much money would your mummy pay to have you back?' She shrugs and bends down to straighten her sock.

'Take a guess!' I insist.

She looks at her shoeless foot and wipes her nose with her sleeve.

'Fifty pence?' she says.

'Tell me. What's your daddy's name?'

'I don't know'

'No?'

The child announces firmly: 'I hate you.'

Then after a long pause, she says, 'Sometimes it's Simon. I don't see him much.'

'Simon…that's nice,'

'Sometimes it's Richard.'

'Richard?'

'Richard tickles me,' she says, pointing under her chin. 'Here!'

I stare at her. The contours of her plump cheeks and glowering eyes are just like my brother's. I imagine that in middle age, she would fill out to become a tall, overweight blob just like him. She's already a bit jowly around the throat.

'The sly old freak!' I say to myself. Freak! That had been my nickname for my brother when he was young, on account of his ring finger and pinkie on his left hand being fused together at birth. I never forgave my parents when Richard had corrective surgery as it closed off a source of amusement for me and made my brother ordinary.

I spread my fingers a few inches from my face. 'Go like that,' I say, and the child does so with uncertainty. I notice that the same two cocktail sausage fingers on her left hand are melded into one. I turn them over slowly.

I give out a low whistle, laughing softly.

Tugging her thick curls at the nape of her neck, until her head tilts back, I bite into her little damask cheek. 'Well, well, well! I might be your aunty, after all!'

'Ow, get off me! You're not my aunty!' she says hotly, trying to stand up, but I hold her down. I get out a plastic bag from my rucksack and tie it over her shoeless foot.

'You might yet be a trend setter.' I say, knotting the plastic around her upper calf. 'People will want to wear one of these when they see yours.' I take the child to the pond, but she thrashes about refusing to hold my hand, and shows no delight in the squawking ducks and gliding moorhens. I buy her an ice cream from an ice cream van, but she turns away in disdain from my outstretched arm.

I force the melting treat into her hand, but she carries it to the bin and drops it in.

'I want to go home,' she demands. The taxi firm sends a message to my phone, telling me where to wait.

******

The Glass of Water is in my room when I get back to the squat. I don't see her straight away as it's so unexpected. It gets my back up that she's hiding in the grey-gloom dark like that. On seeing her, Gracie starts to writhe furiously, letting out a series of grunts like a piglet's. The child knocks off my glasses, and I tip her onto the bed in exasperation so that I can look for them.

On her knees, with one shoe on, her eyes as round as pennies, the child shrieks at The Glass: 'Aunt-ieee! She hit me-eee!' Tiny sobs wrack her body.

'No-one's hit anybody,' I say. 'And *I'm* your aunty—not her!'

Then bounding up to Melanie, standing on her toes, Gracie holds out her arms to the Glass which annoys me as I'm the one the child should be reaching up to, having just spent a pleasant day out together.

'What're you poking around in my room for?' I growl at the Glass of Water. 'How d'you get in?'

The Glass is frozen to the spot with a dazed expression. She clamps her hand over her mouth.

'You *did* take her...' she says at last, her voice tremulous, mouth gaping. 'I told them ...I swore to them that you...hadn't.'

'She tried to kill me-eee!' says Gracie, grasping the folds of Melanie's skirts. Melanie scoops up the child-bundle to her flat unmaternal chest, kissing the back of her head where her curly tresses have lost their shape. 'Shhh, Gracie!' trills the Glass, kissing the child about the neck, breathing her in.

'Tell her to get out!' the child says pointing at me before burying her face in my rival's shoulder.

'Shush, dear, everything's alright,' says The Glass as if she's finishing a bed-time story. I glare at them both, their show of familiarity and ease with each. Has the world gone mad?

******

Chapter 28

The Killjoy gazes out of the bay window, where a stream of light pours over her, catching her silhouette from behind so that she resembles a young girl. It seems an age before she turns around to face me, with the eyes of a boxer in the flagging seconds of the final round.

I could slumber on for a year in this wonderful reclining chair of hers, which wasn't here the last time I was there.

She's been talking a lot of baloney since I got here, going on and on about some anxious dreams she's been having, but because I haven't slept for several days, I can't take in any of her drivel. She hasn't recognised me from my last visit when I'd pretended to be a reporter from the Daily Argos. And when I told her my real name—Sylvie DaSouza— I just as well might have said I was Jerry Springer. I've returned her pink mobile phone on the coffee table from where I'd first taken it. I imagine her 'finding' the phone, staring at it for a long time before saying, 'Would you look at that! The dam* phone's been here all along!'

I lean back in the chair—that's smack in the middle of The Killjoy's living room— preparing to take a five-minute snooze.

Sinbad, the Pit bull, whimpers from the back bedroom, scratching furiously to draw attention to his plight. I'd managed to lock him in after using the bathroom.

'Competing for my husband's attention...now that sure was hard work,' complains The Killjoy (Rosemarie). She's pleased to have an audience as I don't think she's had anyone to talk to in a while. I can't make out why she's telling me this convoluted story about her life. I'm not in the mood to hear who she's waged war with or any of her battle campaigns. Besides, I've been waiting to find the right moment to say what I've come to say to her, so I let her words wash over me, completely unconcerned.

'He was my husband, after all,' she continues, her blue eyes studded with the stars of melancholia.

Did the Killjoy just say she had a husband? I didn't know that. Just like I didn't know I had a sister, a much younger sister. The Glass—Melanie—it turns out, is my sister! Sent to spy on me by my father!

The 'squat' belongs to him! The 'squatters' are art student friends of hers! I have been supported entirely by my father who had sent Melanie to find me after Ron's arrest!

With drooping eyes and half my attention, I listen to her rambling story.

The Killjoy explains how before the couple came to live in this country, she had been in a common-law marriage in Texas. While the state recognised their status as a 'married' couple, they couldn't get a marriage certificate—because they weren't married! The Killjoy's great-aunt had left her a house in the UK, and that's why she and her 'husband' uprooted themselves to come and live here. 'It sucks being a long way from home,' she tells me.

'I know someone from Texas,' I murmur, as sleep batters my eyes, and my vision clouds over. But my left eye's cracked open, in case that beast of a dog should break free, and come looking for me.

'He must've seen me coming,' says The Killjoy, with the haunted look of a woman who had chanced life by jumping out of a secure lifeboat only to find herself clinging onto a useless piece of wreckage. You do that when you're in love, I guess…so I've been told.

'D'you know how he got the house in the first place, Sylvie? The house'—her rooster-red chest puffs out— 'My house! I'd inherited it from *my* aunt who was running it for American girls new to this country, and in need of a place to stay.'

'And when we got here, that…that punk couldn't believe how huge the house was; he skipped and danced through the entire place, you know…rubbing his hands together he was, singing, "We're in the money," and giggling like a lunatic! Now where property was concerned, he didn't see any advantage of being a common-law husband anymore—so we married soon after we arrived. He convinced me to register the title of *my* house in *his* name as he was planning to create a charity—along the same lines of my aunt's charity—that we could both run together as Directors.

'Boy! He saw me coming, alright! He convinced me that we'd have a better chance of obtaining charity funding if everything was titled in his name, and that once government funding came through, the house would later revert to me. In those days…. it was easier for a man to manage all the business dealings. Women weren't supposed to be business-minded! That's just how it was back then! We separated a little later, because of his numerous affairs, but the b*m refused to give me back my house. It was my house! But the deadbeat wouldn't give it back! I went to see his solicitor recently and he still refuses to give it back!'

'That's men for you,' I manage to say, hoping she'll shut up so that I can get some shut-eye!

'The police told me it was a civil matter…I didn't have money to hire a lawyer…I didn't even have money for the plane fare back to the States. My family couldn't understand how an independent, free-spirited, straight-talking woman like me could've let a hustler, a high school drop-out take advantage of me. Did you know he was an army deserter! He couldn't hold down a job because he hated taking orders –he took me for every penny ...and I…I let him! Oh, he saw me coming, alright!' The Killjoy's plaintive cries jolt me awake, and I look up to find her staring down at me; her face, lined with deep grooves, is damp and flushed, her eyes blazing. She then sits on a footstool facing me, her shoulders heaving now and again. I close my eyes again.

'Do you know what it feels like? To be duped like that?'

'Harr-umph,' I mutter, falling asleep again, but she pulls me back to a state of semi-wakefulness.

'D'you know what that *feels* like?'

'Ahhh! For f**k's sake—can't you shut up for five fu**ing minutes? Plee-ase! Plee-ease!' I plead, striking the cushion under my head with my fist. 'Five minutes! Is that too much to ask?'

Her eyes widen, her mouth droops like an unhappy clown's. 'I'm not making it up,' she insists, dabbing her eyes. She goes over to a bureau to retrieve a document folder. 'There!' she says, and sticks a lime-green piece of paper that's covered all over in black fancy scribble right under my nose. It's a marriage certificate. I'd never seen one before.

I take it from her and hold it up to the light; it has a watermark. I stare at the names:

| Ronald Ewing Partridge | Age: Twenty-Nine. |
| Rosemarie Susan Whittington | Age: Thirty-Five. |

They were both living in a property called 'New Horizons' at the time of their marriage.

The cushion under my head falls to the ground. I sit up, shaking my head to clear my vision. I stare at the Killjoy. Ron's ex-wife! I guess the idea of my being a joint tenant is out of the question now. She's my enemy...his and mine.

The pit-bull scratches at the door, growling at an enemy he can't see. On my way out, I leave Bunchee Golding's last letter— unopened and addressed to Rosemarie— on the hallway table. The one Nathan couldn't find.

******

Chapter 29

I think she's playing with me. Ms Chillingsworth. They've got her in from Barnes, Chillingsworth and Mannheim. She'll probably inherit the firm when she grows up. She looks like a schoolgirl on work experience but assures me that only adults can be admitted to the Solicitor's Roll. And no, she isn't a Trainee.

As I sat waiting for her last week, thunder had rumbled in the desolate sky (as I imagined it as I couldn't see the sky from where I was), storm-chills had swept through the interview room, blasting over me— and all this before she had even stepped into the room. It's the same every time she comes to see me, and so I now put on a pair of gloves and a woolly hat.

Yes, she's playing with me. Elspeth Chillingsworth. Waiting for me to slip up. She sucks!

The solicitor's hair is scraped back in a bun, lifting her cheekbones to giddy heights that would make you wince. Although her makeup is immaculate, I wonder whether to tell her that she's got too much rouge on those cheeks, as it draws attention to what is definitely not her best feature. There's a touch of the bohemian about her; long black ruffled skirt, purple velvet jacket softer than a cat, and dark brown wedge-heeled boots. All totally inappropriate, and I wonder if she really might be one of the patients that live here.

Chilspeth (I invent this name for her) seems to follow a checklist when she visits me, one she neither shares with me nor deviates from. She leaves a gap of four feet between us, and the door to the interview room is always propped open by a dazzling red fire extinguisher. A path, clear from all obstruction, leads to a red knob on the lime green wall that's reachable in two—perhaps three— largish strides from her seat. The red knob pulsates like an enormous baked pimple that sends shivers down my spine.

Chilspeth usually comes in clutching the smallest sized bottle of water I've ever seen. It has enough water in it to keep her going during our meeting. Hot beverages are out of the question, although I have a sneaking suspicion that she's a coffeeholic. She's fidgeting with an old stubby pencil, and a couple of sheets of paper torn from an exercise book lie in front of her. No handbag. No phone. Nothing you could use as a missile or an object to club someone with.

She's playing with me, because she keeps asking me questions she knows I don't know the answers to, questions that leave me cold and make my eyes glaze over.

'Do you know what a flight risk is?' 'Do you know what the *mens rea* for murder is?' 'The elements of grievous bodily harm?' 'Kidnapping a child?' She enjoys lording it over me with that fake smile of hers that appears and disappears like a bobbing seal at feeding time.

I inform her that if I knew the answers to her questions, I'd be sitting where she is, and she'd be in my seat, merely suggesting a comedic role reversal between us. But her eyes slant with suspicion, and she says in a tone that can snap a twig in two, 'I don't want to swap chairs, thank you!' She blinks at the red knob on the wall, lost in thought, transfixed by it, transmitting thoughts with it. Yes, lost in thought.

******

But most of all 'Chilspeth' wants to know all about my experiences in New Horizons even though she can see that I get an almighty headache just thinking about it. Spasms dash up and down my spine. But with each visit, she persists in her questioning with the zeal of a starving dog that comes across a fresh bone. She reminds me of that Nathan Newspaperman who was always digging around for a story for his own twisted purposes. I'd initially thought that Chilspeth was acting for the prosecution team until she told me she was, in fact, my *defence* lawyer.

Where did I disappear to after the break-up of New Horizons?

Why did I push a respectable court usher down the stairs?

If I didn't have a motive for killing Bunchee Golding, what motive did Nathan Chudasamar have for killing her?

Why did I pose as a lawyer on a prison visit? What happened to the fake passport that I say was manufactured by a reputable solicitor?

Why did I kidnap the child of my father's housekeeper?

What did I know about Ron Partridge's prison escape? Was I the lead accomplice who provided the gun and planned his escape with unknown persons?

I want to inform her that I can't even read a street map let alone plan murder; that the Glass of Water has to organise my taxis because I get lost easily; that I'm not used to people and crowds after a lifetime spent…indoors. Opening a bank account, making a medical appointment, cooking a nourishing meal are beyond my capabilities! I've never had to do these things! Tears run down my face, and I split my sides laughing so hard…listening to all her tall tales about me— about the stuff I'm supposed to have done!

She wants me to look at some CCTV nonsense or other, but I just writhe in my chair until I fall off, landing in a heap on the floor. I have no idea where I was yesterday let alone all the other places they allege I was at. 'The medication they keep plying me with has eaten away the part of my brain related to memories,' I tell Chilspeth. 'That's all I know.'

******

As Chilspeth throws supercilious smiles at me, shooting off questions with the rapidity of a Kalashnikov, I decide not to answer her tedious, pointless questions. There's no regard for what I'd rather talk about, what my concerns are like the disgusting porridge they serve up daily in here; being thrown into 'the slammer' every five minutes for being 'too slow' or for 'talking back.' I press for an internal inquiry when a chocolate orange from Melanie goes missing but I'm ignored by the powers that be.

How did I manage to track down Bunchee Golding? Where's the sentencing report I claim had her address in it? Why did I kill her? Questions – fu**ing questions!

******

Chilspeth's blunt pencil disappears into her club-like hand, the tip poised to write on a blank sheet of paper that's jagged along the top. I suppose she's earning her keep, hoping to make it through the day, unscathed, just as I hope to do.

'Were any of the women treated worse than the others in New Horizons?' she asks.

'Yeah, me, if I'm honest,' I say, thrusting my chin forward, staring her in the eye in an effort to ignite a spark of life in her before she drives me fu**ing mad…ah! Those splinters of ice she drives through my heart every time she questions me!

She lets me continue.

'You don't know what I had to suffer…what I had to …well…put up with… trying to keep a bunch of insufferable women in order—you have *no idea* what that was like!'

Her chair squeaks as she leans forward, her mouth locked in a snarl as she slams the table with her fist so that the reverberations run up my arm. I nearly jump out of my seat, covering my mouth to suppress a giggle that floats to the top of my throat and lodges there, bursting to get out.

Chilspeth's on her feet now, and replacing chunks of ice with hot bricks from the kiln of inner emotions, she aims them at my head.

'I'm fed up to the back teeth with you!' she shouts. 'Let's not play games! This is *your* life! Your plea hearing's next month and you've given me nothing! You're always sulking like…like…a big bl**dy baby!'

Chilspeth's unexpected outburst expunges my thinking faculties like a flickering flame in snow, and sets my heart racing, ready to explode. My legs tremble like reeds in water, and I don't know if it's the diazepam or her.

My lawyer waves one or two sheets of paper at me—it could be more. 'See this? Hah?' Her voice is strangled and thick. 'This is the charge sheet! And it's all to do with you! That's right –you big baby!' They really ought not to send people like her in here.

Chilspeth throws the document at me, but it flops onto the table like a shot gull. I yank my head away. It's the prosecution's charge sheet, full of baloney allegations— the one she's always shoving in my face, the one I refuse to read or talk about.

I cross my arms, staring at the porthole window high above, where a beam of sunlight streams through, suffusing the lime-green painted room, making it gleam like a bowl of lime jelly. Beautifull!

'Let's just look at the first charge—forget everything else, yeah?—let's just start with *that* one, shall we?' rasps my solicitor .

'But it's nearly time to eat,' I whimper, scraping underneath my fingernails in readiness for meal inspection. 'It's chicken pasta bake…'

Chilspeth bangs the table again. 'No! We're doing this now!'

I bring my arms over my head and close my eyes; my stomach's growling like a low-bending tornado in full throttle. I'd welcome a pillow for a quick snooze, and not have to think about her sh*tty little questions.

I let out a roar that makes my tonsils vibrate. Then I do the unthinkable. Dragging myself out of my chair, with clenched fist, I thump the red bump on the wall that turns out to be a thin plastic hub cap. It shatters on contact to form drops of blood, bejewelling the floor. The noise of the clanging alarm electrocutes the nerve endings in my ears, and I dive for cover under the table. A scuffling noise of footsteps, the dull thud of metal, a door slamming shut. I peep through my fingers to see the lower part of a pair of stocky legs, an apron flapping between them.

'You alright, ma'am?' asks a man, his voice brimming with concern as he tries to switch off the alarm. He thumps it a few times, but it continues its earth-shattering chime. He clucks like a startled hen, and I imagine his eyes full of hot angst, devouring the room.

'Come out, Sylvie!' he barks, 'Don't make me come and get you!' I can make out his sing-song Welsh accent. It's Stephen, one of the orderlies, who helps to dish out the pills in the mornings. He bends low, ape-like, gripping a hand brush towards the floor as if it were a gun. He breaks into a brisk walk like one of those FBI agents you see on American cop shows, as if I'm some kind of cunning high-level offender trying to outsmart him.

'Come out! Come out, wherever you are!' he says in a thunderous voice that conveys a ludicrous sense of his own self-importance and sets me off giggling.

Stephen pretends not to know where I am so that he can eke out this whole sorry saga for when he re-dramatises it for the rest of his staff team in the break room –how he rescued a solicitor from the clutches of a dangerous in-mate. And in any subsequent re-telling, I will grow to be increasingly hideous, like an out-of-control monster, deserving of cruel punishment. Stephen grabs me by the collar and drags me out with a satisfied sounding: 'There you go! Out you come!' He plops me onto a chair like I'm a sack of potatoes, so that I almost slide off. He's wearing a pair of yellow washing up gloves. His brush and dustpan sit on the table and, and as he sees me eyeing them, he snatches them away, taking shallow breaths. I can smell disinfectant and mouthwash on him. I sit in a hunched position, my right arm stitched across my chest, my knuckles sore and bleeding. Without so much as a by-your-leave, the orderly flips over my hand, first one way and then another, and on seeing the damage, he shoots me a withering look. He goes over to my solicitor who's been slumped forward, fingers in her ears, pondering the table's surface all the while.

He crouches down next to her.

'Did she hurt you, love? She's got some blood on her…' His voice is soft and tremulous, but I don't think she can hear him above the din of the alarm.

Stephen steps over the strewn confetti of red plastic hub cap to wrestle again with the alarm which, this time, gurgles to a silence. 'You only had to press it gently,' he says to Chilspeth who nods faintly. Then he turns to me, hissing like a provoked snake.

'You're in enough hot water as it is-ss! I have to record this-ss asss an inss-ident—'

'I didn't start it,' I protest, inviting him to look at the evidence that it was me who had set off the alarm, but he ignores me, turning to Chilspeth again. 'Don't worry, Miss. We'll fix it before your next visit.' And with that he falls to his knees, sweeping up the red globules into his dustpan.

******

I feel like a slug dried out in the sun. My eyelids start to droop and we're only ten minutes in. I swear they send her here to punish me.

When Chilspeth asks the same questions— yesterday's fish and chips wrapped in yesterday's newspaper, as I like to think of them— I shrug my shoulders or mutter some nonsense like: 'Cheese – cheese – ham - s**t – cheese – and cheese.'

'Have you taken your medication?' she asks, peering at my face for the hundredth time.

Chilspeth knows that the staff force medication down my throat three times a day. I had once told the staff team who dished out the pills each day that I knew exactly what a zombie felt like, and I warned them to watch their backs after lights out. I made several jabbing motions with my hand just to see their horrified expressions. They reported me for making threats with menaces, and I had to take 'time-out.' which really meant a spell in the isolation unit—aka The Slammer!

I must do something about her though. 'Dear Sir, Sir, and Sir…'

******

'What the f**k!' I say, within her earshot. They didn't mention it was going to be her! They'd only told me, "Your legal's here." It's not supposed to be her, again!

But today, there's something different about Chilspeth. She doesn't react to my cussing. No chill-winds buffet my ears. She shoots me a warm, sunshiny smile that lingers sweetly like the perfumed soap she uses. She wears her hair down which makes her look more grown up. She forgets to leave the customary distance between us, and even sits with her back to the red pustule of pus (the alarm) that's been fixed since I last demolished it. My shoulders start to stiffen and hunch up. I'm expecting something to kick off any second now…oh, I don't know…perhaps I'm being…dramatic…

'If you don't want to cooperate with me— and God knows I've tried— as has every other lawyer in my office! How else can we –' she breaks off, releasing a stream of breath that can float a toy ship in Baggershott's pond behind this madhouse.

From a hip pack, she takes out a cigarette and lights it— not even bothering to ask me. My eyes water as a mushroom of cloud sails from her cigarette and up my nose, coating the table with a layer of ash.

'We need your instructions on the evidence of the prosecution's case. Are you paying attention, Sylvie?' She pauses to look me squarely in the face, which she knows I hate, and that sets me off yawning. 'We need to work out a defence for you,' she says.

'Can't I plead, "I don't care?"'

'We're awaiting a psychiatric evaluation.'

'Ah...did you hear what happened with the other psychiatrist?'

'—I'm getting someone else now.'

'I'm not going to tell them anything,' I say.

'We thought you might feel more comfortable writing it down,' she says blithely and plops down a WH Smith bag on the table. Her busy hands make the contents spill out: a metallic green A4 Pukka Notepad with a receipt poking out at the top.

'You're good at expressing yourself on paper, Sylvie,' she says, her voice faltering slightly, as she tries to butter me up. A game she thinks she's good at.

Then a dribble of realisation starts to percolate in my mind as I take in her words. My cheek, that's been resting in my cupped palm, flies off its pedestal, and I almost poke myself in the eye. I stare at her, but she avoids eye contact.

'But how would you know that?' I ask, ramming my steely blade of consternation into her. 'About me expressing myself on paper? How would you even—'

Blush spots appear on her high cheeks making them a sweaty pink. 'I read your letter to my firm...'

'They...they showed you *my letter*?' I feel the blood gushing to my throat, and my chest closes in on itself. 'Don't you lot believe in a little matter called privacy?'

'They have to let me see complaints... about me'

'Well clearly my ability to express myself (I mimic her voice at this point) – didn't hold much sway with them...'cos you've turned up again like a fu**ing bad penny!'

'That's not quite right...'

'Well, you're here, aren't you? Or are you a ghost?'

She hesitates, breathing out a puff of smoke. 'I've got to attend a training course...'

'Really? Because of what I wrote?'

'As part of my...um...professional development.'

'Good!' I punch the air and stamp my feet. 'Cos a lot of times, missy, you're bang out of order!'

Chilspeth indicates the writing pad and pen.

Then smiling through clenched teeth. 'This is what I'm proposing,' she says. 'It's *your* story, Sylvie. *You* tell us what life was like in New Horizons...how *you* spent your time with the other women; what they said to you ...what you said to them. Write it down, eh?'

'Bl**dy hell! Homework! Isn't it enough punishment to be locked up here 24/7?' I make a big show of flicking through some hundred virginal pages of the A4 Pukka Notebook, to underline her unreasonable expectations of me.

'I don't expect you to use it all,' she says in measured half-breaths, holding a fist to her chest, as if trying to keep in a powerful force. Her treacly tones return. 'No-oo, dear. Only write as much as you want. D'you think you can manage that for me, Sylvie?'

After a long pause, I clench my eyes to stub her out from my mind like a cigarette.

'Otherwise, how else are we going to defend you? If we don't know your story?' Chilspeth pleads as if to a three-year-old child wanting to go out in the rain in new shoes.

'And how do I know you won't give what I write to the prosecution to hang me with?'

'It would be strictly between us,' she says, patting my arm. 'I promise.'

I'm about to tell her that it's all been a misunderstanding, and that I'm a victim of circumstances beyond my control when my eyes alight on a pink pen that's rolled underneath the WH Smith bag. It has tiny, raised dots along its length that look like chicken pox; and the grip, clip and tip look as if they've been made from gold lathered in butter. I hold up the pen, marvelling at the way the sunlight bounces off it, shooting darts of liquid gold into Chilspeth's eyes. I do this a few times until she turns her head away, her fingers covering her eyes.

'Where to start, though? My childhood?' I ask.

'It's totally up to you, dear.'

'But I've only ever written shopping lists, washing-up rotas and messages for the Message board. I've never written long stuff before—'

At that moment the heady perfume of jasmine rises behind me. Chilspeth's soft fingers move about my neck and shoulders as if she's grappling with putty, massaging the fibrous sinews underneath. I'm reminded of the Edwardian bigamist, George Joseph Smith, who had massaged the genteel egos of a string of wives by giving them cream teas, and jolly outings with scenic views before he drowned them in his deep Edwardian bath. Did they not see the sticky fingers of opportunity about their throats before it was too late?

But there's something else too...pretty soon something will kick off in me, some terror, some disappointment, some future retribution after a touchy-feely moment like this… and, somehow, it's been a familiar pattern ...to do with my past.

'Shut your eyes,' Chilspeth croons softly in my ear. 'Then let the memories come flooding back… like excerpts in a film…as if it's happening now…before your eyes…then think of the happy days you had…the dark days…write it down …does that help?' she asks and anchors me down on the chair as if I'm a delicate package. 'That ought to get you writing!' She's pleased with herself and bends down to scoop up my new pen that's dropped on the floor, before placing it between my flaccid hands.

'But I can't remember when things happened, the time of day, the month...or year...' I say.

'No problem. Leave them out...' She opens her bag and takes out a hairbrush, and her head dips down each time she gives her hair a fierce stroke.

'And I don't want to use street names or the names of places I've been to...'

She stops brushing. 'Oh?'

'...I know there are people out there who organise group tours...pilgrimages, taking members of the public to places associated with me, making money out of me...now that I'm in the news.'

'You can leave them out too.'

'How much description do you want?'

'As much or as little as you like,' says my solicitor

****

PART TWO NEW HORIZONS

By Sylvie DaSouza

Chapter 1

Skin care

I was driving home in the family car thumbing through the pages of 'Frisson,' a fashion and beauty magazine that someone from my French class had discarded. Despite its French name, the magazine was published in America. There was an advert for a new face cream called Peachy-Peach. 'For Girls who like to Glow.' It declared:

"You too can see the difference in two weeks! …or we'll refund your money—no questions asked!" There were two pictures of a pretty model, showing a 'before' and 'after' shot for the benefit of readers who might want to try out the product. The model's complexion was dull and sallow in the first picture; she had dark circles under her eyes set in a blank, unsmiling face. The second is the same model with a blemish-free, satin-like skin, a pink and creamy complexion, looking joyous, smiling. I run my hand over my face and look down at my dark knuckles.

Then just below the pictures, a small advert reads:

NEW HORIZONS

'Looking for a fresh start?
Want to upgrade your skills to prepare for the world of work?
Contact Ron Partridge on: 25* 1858. Limited accommodation available.
ONLY WOMEN NEED APPLY'

There are some people who crave change in their lives, to broaden their minds or to achieve aspirations, yet half-formed, and who are willing to take the necessary steps as easily as you change a pair of shoes.

Was I running away? No. But if I did choose to run away, it would be to somewhere like Paris or …Nairobi... for a few years, anyway. I wanted to embrace change. I had once overheard my father at a dinner party, telling someone about his personal experiences: that you had to have the bal*s, the imagination to change your life –and that if you wanted to 'seize the day' and be someone, you had to do it right away! Tomorrow would be too late.

******

I told my parents that I'd be home later than usual, and not to send the car to fetch me as I was starting a new evening job at a restaurant. But they insisted that a job at that late hour of the day would invite trouble and cause them to worry. They pulled long faces as I had made the job application without first discussing it with them. 'It's not as if you need the money,' my mother implored. 'I would never forgive myself if anything happened to you!'

I told my parents that I would inform the restaurant in person, that evening, that I was unable to take up their job offer, and that would be that. I packed only a few essentials in my rucksack, and I didn't see my family again for the next forty years. And there had been no restaurant job. It was part of an escape plan, to cause confusion and help buy me some time!

******

I didn't use public transport as it seemed too confusing. I'd saved enough for a taxi to take me to a large, sprawling Victorian house at the address I'd been given. It stood over three floors; tall and elegant with picturesque windows, and a white picket fence around it that made it stand out from the other houses. A tall, well-built man opened the door; he stooped slightly as if he feared his head would bump the ceiling.

'You must be Sylvie!' he said. 'Welcome! Welcome to New Horizons,' and with feet crossed, he gave a low, old-fashioned bow, the back of his knuckles almost scraping the ground. I laughed. His green-blue eyes locked with mine, and I knew in that moment that I'd made the right decision.

He introduced himself, and followed this up by what we residents later came to call a "double welcome grip": his right hand gripped mine until I winced, while at the same time, he clenched the top of my right shoulder, pulling and twisting every which way as if he were physically sizing me up, getting a measure of my sinews, the marrow in my bones, while all I could do was let out short gasps. I learned, much later, that it was a ritual Ron did with all newcomers, and he explained that this exercise helped him to 'absorb' everything he needed to know about the person, what they were made of, their proclivities for hard work, whether they would stay or leave.

Ron wasn't that much older than myself; perhaps late twenties to my nineteen years. His eyes were busy, observing, smiling and, above all, being attentive.

'Ah, Rosemarie....Rosie!' he called, and he repeated the name several times until an unsmiling, insipid-looking woman, whom I imagined to be his Secretary, arrived. 'Some refreshments, I think!' Ron said. Rosemarie left us, still unsmiling and grim, returning later with a tea tray before leaving again. I was too excited with my new surroundings to eat or drink. A stone fireplace swept clean, washed-out rugs, faded curtains, and minimal furnishings. Everything about his voice—his bright tone, American accent – had an easy-going and reassuring quality, yet it was commanding at the same time.

At that moment the doorbell rang, and Ron looked out of the laced curtained window to see who it was. Anxious to also see, I stood behind him, and caught a glimpse of an overweight, black girl with a spotty face on the doorstep. She looked up at the house inquiringly, her mouth agape. A red and white striped suitcase stood near her feet. Before Ron could turn around, I plonked down in my seat again, knocking the coffee table in my haste, so that the tea spilled into the saucers.

'No, no, no, no, no!' said Ron shaking his head, and I thought he meant the tea I had just spilled. 'This simply will not do!' he said under his breath, glancing at me half-awkwardly with the expression of a harassed clown. Leaving the door ajar, he left the room to speak to Rosemarie just as she was about to answer the front door. 'We're full, Rosie,' I heard him say. 'There's no more room at the inn...' 'But she's got an appointment,' objected Rosemarie.

'I don't care what you tell her—just handle it, okay?'

Ron swept back into the room, throwing back his golden locks, as if nothing had happened. He explained that the organisation was a charity that helped women residents by providing opportunities through training courses, and at the end of six months (or a year depending on the individual) the residents were expected to move into work. 'Do you think you can manage six months with us?' he asked.

And we both laughed because of the clownish way he'd said it. He gave me a tour of the house and showed me his collection of medals and trophies that he'd won in swimming competitions before he came to live in this country.

******

People said I had a complexion to die for. By the time I was in my late teens, my complexion had as many as four different tones all fighting for supremacy in a whirlpool of white, off-white, yellow and brown. Despite wearing sunglasses and a sun hat, the sun would grill my skin to a nut-brown colour and my school tormentors would tease me endlessly, calling me "Princess Ayesha" or "streaky bacon."

I asked my mother if I could stop going to boarding school, but she said that the fees had been paid and that I was lucky to get a place. After a while, I got used to the banter; it didn't really bother me.

******

At a local school Summer Fair, I came across a tattered-looking book in a box full of junk, called 'The Elizabethan Lady Beauty Book.' The cover was brown, the pages discoloured and desiccated, and it had been withdrawn from a public library that no longer existed. It was full of tips on how to draw out impurities of "the savage blood". There was a recipe I seized upon as a solution to my skin problems, and the name-calling from my tormentors.

I made a creamy mixture of glycerine borax, zinc oxide and witch hazel which I'd managed to source from a local chemist, and the one or two items they didn't have, were ordered in. I daubed my face and neck, the outer ears and tops of my hands and wrists with the chemical blend. The next day my surly headteacher had to call the doctor as my face had grown to twice its normal size. It hurt when I tried to swallow or move my hands. The swelling made my eyes appear shut, and a yellow-white pus-like substance wept from various lesions on my face. The school called my parents who promptly arranged for me to return to Skylarks in a taxi.

'You just couldn't stop yourself, could you?' my father barked as he paced up and down in my bedroom.

'Why do this to yourself?' my mother wailed. 'We love you just as you are!'

They called in our neighbour, whom I secretly called Nutty Nilufer, and as soon as she saw me, she made up a potion from cucumber juice and quince seeds which I assumed was a natural remedy from her own country. It had an instant effect of quelling the horrific bonfire that scorched my face and, if I'm honest, saved me from permanent scarring.

My mother seized the Elizabethan Beauty Book that she found in my school suitcase, along with several of the chemical ingredients I had bought with my pocket money. My father directed me to set a small bonfire in our huge back garden to burn this 'book of mischief', which I did, although I hadn't wanted to. My puffed-up eyes started to stream even more from the smoke and ashes that blew into my face.

My little brother, Richie, afraid to come near me, called me a witch from a safe distance, his eyes burning like two flickering flames.

******

While living at New Horizons, I came across 'Bella's Beauty Emporium.' There was floor-to-ceiling shelving full of beauty remedies; some shelves sagged in the middle from the weight of jars and bottles of skin emollients, hair unguents, make-up and wigs of varying length and styles. My eyes scoured the labels on the jars, scrutinising the ingredients I was looking for. I was stunned to find a tub of Peachy-Peach face cream as advertised in 'Frisson' magazine: 'For Girls Who Like to Glow.'

In the early days, leaving the cream on overnight, I would wake to a lobster-red face looking back at me in the mirror. My crimson nose resembled a throbbing mass of insect stings, and my eyes looked as if I'd been crying all night. Tiny blisters like sticky, burst pomegranate seeds had formed on the rims and lobes of my ears. The skin peeled away from the top of my hands, highlighting tributaries of silver-blue veins that glinted under the light. I kept out of Ron's way as much as possible, pulling up my turtleneck as far as it would stretch. After a few days, the sore patches of red skin diminished, gradually being replaced—if you squinted hard enough—by tiny flecks of lily-white skin. Then after a week, a longing would draw over me like a curtain, opening an inch at a time, and when fully drawn open, I was compelled to apply the cream all over again.

******

Chapter 2

Tea at the Ritz - well almost!

After two years at New Horizons, Ron asked to see me in his 'study/bedroom' on the top floor of the house. 'Twelve sharp and don't be late,' said his note that was handed to me by Green-Fingers, a boxy little resident in her thirties, who had never grown to full height. She would often be found working in our back yard, assigned to the task of saving on the weekly shop with her skilful, but calloused fingers. Green–Fingers often affixed a see-through plaster on the bridge of her nose, where the sun had caught and beaten it a purple pulp. Ron had tasked this dwarf with vegetable production so that we could economise on the food bill, which was astronomical, he said. That summer, Green-Fingers had only managed to grow a few worm infested green tomatoes, and runner beans as thin as shoelaces; she never fulfilled Ron's ambitions of producing and running our own market garden. She was an abject failure in this respect, but she had wanted to make it work, and that was what I liked about her. The tip of my nose buzzed when I read the note Green- Fingers gave me with her mud-streaked fingers, without any curiosity on her part. I couldn't help feeling a little pleased that the badge of privilege –a special invitation to Ron's 'quarters'—had been extended to me. I'd never been invited before. In fact, I seldom ran into him in the house. None of us did, except those who took it in turns to take up his meals. I wasn't on this 'Ron's Rota' as we called it, but it was my job to prepare the written rotas, which I did on a weekly basis. Ron had advised that I needn't put myself down for 'Ron's Rota' AND the writing up the rotas—otherwise I'd be doing two jobs at once. Besides, Ron had advised, that as a senior member of New Horizons, I should not have to do any of the menial jobs. Only 'freshers' or 'newcomers,' he said, must do all the carrying and fetching jobs, including bringing his food up to him.

    I practised a few deft twirls and curtsies that I had learned in ballet class as an awkward schoolchild. I used loose powder to cover up my cheeks that resembled burst cranberries. I styled my hair loose over my ears to cover my neck as it was darker than the rest of me.

******

I took my Rubik's cube to the meeting so that I could have a familiar object to help with my anxieties. The light from his room spilled through his open door when I got there, and passing a hand over my head, I tucked in any 'flyaways.' I gave a little leap and a twirl on entering, curtsying low to add humour to the proceedings, as if to say, "Ta-da! Here I am!"

But Ron missed my playful entry. He was sitting at a majestic oak desk that faced the door, his eyes fixed intently on a television screen no larger than a briefcase. He was bathed in a white light from the screen's reflection, giving him the appearance of bleached skin. A pair of headphones was perched firmly on his head, the type you see in military films where both sides are trying to bomb the hell out of each other. The room—his room—was gi-normous: the entire width and breadth of the house. It was divided into sections like a self-contained studio. We were in the study area, where he did all the work for New Horizons: collating statistics, devising study programmes, writing funding applications. There was a decorative seating area in muted colours opposite his desk near a gilt-edged mantelpiece. I peered into the rest of the room which had the atmosphere of a glorious fairy tale. The sleeping area was awash with swirling materials with bows of red, gold, silver and blue silk, the walls decorated with yellow crepe patterned paper. The thick pile of a wine-red carpet swallowed my feet.

I could make out the outline of a high-off-the-floor four-poster bed draped in luxurious satin material. On the farthest corner was an 'interior garden', a slice of the tropical Amazonian rainforest that I had never imagined could thrive in a polluted area such as ours. An entire wall was lined with blue and pink blooms, interspersed with tall leafy plants with ticklish fronds. A pleasant sensation ran down my back. I'd never seen anything so pretty — so revitalizing!

In those early days, the residents at New Horizon would sometimes play a game involving a high-end furnishing catalogue that was pushed through our front door from time to time. I remembered that six months earlier while playing my favourite game —'This is What I'd Get You if I Could Afford it'— I had chosen a splendid glass chandelier for Bunchee Golding. She had chosen a king-sized bed for me.

And here was that very same chandelier (or one remarkably similar) in Ron's very own bedroom.

At that moment Ron looked up, our gaze locked and then bounced away like two marbles struck in a game. He jumped to his feet, forgetting the headphones that now smacked noisily to the floor. They became dislodged and separated from the television itself and I could now hear some strange noises, of animals rasping... primitive grunting...sounds of choking, slurping ...all coming from the direction of the screen that I couldn't see. The stripes on Ron's pyjamas seemed to flow endlessly down his long legs, hidden behind the desk. He peered at the television screen, hunched over, and with fumbling fingers, he adjusted something on its underside to make the sound cut out.

'Midday already!' he gave a low whistle. His eyes wandered over the landscape of his desk before alighting on a formal-looking envelope, square and solid—similar to the ones I used to receive when I was at boarding school. Ron slid the letter across the table towards me. The letter had been opened, although you couldn't tell that it had. I recognised my father's writing: fanciful loops and swirls, right forward sloping letters in both thick and thin pen strokes. The letter was addressed to me.

'Sylvie—' the letter began and that was enough for me. I couldn't bring myself to read any further—I could feel an ominous heat coming off from that one word alone, as if the bitter man who had written it were here in the same room –breathing menacingly: 'Sylvie—'

I shifted in my chair and one of my flip flops fell off. I imagined to myself that 'Sylvie—' was probably followed by: 'Don't upset your family like this. Come home at once. Now!'

I was about to read the rest of it when Ron leaned over to snatch it from my fingers. 'I can read it if you like,' he offered kindly, but I shook my head, swiping the air dismissively with my hand. I slid back in my chair, lifting the fallen flip-flop with my big toe so that it fell back into place. I bent over the shiny oak table, my reflection looking back at me. My throat was dry, and I trembled like a wild bird in a cage. I was annoyed with myself for being so weak. After all, words on a page couldn't hurt you.

My father had found me. He had the resources and the 'know-how' to have me retrieved.

Ron glanced over the letter as if reading it for the first time. 'Ah, there you go! It's alright. See? He only wants to meet for tea,' he crooned gently as if I were an unreasonable child. 'He's naturally missing you—'

'Let's not, Ron,' I interrupted, my eyes blinking like moth wings, trying not to cry. At the same time, a mountain–fast anger, intense and infinite, welled up inside me, rooting me to the chair. 'You don't know my father, Ron. He can use stuff you say against you. Against both of us. I know it! Oh, I know!'

'Sylvi-ee!' he clucked gently, holding up the letter to the light. 'He isn't just any old Tom, Dick or Harry.' A knot had sprouted in the middle of his smooth, broad forehead which happened whenever the subject of my father came up. 'He's your dad, Sylvie. Whatever we think of him, we've gotta respect the fact that he's our blood.'

'Don't send me home, Ron!' I said, rubbing my elbow where the skin was flaky. 'Please don't...home sucks!'

At that moment he leaned over, a sickly-sweet smell of aftershave hung on him. He squeezed my hand gently before bringing it to his lips. 'He-yy!' His voice was both low and reprimanding. 'Who said anything about sending you home?' and he paused as if considering my deep-rooted apprehension for the first time. 'No one can force you to do stuff you don't wanna do, okay?' he said, narrowing his eyes. 'D'you get my meaning, hun?'

'Sure,' I said, averting my gaze from his lustrous, aquamarine eyes that could swallow you whole.

'Hey, Sylvie! What would you say if we treated your father to tea at the Ritz?'

'But it's so ....expensive…!' I began to say, feeling the colour rising above my collar.

'This is your father we're talking about, right? He's coming to see you, and we wanna make sure he gets a darned good impression of us!'

I nodded, making a mental list of all the household essentials we would need to cut back on afterwards.

'There! Happy?' he asked grinning at me, stuffing the letter back into the envelope that now appeared too small for it. A dull 'ping' rang out as he tossed it in the bin, resounding loudly as if to announce: "Yesterday's news is officially buried!"

I forced a smile, with eyes glued to the floor; yet part of me wished that I had not handed over my father's letter without reading it.

'Well—that's something to look forward to!' he said, his hand stroking the area above his groin. 'Oh, and hun? Could you tell Sarsaparilla it's time for her English Language Progress test?'

I left him seated in his chair, his chin cupped in his hand, lips drawn thin, headphones fixed firmly on his head. His eyes, full of mesmerised fury, meandered over the screen, absorbing the images like sponges.

And after that day, the words, 'The Ritz', 'tea' and 'father' were never mentioned in the same sentence again.

******

Fishtank was a resident who resembled a boy in all respects except when she opened her mouth to speak. I told her about my boarding school days, the holidays abroad spent with my family which I rarely did with anyone else, except Bunchee Golding, who at the time was in hospital with a severe stomach cramp.

Fishtank's eyes turned round in astonishment. 'Oh, but why, Sylvie? Why? she asked, her tone querulous, disbelieving. 'I would never have swapped *that* life for *this*!'

She started to hum a melody before bursting into song, a song I half knew but not well enough to join in.

'Don't it always seem to go... that you don't know what you've got 'til it's gone...they paved paradise, put up a parking lot...'

******

'Dressing-up-Nights' were held on the last Friday of the month. Everyone, except surly old Rosemarie Whittington, would get dressed in their best clothes made from an array of different fabrics: soft taffeta, flowing silks, and smooth satin materials. Chests and arms were modestly covered, hemlines of an acceptable length. We would dance to 'easy listening' music from Ron's record collection. Ron would nod at us in appreciation, making sure not to leave anyone out as he dished out praise, in his usual kind and jocular way: 'What a fine bevy of beauties!' he would say, clasping his hands in awe—'I'm a truly lucky guy!'

'Honey! You look like a fabulous angel!' And whoever the girl was that he directed this towards, she would swoop away from him, squealing like crazy, hands over her flushed face. Ron would pounce on jewellery with glittering stones, making the wearer take them off. He would weigh the 'piece' in the palm of his hand, or delicately run his fingers over the lumps and bumps of the jewelled surfaces like an expert appraiser. Sometimes he would hold up a stunning stone to the light. 'Ah, this one's paste; it belongs in the junk category,' he would say, promptly handing the item back, or 'This is a genuine *emerald*!' Ron would offer to keep the 'good stuff' for safekeeping in his office safe, and if anyone refused he'd mutter, grimacing, 'If you lose it— just don't say I didn't warn you.' After a while, the residents stopped wearing their flash jewellery as they were loath to part with them. I once borrowed an evening dress from an encouraging Bunchee Golding; it was an orangey-crepe Chinese affair with a bare back, and a slash down the side as if sliced with a barbarian's sword. I sewed up part of the gap leaving five inches unsewn. Bunchee didn't enjoy these special evenings, and she went around handing out orange squash and an overly sweet drink called Sarsaparilla in a quiet, stiff manner. Ron's eyes lit up on seeing me with my borrowed dress and he beckoned for me to approach. 'Why! You sure look mighty purdy, sweetheart,' he said with his usual old– fashioned Texan charm and courtesy, smiling down at me. Then placing a strong arm about my waist, we strutted up and down in a mock foxtrot. But I stumbled and stood on his foot a couple of times, so he slowed down, finally waltzing out the room, tugging me after him like a sack of potatoes. I blushed as ten pairs of eyes followed my two left feet. 'She's as pleased as punch…that one thinks—!' I heard someone whisper. A long and lingering 'shush' went up in unison, drowning out the end of the sentence. 'She hear you!' This was Bunchee. Ron closed the door firmly behind us. He held me by my wrist and sniffed the inner part of it, enjoying the 'Midnight Oil' perfume I had sprayed there. He closed his eyes and took another sniff, deeper than the first. His Adam's apple went into convulsions, his eyes narrowed as he asked, accusingly.

'Hey, isn't that the same perfume as Sarsaparilla's?'

I nodded, looking away. Then tapping the side of his nose with his finger, he pushed a crisp five-pound note in my hand. 'Do us a favour, Sylvie, and get me some tobacco for my roll-ups… and some of those um… rubbers…balloons that I showed you in Lythams, right?…leave 'em there… along with the change,' he said, pointing to his coat hanging up in the hallway. He looked me up and down, his smile long gone. 'You might need to change first…but that's entirely up to you, hun…'

******

Chapter 3

The 'Polish' girl

People should keep out of other people's business. This was a lesson a visitor learned shortly after her arrival at New Horizons well after midnight, inconveniencing everyone. She was in her early twenties and sounded Eastern European...perhaps Russian. Strings of golden red hair tumbled down from underneath a woollen hat with a bobble. Her name was "Treblinka" or "Malinka" or something like that. I can't remember exactly. Her English was worse than Bunchee Golding's, and every time she would address me, I turned to Bunchee to help deal with her, as for some reason, hard to explain, our visitor's heavily accented speech struck terror in me. Ron, who could never turn away anyone in need, and Bunchee had to point or use gestures to 'converse' with her, but all the newcomer managed to say was "yes" and "no." I tried to join in but met with no success.

'How–long–doo-yoo-uu want to st-aaay?' Ron asked her, measuring a two-foot gap with his hands to signify the length of time she might want to stay, before pointing at her, and then at the ceiling above.

'Ah, yes,' said the youngster, nodding at everybody.

'You are Polish?' asked Bunchee.

'Ah…no. Happy...me happy.'

We checked her passport. She was Polish.

We stood her in front of our cavernous but bare fridge, and gesticulated like apes on speed, but she refused all offers of food although her eyes screamed, "I need nourishment!" Her belly bellowed like a goat's. We took her to the bathroom and shut the door on her. Having nowhere to put our guest, Ron asked us to deal with her which was his way of asking me to give up my basement room for the night. I shared Bunchee's bed that night and got a rotten night's sleep as she was a real kicker.

The next morning Bunchee and I went to wake up the Polish Girl. Bunchee had a large torch that doubled up as a table lamp. The girl lay still as a stone, and try as we might, we couldn't rouse her. 'Hey, there! It's time to get up!' I cried.

On raising the duvet, we saw a trickle of blood running out of her nose and cuts and bruises on her blue-black brow. Clumps of bright copper-coloured hair were lying on a blood-soaked pillow, and on the ground at the head of the bed. Bunchee shook her by the shoulders. She appeared dead. We put my compact mirror in front of her bruised mouth, swollen to twice its size. The mirror misted over faintly, and we heaved a sigh of relief.

We surmised that she had stumbled in the dark while walking around in unfamiliar surroundings. The bulb in my room had fused a long time ago, had never been replaced. The night before, I had taken pains to explain to her not to get out of bed because of the situation with the light, and the fact that the room was filled with all sorts of dangerous junk: a lawnmower with a broken blade that jutted out, bottles and cracked glasses in a box, dust covered vacuum cleaners, rusty pairs of ice skates, charred cutlery and china, broken kitchen equipment—toasters, kettles, microwave ovens of every description. 'Why can't people just do as they're told?' I grumbled to Bunchee who had grown pale and quiet.

When apprised of the situation, Ron squawked like a hen that's seen a kitchen knife coming towards it. 'Fu*k! F**k! F**k!' he yelled. He wrung his hands until his knuckles shone through; half collapsing and sobbing, shaking his fist at the sky, he bawled: 'Why me? Oh,

Gaa—hhhd! Why does this have to happen to me?'

I wondered why the commotion he was making did not rouse the other New Horizon residents.

The injured girl regained consciousness and as soon as she was able to sit up, Bunchee and I knew what we had to do.

'Not one too close to home,' Ron warned us.

******

While I was in the kitchen getting a wet cloth to wipe off the blood from our visitor's face, I heard raised voices coming from my basement room through the air vent. I had not realised that the acoustics in the house allowed you to hear people squabbling in my room in this way. I made my way downstairs, wondering where everybody was.

Bunchee was giving Ron a tongue-lashing in both English and Chinese, which she was sometimes prone to do when she wasn't coping very well. I hovered outside my room. Something about a passport.

'...I don't think I could do that young lady!' Ron was saying. 'I can't have you disappearing on me...' I couldn't work out how the mention of a passport was relevant to a situation where we had a girl who looked as if she'd been tossed down a ravine. Polish Girl was sitting up in my bed, clutching her head and bleating like a new-born lamb.

I turned to the noisy pair. 'Plee-ase,' I snapped, nodding in Polish Girl's direction, and as soon as Ron and Bunchee noticed me, the argument melted away and order was restored.

Then Ron muttered something under his breath that I didn't quite catch as I waited outside my own cramped sleeping quarters.

With a grimace, Bunchee let out a piercing scream, jumped on Ron's back, her stick insect arms around his neck, her short legs thrashing the air. He prised apart her arms as if they were rubber bands, leaving her slumped on the ground, groaning. Purple with rage, he shook Bunchee by her hair. 'Get a grip for f**k's sake!' Leaning down, he murmured in Polish Girl's pink, bloodied ear, shoving something inside her pocket, but I couldn't see what it was. Ron didn't look at me or speak to me as he left my room, leaving Bunchee sprawled on the floor.

The other Residents were still not up at that late hour in the morning, but I didn't have time to sort them out.

******

'An accident,' I told Polish Girl when we were in the taxi. 'You had an accident.' I pointed to her chest and then to her head. 'Yoo-u... had... an... ac-ci-dd-ent.'

'Okay? Understand? You have accident,' said Bunchee, shaking the drowsy girl by the arm, rubbing her shoulders brusquely, to keep her awake.

'Accident,' the youngster nodded, as if adding a new word to her English vocabulary. She chewed her lips trying not to cry. Her eyelids fluttered as her pupils roamed from side to side. We had left her woolly hat behind in our haste, and which we now regretted, as the moist gashes on her brow and scalp glistened noticeably under the lights of the taxi, glowing like the ruby brooch that Bunchee had kept hidden from Ron since she'd arrived.

'I ... accident,' repeated the Polish Girl mechanically. I tried to exchange a hopeful glance with Bunchee, but she held her head in her hands, refusing to look at me. Beaming a wide smile like the proud parent of a child who had uttered their first word, I gave Polish Girl an effusive thumbs-up. 'Good girl! Accident. Keep saying it, okay?' I told her, squeezing her arm.

******

I pointed to the 'Ladies' restroom. 'Time for a p*s—then you see the doctor, okay?' I said, nodding to encourage Polish Girl. 'Doc-tor, okay?' I said, raising my voice as she did not respond.

Little shiny tears began to fall like droplets of rain, and Polish Girl started to shake her head. 'No, no, no...please!' Her breath was hot, her chest heaving as she clutched at our sleeves, our hair, scratching our hands, until I had to whack her hand away...which made her step back. 'Please, no go,' she whispered, her left eye swollen shut, and, although we had washed her face with care, the left side had bloated to twice its size. It wasn't the rawness of her gaping cuts that attracted people's attention as they passed, but her delicate presence, the vulnerability of her small stature, her piteous whimpering.

Silver tracks of tears snaked down Bunchee's nose. She went inside a toilet cubicle, scuffled with the toilet roll holder before blowing her nose. I finally managed to get Polish Girl to enter a toilet cubicle, gesturing to her that we'd be waiting outside; all the while the stupid bi*ch pawed at us, her eyes pleading with us. As soon as the cubicle door was shut, Bunchee and I bounded out of the hospital grounds like gazelles being chased by their most feared predator. I hadn't known that Bunchee could race like the wind. I watched her as she ran, her tongue lolling in her mouth, panting all the way to the taxi rank.

******

Bunchee Golding squeezed her eyes together that made her look like a wrestler psyching themself up before a big match. She whimpered,
    'Poor girl!'
    She rocked herself. 'She just get here…no time to put down roots ….' she paused before continuing, '...and she is attacked like that!'
    I looked at her in surprise. 'What attack?'

'She is attacked—'

'Attacked, my ar*e!' I scoffed, rolling my eyes. 'You've been watching too many fu**ing crime dramas.' The taxi-driver glowered at us through his rear-view mirror.

Bunchee slaps my thigh sharply. 'Shut up! Think about it, Stoopid. Nobody in the New Horizon know you sleeping in my bed!'

The sing-song intonation of her voice was beginning to grate on my nerves—and she had just called me "stupid." Bunchee's cheeks flushed crimson as she clapped the air. 'And this poor foreigner girl comes in your room—only me...only you know she is there!' Her eyes gleamed as if they had been dipped in glitter and put back in. Every now and again the taxi driver would glance at her surreptitiously through his rear-view mirror. Bunchee pushed my shoulders back, pinning me down, so that she could look me in the eyes. 'Do you see? Do you see?' she asked.

'All I see is that Polish Girl shouldn't have been snooping around in my room,' I insisted.

'You so...so thick, I want to cry!'

'No, you're the thickie!' I say, pushing her hands away.

'None come down today! Do you see?'

'Stop chatting sh**' I told her, delving into my jean's pocket.

'You so stoopid...'

'I don't know about you but I'm starving. We could get a McDonalds,' I said, holding out a ten-pound note to her. 'We could have everything on the menu we've ever wanted with this...we don't have to play some stupid pretend wish game...'

She stared at the money, transfixed. 'Where you find that?'

'It's alright. The hospital's gonna look after her, aren't they? She won't—'

'You dirty thief!' she roared, leaning away from me as if I had a contaminating disease. 'Oh, Gah-had! You take the money Ron give her! Thief! Why you not — just die?' As we were nearing home, she muttered stuff in Chinese, which she always did when she got mad.

She got out of the taxi, slamming the door behind her, continuing to cuss, but instead of landing like real English swearwords, real English bullets like "Sh**head" or "Pr**k," the topsy-turvy sounding nature of her swear words—that you didn't know were coming or going,— the up-and-down tinkling sound of her intonation had me in stitches. Judging by past experiences, I think she had called me a "heartless bit*h."

'By the way—it's "New Horizons",' I shouted after her, sticking my head out the taxi window. 'There's no definite article!— and there's an "s" at the end—"New Horizons!" D'you hear me? It's New Horizons! –you language-murdering freak!' I sat back to enjoy the rest of the ride home.

******

Chapter 4

Training Week with Wilbur

Not long after the incident with the Polish Girl, Ron made an announcement at TableTalk. He playfully threw a glossy catalogue at me, and then half crouching behind me, his arms around my neck, he held me close, as we flicked through the pages together. The catalogue showed people dressed in army fatigues, carrying rifles and aiming them at targets. Men and women, carrying backpacks, were shown tackling assault courses and taking part in combat activities.

'You—young lady,' he said to me joyfully, 'are going on an all-expenses trip to Arlington—my hometown—to attend army boot camp!'

The other residents looked at one another, their watery smiles dribbled away like newly laid snow on rooftops, their eyes like dead birds, hard and glassy. A week-old snowman exuded more warmth than this lot. Bunchee left the room. We had not been on speaking terms since our quarrel over Polish Girl. Roly-Poly, a girl who ate other people's puddings behind their backs, rolled her eyes and made a small circular motion near her temple with her finger when Ron wasn't looking.

When Buttons, a girl with broad shoulders strong enough to pull an elephant, asked why I had been specifically chosen for this exceptional advantage, adding that she, too, wouldn't mind going to Arlington... Ron put up a warning finger and her voice dribbled away at once. 'Sylvie has shown exemplary behaviour during her time here.' He paused to consider the effect of his own statement, before continuing: '...the only one who has consistently and sincerely placed the needs of others before her own.' His chest puffed out with pride.

And then he pulled me towards him, ruffling my hair. Roly-Poly pretended to shove a finger down her throat to fake throwing up, with Pigtails following suit.

Later in the kitchen or on the landing, they would say things like, '...Ron's seen your potential! You'd make a great assassin...' or 'Don't forget to wash and press your fatigues while you're in Arlington, Sylvie...they like people to look smart at bootcamp...'

'I'll believe it when we see it,' said Arora, the corners of her mouth pointing down towards her boots.

I'd never been abroad since family holidays when I was still living at home. I felt nauseous and excited at the prospect of going to Texas, but over time, I started to relax more, daydreaming about army training. I went to the library to read up on army life and found a book on bodybuilding exercises, and one with the title, 'Eating for Stamina and Strength'. I took out a book called 'Building the Body' published by Nigerian Press-Nigeria, but discovered it was full of biblical scripture and guidance on how to lead an exemplary Christian life.

When Ron was running errands or attending one of his week-long conferences to do with New Horizons 'business,' as he called it, with one or two of the residents in tow for administrative support, I would sneak into Ron's room to use the only full-length mirror in the house. The key to his bedroom was left in Bunchee's safe-keeping, but she would hand it over to me just to get a quiet life. I practised military and karate poses as shown in the library books. Back then, I was a picture of health, flat-chested, not pretty but slim and sturdy on my feet; possessing shiny pink gums, and a creamy complexion, except for my cheeks, chin, and the area around my nose and eyes.

I began to help more in the kitchen, joined the others for breakfast, contributed to their crafty jokes and garrulous small talk. I got to hear about their hang-ups and frustrations without taking them too seriously. I even risked a boll**king from Ron when I allowed them to watch late-night TV shows, past curfew hours. I threw my head back to join in with their laughter, watching programmes that Ron described as 'televisual b*m-fluff.' Despite being singled out for an once-in-a-lifetime trip, I wasn't going to lord it over them. I was still the same Sylvie DaSouza, aged twenty-five, worthy of charitable investment that would help me reach my full potential.

As I waited to be 'called up' to boot camp, I made things happen at New Horizons: a trip to the children's zoo, the cinema, the County Fair Market. I also helped peel potatoes in abundance, washed the windows with an extendable brush, including the ones on the upper floors, hung out the washing and took them in. I took Ron's shirts to the drycleaners and wheeled out the bins on bin day. In this way, I draped a cosy blanket around me to keep the chill off my bones as I waited for my big day to arrive. I would often go into the garden in the evening to let the cool breeze race over my cheeks and play with my hair. Sometimes I would stand in a thunderstorm, letting the rain pelt me with 'pennies from heaven'—oh! The wonderful rain!

One evening, long after bedtime, as I was undertaking a random inspection of the house, I heard muffled voices coming from the kitchen. The door stood ajar like an open book, and I heard fragments of hushed talk.

'....this way ...his hands stay clean...'

'....pushed around enough as it is...'

'...the charity commission (voice is muffled here) has to say about bodyguards...'

'Wait! Who's there? I can hear...' someone had called out. I scurried back to my basement room. Four against one. I'd have been outnumbered.

******

Bunchee was the only one excited about my impending trip. We prattled away like garden birds comparing notes at a seed festival. She drew up a list— "Sylvie's Packing List"—of all the essentials I'd need. We wrote on two sheets of kitchen towel: passport, sleeping bag, green household soap, torch, Swiss army knife, compass, nail file, waterproofs, medication, Savlon, First Aid basic kit, sewing kit, mosquito repellent, durable underwear, maps, swimsuit, walking boots, gloves, toothpaste...and toothbrush etc.

"Sylvie's Packing List" was given pride of place on the New Horizon's general notice board, and further items would be added as we thought of them. One morning, I woke to find Bunchee Golding punching my arm, gasping and gnashing her teeth.

'It's gone, Sylv—ieee! Wake up!' She grabbed my hand, not slowing down once until she had dragged me upstairs to the notice board, where a stark, blank space screamed out at us. "Sylvie's Packing List" had disappeared.

At our TurnTable meeting, Ron's lips were pursed so tightly you couldn't push a penny past them; his eyes were like a panther's scouring the landscape for prey. He spoke in a low growl that made us all aware that this was a serious matter.

'I want to get to the bottom of this whole darned thing!' he said. 'Girls should not behave badly with each other. I want you to think carefully before you speak.' He scrutinised each of the women in turn, as if he and he alone could detect a sign that would give the guilty culprit away. Some of the girls— there were ten of us — looked blank, some weary, or indifferent, and some were simply intrigued by the whole incident. I think Ron was referring to my packing list, but why was he taking it so seriously? I could always write another one.

Nobody said anything.

Then like a conjuror, Ron made the packing list—"Sylvie's Packing List" materialise from underneath a copy of Ron's monthly newsletter called 'The Bulletin Board.'

I stared into my lap. Bunchee squeezed my hand underneath the table, her eyes a murky sea of stillness.

'I'm gonna pass this round for you to read,' Ron said grimly, and slid "Sylvie's Packing List" under the first person's nose to his left, who responded by pulling a face. 'And then I want whoever's responsible for this mindless atrocity to own up, and say why she did it,' he continued. The list was passed around in this fashion making the girls either grin, snigger or re-direct their gaze. I was the last to see it...and the offending words that had been written in a different hand to the rest of the list, was in red ink; bleeding all over the lower half of the kitchen towel, someone had added the word, 'CHASTITY BELT.'

******

Not long after, Bunchee told me that my trip had been put 'on hold'. Chastity-Belt-Gate (as the others called it) had made Ron think twice about my personal safety abroad as I would be a long way from home.

******

'Boy, do I have a surprise for you, Sylvie,' Ron said, beaming at me. 'My brother Wilbur is visiting us this summer. He's a former marine who's trained in similar training camps that you were supposed to have visited in Texas. He tugged my hair at the nape of my neck. 'Now, tell me ...if this is a good idea— just let me know...but I've suggested he organises a basic course in military training when he gets here. You'll be covering essentially the same ground as if you'd attended boot camp in Arlington.' His blue eyes shimmered as he gazed into mine. 'Is that gonna suit you, my darling girl?'

'Sure. That's fine,' I said, after a long pause, trying to keep the flatness out of my voice.

His face fell like a pile of wood logs, disappointed at my low key, unsmiling response.

'I love the sound of that, really, I do, Ron—really, I do! I can't wait!'

'That's swell! Real swell, Sylvie. You're a trooper!' The tips of my ears glowed as I felt them redden. A 'trooper' was the highest praise he could confer on anyone. 'You'll have a blast—I promise!'

At least I'd get a tailored course from a qualified trainer. It was better than nothing, and this way I'd save face with the others. I had a burning question that I wanted to ask but it stuck in my throat like a fish bone. 'Yes?' he enquired, sensing my hesitation.

'I don't want to sound like a...cretin Ron...but what's the training *for* exactly?' I asked.

He straightened himself, scratching the side of his head and neck.

I continued. 'It's just that ...the girls are saying that you ...you want me to leave ....to go and join the army, instead.'

'What the devil—? he said, startled at first, staring at me as if I'd gone mad. 'Oh, they're joshing with you!' He burst out laughing. 'I just thought you'd be the kinda gal to enjoy something...well you know...some structured activity. You'll have the chance to improve your mental and physical stamina...and I... just thought...'

His mouth kept moving, but no other discernible words followed. 'Can the others join me?' I continued, wiping my nostrils with the sleeve of my jumper rolled over my hand. 'I think I'd appreciate some company.'

Ron looked at me and rubbed the side of his nose, his voice jaunty and light. 'Don't make me smack your bottom—you sissy! The training programme's for you and you alone!'

A pang of something strange and imperceptible, rippled through my tummy, and turned my brain to mush. I put it down to the stale cheese that we'd scraped over the pasta dish at lunch.

******

Ron's brother didn't come to us until a year later. His name was Wilbur. Wilbur Partridge. It seemed as if he had been drawn in five rounded brushstrokes that made him look babyish. His hair was cropped short, his multiple chins looked like steps that led to the rest of his misshapen, sponge-like face.

Wilbur looked nothing like Ron, and there were whispers in the kitchen that they weren't actually related. Wilbur twanged his braces and broke out into an ear-splitting laugh every now and then, even if there was nothing funny to laugh about. Some of the girls wondered if he took those 'happy pills', the sort you could get freely in America.

Captain Wilbur Partridge told me about his army days, how he used to play the reveille at dawn. When I looked up enquiringly, Wilbur explained, 'It's a soldier's duty call—to stir him...or her into action, to fight the battle for the loyal cause.'

'The loyal call! Yessir!' I barked in the manner of soldiers in US television movies, and at this, his cheeks suffused with colour.

But Wilbur hadn't packed his bugle, as in his haste, he'd forgotten to put it on his packing list. I wanted to tell him about my packing list for Arlington but decided against it.

He gave me our training timetable, and I was immediately struck by the scope and breadth of the different activities.

The workshop shed in the garden measured ten feet by eight, and everyone helped to clear out the clutter for our...my training programme. A foam mat filled two-thirds of the room. Wilbur used a sack of wheat flour from the kitchen, the size of a large child's torso, which he hung from the wooden rafters. Our punch bag. Wilbur handed me a pair of weighty boxing gloves, and asked me to throw punches into his open hands that he outstretched in front of him. When I gave out puny punches, I would have to take off the gloves so that he could then put them on to demonstrate the correct way to punch; in this way we shared the boxing gloves between us.

'Try and punch rather than push! Like this, DaSouza! Bend your knees slightly—like this— and dance about, see? See my footwork...one...two...three!' Wilbur instructed, bouncing from one foot to another; a "hot-shoe shuffle," he called it.

'Yessir!'

'Got anything we can use for reveille, DaSouza?'

'No, sir!'

'Hmm. We need... something for reveille'

'There's an old dinner gong, sir, that I could get hold of,' I said.

'You do that, DaSouza. That'll be just dandy,' he said, letting out a loud guffaw, nodding his head in appreciation.

I would have preferred a bugle but a series of rapid strikes on the gong each morning at 8.00am outside my basement window did just as well, setting us up for the rest of the day. I kept the gong under my bed long after Wilbur had left us.

My commanding officer showed me how to do push-ups, pull-ups, sit-ups, squats, lounges and abdominal crunches. He taught me how to salute, use a skipping rope for exercise, and how to tie someone up with the same skipping rope. I learned about the different types of knots depending on whether you were a soldier or a marine, and how to check your immediate environment for 'booby' traps.

On our second day Wilbur managed to buy a mannequin doll from a local fashion store. Jo-Jo, a new arrival, claimed to have seen the same mannequin on a rubbish dump in the woods at the back of our house, just to make me mad.

******

'If you're dealing with more than one assailant,' advised Wilbur, demonstrating with the mannequin doll, 'you can tie one of 'em up in a separate room...like this, gag 'em...then stack plates on their back. That way you'll have time to deal with a second assailant... or to deal with other urgent situations as they arise,' Under Wilbur's guidance, I bound his hands and feet, gagged him with one of my clean socks, and piled plates on his back. I checked the room (the shed) for booby 'traps' he had laid for me but was distracted by a spider dangling from the door frame. It took me a while trying to guide the spider down before I squelched it underfoot. As I hadn't released Wilbur in good time, he wriggled in discomfort so that our kitchen plates chipped or cracked when they fell off his back. He gasped as if he were dying once I'd taken the gag off.

Weight training consisted of sugar bags of varying weights stuffed into ASDA shopping bags, and suspended, on either end, from a sturdy tree branch. Wilbur laid the branch—with shopping bags swinging from it—across my shoulders, while I worked my arms up and down to lift them.

On one occasion, Chilblains, a Resident flirt, came over from the house saying that they had run out of sugar, and please could they borrow a bag from us? In this way, she slaked her curiosity about my military trainer. Grabbing her by the scruff of her neck, I shoved her out of the work shed, despite Wilbur shouting at me to 'Cool it!'

Wilbur took a bag of sugar out of our ASDA bag, ran out after Chilblains, and handed it to her. She put her finger in one corner of her mouth, simpering. The two of them spent the next five minutes chatting, which incensed me as it was eating into my valuable training schedule. With a bag of sugar gone, the 'weights' were now uneven, and when I brought them up and down, the lighter bag would spin, first one way and then another—ruining everything!

Wilbur also demonstrated key combat techniques. He stood behind the mannequin bringing it down to the ground in what he called a 'near-naked chokehold.'

'You get the assailant—or aggressor— like this, and transition into a "seatbelt grip" like this!' With the mannequin face up, lying on top of him, placed in a chokehold, Wilbur's legs wrapped around the body of the doll, his arms around its torso, squeezing like a snake.

'See? You don't want to hurt the subject—just subdue her.... Priority must always be given to *de-escalating* a situation, to keep everybody safe and not hurt them,' he panted heavily from the floor.

'Yessir!'

As Wilbur lay on the mat, his hips started to gyrate, thrusting to maintain 'control' of the mannequin. I absorbed every part of his demonstration, preparing to re-enact the exercise. I counted each pelvic thrust, each throttling motion, working out how I would replicate the same.

Wilbur's eyes were clenched shut now—I must remember to do the same. The rhythmic pelvic thrusts were becoming stronger, as he subdued the enemy, for the last time, his legs thrashing about him. Eventually, with eyes still closed, he dropped his head back, and let out an intense moan, his hot breath reaching me as I stood over him. With face twitching, his eyes fell open, the whites rolling to the back of his head. His arms dropped languidly to their side like rag bundles coming undone.

The mannequin doll glided off him, still facing upwards, rebounding ignominiously on the floor where there was no safety mat. Entirely subdued, it had nothing to say. Wilbur remained where he was, continuing to moan, the tip of his tongue poking out: 'Oh-oh-ohoh! Jeez-oh- jeez-oh-jeee-eeez!' The growing intensity of his cries, his out of control, fat tongue, and his feverish demeanour made me wonder if he was having a fit.

'Shall I get help, sir? Tell me what to do, Sir!...Sir?' Wilbur held up a bony finger, holding it there until his senses recalled him. 'DaSouza....d'you think…I've come over a bit queer… d'you think we could stop there?' he gasped, clasping his throat.

It was still early afternoon. 'Sure...that's fine, we can finish...' I said, trying to sound nonchalant.

He leaped off the floor to his feet like a graceful gymnast finishing a routine, but some realisation, on his part, turned his elegance into a lumpiness. And like a saddle-sore cowboy, Wilbur Partridge made his way back to the house, leaving me with my head bowed and alone.

******

'I don't think you wanna do this, okay? I don't think you do!' said my instructor as I brandished a potato peeler at him. A potato peeler was the least innocuous weapon we could find, but it could also do real damage if needed. We wanted a frisson of risk, an element of danger for the role-play we were now engaged in.

As he grasped my arm, bending it to get me to drop the peeler, the sound of ripping material filled the ten-by-eight foot space of the training shed. Thwa- acck! I could see a four- inch gap in the seat of his pants, his off-white underpants showing underneath. Before I could blink, he had whipped off his trousers, as if we were fellow comrades in a changing room, two souls stitched and bonded together by shared military experience. 'I'll wait for you,' he grinned, throwing his pants at me so that they landed over my head.

We had to stop our exercises while I sewed up the jagged tear back at the house. My fingers trembled as I darned with a blunt needle and thread, closing the gap in my superior officer's pants.

The other residents exchanged looks, giggling behind their wrists. 'How did *that* tear happen in *that* place?'

On learning that Wilbur was alone in the training shed, a three-girl band formed instantly, almost falling over themselves to prepare and serve him tea, using the china plates reserved for guests we'd always hoped to have but never did. I didn't want them eating into my precious training time and was about to warn them off—that the first person to walk into that bl**dy training room might not wake up to see a bl**dy new day!

But when I saw their bright, excited faces, their anticipation of mingling with rare male company, sharing his space, their collective breath hotter than the tea they longed to dish up, I decided to let them have their way.

When Ron had insisted that his brother take up external lodgings, the residents had wrinkled up their noses at Ron. Part of the challenge left to them was to try to bend the rules a little, to get Wilbur's attention for a minute or two— just for the sake of it, to see if they could!

But within five minutes, the women had stomped back to the kitchen, their faces ugly and frumpy, their lips drawn back exposing teeth, noses flaring like nervous mares.

They washed and dried the tea things in silence. They'd left uneaten the brick of home-made cake and wonky biscuits they had taken out to Wilbur.

'Lost your appetite?' I asked, smoothing down the reinforced stitching I had carefully sewn into the seat of Wilbur's pants, hoping he'd notice the effort I'd made when I presented them to him.

'He was wearing Snoopy underpants!' said Aqua, our youngest resident. 'Snoopy, *the dog*, for f**k's sake!'

******

'What's the matter DaSouza?' Wilbur asked me on the third day.

'I feel a bit...woozy, sir,' I said.

'You're not used to strenuous exercise—that's what it is. We'll soon knock you into shape— make you fit for purpose. Okay?' Then standing behind me, he punched me between the shoulder blades that made me stand taller, and in the same movement, lunged at me, wrapping his stocky arms around my legs. The element of surprise he had always spoken about! He chortled as I went down like a bowling pin, face down on the mat, dazed and bruised.

******

Our afternoon training sessions were taken up with practical activities: how to set traps so that you can detect if someone's been messing about in your room. Wilbur took me down to my basement room, asking me to detect any of the changes he had made without my knowledge. He'd switched things around while I was having breakfast.

'This game requires you to have a good memory.'

'I could recite large chunks of poetry ...at school,' I said, trying not to sound boastful.

'That's a bit different...this is observational. You need to recall where everything was before I switched things up. Got that?' asked Wilbur.

'Yessir!'

I only managed to get one of Wilbur's "switches" correctly. The books on army training, paraded along the mantel shelf, had been muddled up and rearranged by him. I didn't get the other two changes: my toothbrush had been 'left' on the bedside table; the pillow had been placed at the foot of the bed instead of at its head. I swore to myself that I'd be more observant in future.

Wilbur shared tips on how to strengthen memory by using word association games, and repetition through the rhythms found in word patterns.

He also showed me how a tiny slip of paper closed in the crack of the door (placed low) could alert me to a potential intruder.

'Why don't any of the doors in this god**mned place have any locks on 'em?' he asked.

I shrugged my shoulders. It didn't bother me. I was used to it.

Wilbur showed me the tricks of interrogation: how a liar will stare to the left when making things up, and to the right when remembering true events. Wilbur turned to me, clapping his hands, speaking all of a sudden in a serious, no-nonsense voice.

'DaSouza! Tell me three things about yourself! One of 'em has gotta be an outright lie, yeah,...then I'll tell you which one's the lie,' he said. 'I'm gonna be 'reading' you, to show you how it's done...'

I looked at him, my eyes flicking from the walls to the ceiling, to the ground.

'Be quick about it!'

'Er...well...' I coughed

'Come on!' he growled near my ear. 'Jump to it!' He started to circle me as I sat transfixed to the spot, panting and sweating. 'This is about the truth! You're ruining the task!'

'But I—' I said in a quivering voice, slouched over the table, shoulders hunched.

'Three things! Don't make me snap your fu**ing neck!' Hot splashes of saliva rained down on me, and any confidence I had buckled like a house of cards in the wind.

So unexpected was his anger that I had to blink hard to oust the tears that threatened to spring up. I looked up at the ceiling, and as I started to speak, I remembered to let my gaze hover to the right—over his left ear: the truth lay there.

'Sir, I've never been in love! Sir, I cannot tell a lie! Sir, I think I might kill someone, someday!'

After a pause, Wilbur shook my hand until my fingers grew numb; his grin fixed, his pupils like black pebbles. 'Gee! That sure was swell, DaSouza!' he said. 'You coped real well under pressure!'

'Thank you, sir!

'Apart from the beginning ...when your eyes were rolling all over the place—ah… you definitely *did* look shifty there— but you swung it around, you soon got into the swing of things. You spoke with such confidence –with a hint of bravado, dare I say?—that I couldn't tell which one of your god**mned statement's the lie! Dang! That's terrific!' His mouth was suddenly full of shimmering teeth, his head bobbing up and down in admiration. 'Da*n! I've been tagged out!'

A series of hiccups, like a stone creating ripples as it skims water, dislodged from my throat, making my eyes burn.

'Hm-mm. I think the lie was the last one—I can't imagine you'd want to kill anyone, DaSouza!'

'Oh yes, sir,' I said. 'I do intend to kill ....eventually...when the opportunity arises...! '

'Hmm. That's mighty complex.' He paused and wiped his hands on his trousers. 'So, which was the lie?'

'Sir...I'd rather not say.'

'Why not?'

'It would destroy the integrity of the task, sir!'

Wilbur stopped smiling. He leaned back in his chair mulling over what I'd said. Then without a word, he went into the garden, lit up a cigarette, sweating profusely as he blew circles of wispy smoke.

******

We continued our training into the following week. I woke up late. There'd been no gong call outside my window. The punch bag was still there, hovering between heaven and earth, but the boxing gloves were missing from the hook where they had not long been swinging. I went to find Ron, tripping over my legs, now useless and unsteady.

From the door to his room, slightly ajar, I watched Bunchee shovelling a clump of sausage and egg into his mouth, wiping his greasy chin with an elegant mauve napkin. Ron stopped chewing as soon as he saw me. Bunchee jerked away from Ron as if he had bad breath, pulling out one of her watery smiles for me. Picking up a sausage, he resumed eating, munching noisily. 'His house is in foreclosure, and he's had to go back home,' said Ron. 'He asked me to thank you for being a good sport, and to say "goodbye," for him,' and with that Ron waggled his fingers at me.

I walked aimlessly through the house, and the desolate training shed, lifting objects, peering into bins, boxes and laundry baskets, not really sure what I was looking for. I had planned to ask Wilbur for his magnificent golden training whistle—something to remember him by, but now I had nothing. My training was incomplete, and the loss of it filtered through my bones like iced blood. I felt that I had lost a close confidante in Wilbur, although sewing up his pants was the nearest we'd ever come to sharing a real moment of connection, a moment that had meant everything and nothing to me.

I had found someone prepared to horse around with me, but with whom I'd never ventured an opinion on any subject or shared an emotional exchange. I didn't even have an address to write him, and I didn't want to ask Ron.

My arms grew heavy, my ears filled with the noise of popping corn. Shooting pains traversed my entire body and got so bad that I had to spend the rest of the day in bed. Bunchee, with a soft, rested face, silky, flowing hair, came to lie next to me on my tombstone-mattress-that-was-my-bed. Wiping away my tears with the palms of her hands, she sang to me in Chinese, but her high-pitched voice hurt my ears. I didn't want her to leave, so I let her stroke my hair, croon gently in my ear like a Chinese mother would to her sad Chinese child.

My carefully tailored training from Wilbur stood me in good stead in the years that followed. I paid more attention to fitness and exercise, increased my intake of whole grains and pulses to keep the weight off, and made sure everyone else did the same. There was an occasion when one of the New Horizon residents, an older lady with thick braided hair, tried to hit me over the head with a frying pan. I was able to bring her to her knees by tugging at her braid and placing her in a chokehold to disarm her. In this way, I learned to keep order within the house for the benefit and safety of all the residents that came through our doors.

******

Chapter 5

PastaPlates- a Vegan Job

PastaPlates was a restaurant for vegans and vegetarians, using imitation meat products at a time when going meatless was a growing fad. During this time, people were declaring war on their bodies, using language to match: fighting the flab, the battle of the bulge, going at the punch ball—hammer and tongs! I was glued to television programmes where celebrities gave advice on exercise, fitness and weight-loss training. New Horizon residents did an hour's exercise together before having boiled oats for breakfast.

PastaPlates was a popular restaurant, in the heart of the busy town centre. I worked the morning shift from 8.00pm to 12.00pm, washing plates from breakfast time as well as from the evening before. Mr Economides, the owner-manager, thought dishwashers were too expensive to run, and would only use them for heavily soiled pots and pans. The crockery, cutlery, ovenware were all washed in a washing-up bowl in the sink—by me!

'If we had a hundred cats, they could lick the plates clean at the end of each day,' said our owner-manager to me with a twinkle in his eye. The chef, a morose-looking woman called Marta, pointed out to Mr Economides, that cats weren't vegans. 'You'd need to smear a bit of meat or fish on the dishes, and they'd soon do the job in record time. You wouldn't need any washer-uppers—!' she'd say, throwing a crafty look in my direction.

I looked at her with consternation, but when she broke into a cackle, I laughed, flicking some water at her head.

Mr Economides, a bear of a man, wore a cream-coloured suit, and a spotted bow tie at all times of the day. His English was flawless, but he would exaggerate his faint Greek accent at times. While I worked at the sink, he would sometimes grip my chin between two fingers, look deep into my eyes, before singing my praises to the skies! I was one of the best human dishwashers he'd ever had, and this burly man, my kindly manager, wanted me to work the evening shift as well. But Ron had ruled it out because of my commitments to keeping order at New Horizons.

I loved my job, the food even more, as at the end of my shift, the chef would place a hot nutritious meal in front of me. The joys of working in a spacious, well-equipped kitchen were endless. The washing-up liquid bottles had Greek writing on them which I couldn't read. The name of the soap translated into English meant 'Knockout,' or something like that. Hella informed me that her father-owner-manager had the washing up liquid flown in by members of his family whenever they came to visit from abroad. It had a crisp, sparkling smell of honeysuckle and mint and produced three times as many bubbles than anything you could get over here. When alone in the kitchen, I'd pour some of the washing-up liquid into a small jam-jar brought from home. I shoved it right down into the bottom of my rucksack as a treat for Bunchee and our allies to enjoy. I allowed them exclusive use of 'Knockout' whenever I organised the washing- up rota.

The liquid soap made my skin condition flare up, and by the time my shift came to an end, my hands resembled a mass of potholes and craters. I didn't use the washing-up gloves provided as they were full of holes. Best of all I enjoyed the lashings of hot water that came with my job. Hot water and heating were luxuries in New Horizons and only available at fixed times of the day.

With eyes closed, I swayed on the balls of my feet to the sound of music played over the sound system. I 'played soft drums' with the cutlery, sponging, scrubbing, and drying in between playing.

I single-handedly kept the restaurant going. People needed clean plates and cutlery to eat their food. I looked forward to my job and served up numerous tales about my experiences at PastaPlates to the other residents. I cheered them with my story offerings, their mouths agape, 'starting little fires within,' as Bunchee described it. None of the other women were allowed to work except me.

Within a month of my arrival, Mr Economides, who took to calling me the "Mama Poppins of PastaPlates," trusted me enough to take on additional responsibilities. I was happy refilling the salt and pepper grinders, wiping down twelve tables covered with checked green plastic tablecloths in the dining area, or running a steaming hot cloth over the laminated menus.

******

My manager explained to us that his daughter, Hella, the "Unmarriageable One" was the "brains" of the family who had shown a flair for numbers at school. She did the business accounts after spending two years learning book-keeping at college. Mr Economides openly despaired, to anyone who'd listen, that Hella, due to turn thirtyone that year, would in all likelihood be left on the shelf, on account of her selfishness and unhealthy opinions about men.

'Ah, this Hella! She doesn't know what she's blo**y talking about,' Mr Economides complained, putting on a heavily-accented Greek voice, which made him appear, to my mind anyway, like one of those TV stand-up comics: affable yet knowing, cheeky but a tad malevolent. 'She says, "The man must be a good man." He must be this—he must be that—this-and-that-this-and-that! Conditions! Always conditions!' he'd exclaim, forgetting that he had shared these sentiments with us several times before. 'She says, "Oh, Papa! He must be honest, loyal— and, above all, he must be willing to come home to me at the end of each day!"' Mr Economides stopped to mop his brow. 'Everything is "it must be... must, must!" So I say to this Hella— "Why don't you settle down with a bl**dy dog then? You don't need a man!"'

Hella rolled her eyes as we looked at her in mock sympathy. 'I have no desire to be ruled by a man, and that's just a simple fact my father will have to get used to,' she said. 'I'm perfectly capable of making my own decisions, Papa, dear!' She faked irritation in her voice, but we could tell she was pleased to have this comedic routine with her father.

Mr Economides threw a tea towel at her, pretending to be annoyed.

'Ah! I'm thankful your mother's no longer alive—God have mercy on her soul— to have to listen to your bull**it,' said Mr Economides. Then he came over to the sink to appeal to me, 'Speak to her, please Syl-vie! Knock some sense into her! I beg of you! Tell her: if the husband's got his own hair AND his own teeth—Rejoice! Two marks out of five is fine! Tell her! Two out of five is *do-able*!' He lumbered off to an adjoining storeroom as he was wont to do whenever he got excited.

'She's blessed with good fortune and will find exactly who she wants without your help,' Marta called after him.

'Don't mind Dad,' Hella said, grinning at me without any ill-will. 'He just wants me to bring in an extra pair of hands for the business, and when my father's gone, he wants the man—the husband— to make all the business decisions. He doesn't have a son– just little old me!'

'When he's gone?' I asked.

Hella's forehead resembled a rivulet of wrinkles. 'When he must ...you know...give up the business...'

'But a man can help his wife without dominating her,' I interceded, feeling some loyalty towards my silver-haired boss. 'Besides, two heads *are* better than one!'

Mr Economides stormed into the kitchen again, and hearing the tail end of what I've said, he patted my shoulder which made me wince. 'Good girl, Sylvie! Good girl! Two heads are indeed better than one! The man is the controlling mind of the operation...the business, while the woman does things –let us call her—"the do-er," the one who makes things happen...that's how it's always been—and will be for evermore!' He went off to bring up the wine bottles for the evening custom.

'And which one are you?' Hella asked me, untying an apron from her well-padded waist.

I looked up, puzzled.

'You seem to agree with my Dad. Are you the "controller" or the "do-er" in your household?'

The glass I was rinsing tinkled merrily in the sink as it shattered. My neck muscles tensed up, my lips stuck fast. Her not-so-friendly honey-brown eyes were watching me as I held up my hand to reveal a wine-coloured drop of blood running down my wet finger. I scrabbled around for a plaster in the First Aid Box pretending to be more concerned about my finger than her questions.

''I don't know...maybe I'm a bit of both?' I said.

'Ron was here last night—' Hella began, a smirk playing on her lips.

Suddenly, I didn't like her anymore.

I tried to control my shaky voice. 'Ron? Here?'

'There was a question to be asked....and so... my father did it in the Greek way. We had a celebratory feast all planned...'

'Ron had a feast—?'

'No, silly! My father!'

I picked up the dishcloth and began to wipe down the worktops with an attention that I'd never before given to worktops.

'What...what did he want?'

'Your hand in marriage...'

My heart skipped a beat, my legs wobbled so that I had to sit down. 'Who? Ron?' I gasped.

Hella whinnied like a horse. 'No, silly! My dad. My dad wants to marry you!'

'Oh,' I said, snapping shut the First Aid Box.

'Don't you want to know what Ron said?'

'I already know,' I said, throwing the dishcloth at her head.

******

Ron had always told us that disappointments made us better people, left us stronger and wiser to meet any future problems head on. He often related an incident when he was due to be called up for national service in the States, but the army had sent his papers to the wrong address—or was it that they had mislaid them?—which led to Ron missing military action in Vietnam.

'I was real disappointed about that! But the army had to do without Private Partridge I guess,' he said with a smidgen of pride. And at each re-telling, the chuckle he emitted was longer and more ear-splitting than the last.

******

Chapter 6

Sleepy-Head

When I got home after work, two residents (whose names escape me) were sitting on the stairs, one smoothing the other's hair with her hands, twisting a mound of locks to form a bun. The one having her hair styled, mouthed something to me and gestured in a way that made as much sense to me as the bookies I'd seen on the horse racing tracks on TV. The girl pressed one finger to her lips, then made a jabbing motion like a woodpecker's beak towards the TV room where two distinct voices were screaming at each other like a married couple.

I approached the open door and peered inside. Ron's long, broad back was turned at a slight angle away from me. The mirror over the mantelpiece reflected his thunderous expression, his face the colour of burnt-red brick.

'Why can't you be a *good* girl?' he asked, his tone tender, cajoling.

He towered over a wispy-looking girl in lobster-pink pumps, and a matching thinly-meshed sleeveless top, that showed her bra straps underneath. Her milky arms were thrown across her fulsome chest, her chestnut hair falling about her neck, I knew instantly that she was in the wrong.

I had named the girl Sleepy-Head because of her resemblance to Marilyn Monroe— only her eyes, that is— as if she'd been pulled out from a deep slumber. This resident was, if I remember correctly, a bl**dy nuisance. She used to forever run herself ragged doing things for Ron, anticipating his every need, chasing after him with cups of tea or milk and cookies. She even volunteered to cook his favourite meatloaf dish or iron his silk shirts—ironing her tender feelings for him into each cuff, sleeve and collar.

'I was only a few minutes,' Sleepy-Head was remonstrating, her chin tugged down towards her curvy, solid chest. A burgundy scarf that usually hung on the hallway coat stand, was lying at her feet like a wine-filled puddle. The TV rumbled low in the corner, showing an excitable man, thrashing about in a television studio, calling out, 'Higher or lower?' to an appreciative audience who conveyed their adulation of him by emitting shrieks of laughter and squeals of delight.

The cushions on the sofa were bent out of shape, delineating a spot that had recently been vacated. The aimless pair on the stairs, were hoping to return to watch their programme.

'God**mnit! You look like you're off to some honky-tonk bar!' Ron's upbraiding of her tore off in mid-sentence, as he did a double take on seeing me in the doorway.

His face softened at once, and a sigh burst from his lips; his eyes swivelled towards the ceiling and he sighed again, more loudly this time. With head cocked to one side, he beckoned me to him.

'Ah! There you are!'

With all that sighing like a wind at high tide, his petulant tone, the way he glanced at his watch with narrowed eyes, were intended to convey a rebuke along the lines of: 'And about time too, Sylvie! Where the hell have you been?' My heart skittered across my chest, a premonition of things to come.

Ron turned towards me, one hand on his hip, the other over his mouth, his passions subsiding to a low simmer. The high colour drained from his neck and was replaced by an attractive pink bloom.

His voice was now soft, half-jeering, half playful.

'Our new dress code,' he said, indicating Sleepy Head with a nod of his head.

I was now involved. I'd been drawn in.

Ron picked up the fallen scarf, casting it over Sleepy-Head like a net, to help cover the large expanse of her chest. A scowl fixed on her darkening face, she turned to face him. 'I'm a big girl now,' she asserted. 'I can do as I please…'

Ron gave the girl a once-over, his sculpted hands flying up in the air. 'Stinking of cheap perfume – buying trailer trash stuff from god knows where!'

He picked up several packets of crisps that were strewn on the settee, their shiny gaping openings revealing their empty contents.

'Where the hell do they get the money to buy this stuff?' he asked me as if I knew. Sleepy-Head threw off the scarf with contempt, where it cascaded to the floor to form another lifeless puddle. The air crackled with an explosive current as she flounced out of the room with a determined step.

******

As soon as the door slammed shut behind Sleepy Head, the hairs on the back of my neck stood up, an inkling– as sure as day follows night!

Hoping to get a clue of what the inevitable torment might look like, I stared at the pillows of clouds floating in a trench-coat-grey sky visible through the stretched bay window.

'They're getting out of hand—' Ron whispered.

He expected me to say something, but attending to his problems like some mother-hen was the last thing I wanted to do.

He continued, short of breath, his tone harsh, unwavering. 'They talk back... there's no-one to keep an eye on 'em!'

'Please, don't Ron'

'They even play poker for f**k's sake!'

'Strip-poker…it's just for laughs…' I said, hotly.

His eyes widened, his arms dropping to his side. 'We risk losing this place!'

'We haven't done so …'

'The girls don't stay long enough ...so we can't claim them.'

'Claim them?'

'Come off it, Sylvie! You know the drill!'

I did know the drill. If residents left before their six months were up, Ron couldn't claim them in his funding returns. New Horizons would lose a whole bunch of money if our retention rates were low.

'It's all I have,' I murmured, trying to keep calm.

My guts were spilling and slithering noiselessly to the floor, his boots sloshing about in the mess.

He fixed me with a stare. 'We can't ...Sylvie—'

'That job's all I've got.' My lips were bleeding now since I'd been chewing them the moment I'd first glimpsed his broad back reflected in the mirror.

'PastaPlates can spare you...' He blew into his hands and rubbed them together. 'The thing is, I need you here,' he whispered, standing tentatively behind me, slipping his hot hands under the looseness of my shirt collar, massaging my shoulders. As my stomach tightened, my head dropped back, eyes shut tight. The sickly-sweet smell of aftershave that he has shipped over from the States, now nauseated me.

'It's only four hours,' I wanted to say but the words came out garbled.

He warbled some nonsense in my ear, his hands gently pummelling the nape of my neck.

'They treat it as a holiday—from the time you leave for work—they sit around doing bug**r all!'

I moved away from him, his curled fingers suspended in the air. 'I can't suckle 'em every five minutes!' I said, adjusting my collar.

'Sylvie… '

The reverberations of the slammed front door shook the house, fixing us to the spot. We stared at each other, and in three strides, Ron had reached the window.

'Godda**nit! She – she's got that shi**y little suitcase of hers —' he croaked. The sun's rays bounced off the beads of sweat on his forehead making it shine. 'I don't—that shi**y little suitcase!'

'We don't need her, Ron—!'

He flopped over at the waist, holding onto me, pleading. 'I...no, we... please, Sylvie...' He jerked his head towards the window. 'She's getting away—!'

'Good riddance, I say!' I continued, watching in disbelief, his disintegration, like cigarette ash underfoot. My stomach pumped up a vinegary taste so sour that I had to spit into an aspidistra plant pot near the door, a plant that had long ago been plunged into soil as dry as the desert.

'Haul her carcass back here!'

'What does it matter? I mean... who's going to check, Ron?'

'What?'

'We can still include her on our returns!' I insisted. 'I mean, *who's gonna know?* No-one's ever come to inspect us!'

His lips were moving as if gripped by fever. Unsteady on his feet, he glared at me with moist eyes, his breathing laboured.

I strode across the threadbare carpet that had lost its geometrical pattern long ago. The smell of cremated cabbage emanating from the kitchen filled the whole house, and one of the girls on the stairs, still waiting, asked, 'Can we finish watching our programme?' I sailed past them, past the coat-stand in the hall; past the tapestry of clematis with its star-like blooms, an assortment of pink, red and purply-blue, that had been creeping up the front-facing walls of the house since I first lived there.

Sleepy-Head was further up the street than I thought. Her fly-away golden hair, blown back by a light breeze showed off her chiselled features. Weighed down by a small green suitcase, her jacket sloping off her shoulders, she bounced along the road like a cat. Holding a mobile phone to her ear, she ran towards a parked black taxi in the middle of the street. A phone.... I had no idea— the sneaky bi**h!

I made a mental note to search all the rooms when I got back.

I stopped in my tracks. Hell! Why can't *he* run after her? If he wanted her back for his miserable figures, then why can't *he* be the one to coax her back? I looked at the house. Ron's white serpent-like face was pressed up against the window, his expression like that of a child who had just seen a favourite toy splinter into a thousand pieces.

I was soon within spitting distance of Sleepy-Head who had slowed down. The game was up. As I spun her around, a high-pitched squeal escaped her throat.

'Hit me!' I gasped, clutching her arms as if to detain her, pulling her from side-to-side. 'It's gotta look good!'

She looked confused at my request, her normally beady eyes were now fully opened so that I could see my reflection in them.

'What?' she asked, gasping for breath.

'If you want to leave, that's fine with me, but you've gotta make it look real!' I tugged her viciously by the collar.

'I don't...understand,' she panted.

'For fu** sake— throw a few punches at me —'

A flash of sulphury light blurred my vision at the same time an enormous crack split the air near my left ear; the pain seeped through slowly. I staggered like an ice-skater about to fall headlong, veering one way and then the other, as in a drunken fox-trot. Another flash of blinding light, the pain has arrived, and I instinctively pulled my arms over my head, protecting myself from an unknown attacker. I let out a mighty roar deep from the back of the throat, at a pitch I never knew I had the strength to make. I tumbled to the ground, rolling in all directions, the pain splitting my head open. Knees up to my chin, I lay on my side, rocking myself. The sound of whimpering, the sucking of air between teeth, grated on my nerves before I realised that the sounds were coming from me!

'You've killed her!' moaned Sleepy-Head to the person who had just whacked me across the head in a mean and sneaky fashion; she sounded dazed, her voice coated with hysteria

'The bi**h got what was coming to her!' said a man who sounded a bit like Timothy from next door who was always trying to speak to Bunchee Golding.

And Ron would be watching from the spot where I'd left him, his eyes filled with a dry rage that would hang over him for some time to come.

******

Chapter 7

The End of the Road

I flex my aching fingers, inky and black. A deep-rooted hollowness grips my heart, my throat; dirt lodges under my fingernails, in my nose, my ears; bugs crawl under my rough, fetid skin. I walk gingerly past the patients whose eyes track me *all the time!* I know that they'd love to tip the contents of their overnight bedpans over me.

This whole writing exercise set by Chilspeth about my life in New Horizons has thrown up stuff I've never considered before. How did that happen? What was really going on there? Why didn't I say something? What did she…he mean by that? Why didn't anyone say anything?

Did I really just let *that* happen?

I don't want to do this anymore. I tear up the chapters I've written so far with my splotchy fingers, and I later burn them at the back of this building with the help of Monkey Boden-Leap, a bearded man with kind eyes, who feeds the blue-red flames that leap up inside the gaping mouth of the waste incinerator.

******

Melanie comes to visit me. I've stopped calling her a Glass of Water. She's a DaSouza…my own flesh and blood sent to spy on me by our father! It transpires that my brother, Tricky Dickie, (Richard) had tried to turf us out of the squat owned by my father as soon as he realised that I was living there. Richard had managed to get Power of Attorney over my father's affairs on the grounds that father was going gaga. With the incident of the breast feeding that I'd seen with my own eyes, and which gives me goosebumps even now, I had to agree with my brother: the old fruitcake's stark staring bonkers…entirely off his rocker!

My preliminary court hearing is tomorrow, and Melanie's bought me a fancy blouse and a trouser suit…with father's money. I take out the badge from Unchained, depicting a woman without features, wearing a chain around her neck. It gives off a comforting pinkish red gleam that lifts your mood.

'Could you see Gracie gets this...?' I ask, pressing the badge into Melanie's soft yielding hand, not daring to look at the flamboyant bauble in case I change my mind.

'Gracie?'

'Our niece...'

'She's not our niece...I don't know why you...'

'She's Richard's offspring—look at her fingers!'

'—she's not...'

'It's in the blood! I'd stake my life on it,' I hiss. 'That child's just like *me*! She's crafty...she gives as good as she gets...and she's totally fearless. I may not be sure about you, but I'm sure as hell sure about her! And d'you know what, Mel? I hope she unchains herself from that family before they end up stifling her...like I was...so please...see that she gets this...'

I stare into her serious grey-blue eyes, thanking her for all her help, and that if she can find out who it was that got Ron Partridge arrested, who made that fatal telephone call that ended my life, I'd be eternally in her debt. 'It wasn't Bunchee ... she didn't have the guts.' I say.

Melanie's shoulders droop, and her forehead wrinkles over like the skin forming on the surface of hot milk left out to cool. Her eyes fill with tears, and I reproach myself for setting off the old waterworks in her just by thanking her. I pass her a box of tissues and yanking one out, she presses it to her nose, squawking: 'Oh Sylvie! Sylvie!' No, I've never thanked her for her many acts of kindness. As I scratch my head and smooth my hair, her watery eyes bulge, as if anticipating what I'm about to say.

'Has he...has he... tried to get hold of me? I ask, trying to sound casual, as if I couldn't care less one way what her answer might be. I scratch the underside of my chin where a boil erupted. My cheeks are red and raw. I'm mindful not to scratch my face as it upsets Mel; she believes that I've bribed one of the staff to sneak me in a tub of Peachy-Peach to lighten my skin.

'Who? Dad?'

'Dad?'

'Of course, he wants to see you' she says

'No-oo! I meant Ron. Has he ...tried to...?'

Melanie catches her breath. 'Sylvie!' Her chest rises and falls in spurts, her expression crestfallen.

'No but…you know, he might have sent…a message—?' I say hopefully.

'Sylvie…don't say that!' she hisses like a thousand snakes. 'Ron's the reason you're here!'

'That's not …strictly true…' I say, using "strictly" so as not to flatly contradict her. 'I feel that he …well…you know…'

'No, I don't know! And I don't think I ever will!' she snaps. 'He's the reason why you're being tried for murder! Are you thick or something?' The colour rises in her cheeks, her voice excitable and shrill. Her complexion …has actually darkened!

I tug my ear and turn to stare at her. 'Then why is it Mel… why is it that if I had the chance to do it all again, I would… yeah? Yeah! I would…I wouldn't change a godda**ned thing! He was my friend and he looked after me … looked out for me…No! Honestly, he did…no matter how much you sneer and shake your head…he was my dearest… friend— can you understand that?'

The corners of her mouth start to dip, her shoulders slump.

I ask her to get me a copy of Ron's Pre-Sentence Report from Irene Cotter, as I'm ready to read it now.

'Anyway,' I say as brightly as I can, that makes her wince. 'Thanks for everything, Mel—I'm glad if you're my sister…but the jury's still out on that one. I look like Dad—but you're so much lighter than…'

'It's genetics… I'd rather be like you…' she lies.

'And yes, I will see Dad but only when… I don't want him to see me in here…you know…he'll be crushed…to see me like this.'

Mel's about to say something, but I don't let her as I'm suddenly feeling tired.

'Don't you worry about me. I'll come through this—just you wait and see!' I plant a kiss on her little clammy forehead.

And with that, the Glass of Water bursts into tears.

******

APPENDIX

1 Chapter 1, page 7: Note from Sylvie DaSouza to Ron Partridge's defence barrister/team

To: Ronald Partridge's Defence team Dear Sir/Madam
I write to let you know that I, Sylvie DaSouza, am present today at the Criminal Courts. I am prepared to give evidence on behalf of Ron Partridge of my own free will. I promise to tell the whole truth and nothing but the truth. I am sorry I have not come forward before, but I was hitherto indisposed.

Yours sincerely
Sylvie DaSouza

2 Chapter 8, page 64: Hospital letter to Bunchee Golding

Dear Ms Golding
My apologies for the delay in arranging this appointment. We were unable to locate your medical files at the Medical Centre you had referred to on your registration form.
Please report to the Psychiatric Unit at the hospital on Monday 12 May at 12.00.

Yours sincerely
Cameron Duguid
Registrar

3 Chapter 9, page 71: Notes from Ana Buchwald's initial meeting with Sylvie DaSouza that were snatched by Sylvie Da Souza.

Sylvie DeSouza: referred to service by Melanie DaSouza, next of kin; father Bernard DaSouza to pay for client's treatment
Client...observant, alert, intelligent...insensitive, awkward; deep-rooted disdain towards authority ...e.g. seen in ice breaker

Hears voices. 'Gingerbread Man' Freudian perhaps (?) Possible diagnosis of schizophrenia? BPD ...
Potentially interesting case study for a good paper. Long-term.

4 **Chapter 10, page 76: Master/ Slave contract**

I (name) promise to obey ONE master I will work wholeheartedly for him
I will be good to him
I will share my life with others without jealousy
I will not take part in tittle-tattle or subversive topics I will not take sides against my master
I will not break any House Rules
I will not do anything to harm my master.

   Signed: Date:
   Signed: Date:

5 **Chapter 11, page 79: Concluding part of TV interview with Bunchee Golding at the television studios that Sylvie Da Souza missed.**

Maisie Small peers at Bunchee Golding with a great deal of interest.
'I'm sorry if I keep returning to this point, but I feel many viewers will be intrigued by this aspect of your story…what made you stay for that length of—?'
'I think that's been answered, already,' interrupts Annie Lederer.
The presenter raps the table with her pen. 'No wait...let her answer... let Bunchee speak!'
'In my heart…I think… I am in love with him,' says Bunchee Golding.
'In love...with your perpetrator?' Maisie Small's mouth hangs opens as the broom of nausea sweeps across her face, her fingers twitching at her throat.
'To start with...yes. I- I ...do not know that… '
'Didn't know what?'
'That he want so many girlfriends…'

6 Chapter 12, page 86: Email to Bunchee Golding from Victor Runcible

'My Darling Bunchee, my heart, my love.
My heart wilts for you, my most precious one. I grow wistful...daily. The cruelty of our seperation is too grate to bear. Our new beginnings await, our new spring! My braggart heart boasts nothing and no-one but you.
...do not wound me with more delay, or I die, my love, truly I die. Without our profound moment, we are incomplete, each without the other. Please complete me my love, no more delays, or by my grave weep for you have killed me.
I send you details of the Western Union yesterday, dearest intended. This is where you must send the money.

Victor Runcible, forever yours.
(your ardent and sincere fiancée who loves you as his civic duty).

7. Chapter 14, page 96: Letter from Bernard DaSouza to Ron Partridge

"....my wife and I would like to see our daughter alone. Have some compassion! We haven't seen her in two years. My wife's nerves are not good at present and denying her the right to see Sylvie is tantamount to killing her...don't take away the mother of my son and younger daughter...
Is Sylvie getting the monthly allowance I send her? Please see she goes for dental check-ups"

Bernard DaSouza

8. Chapter 14, page 104: Picture of Sylvie DaSouza by her mother, Alice DaSouza

9. Chapter 23, page 147: The 'korpse' picture

10. Chapter 27, page 169 Extract: Telephone call placed by Sylvie DaSouza to Mr Bubbles' Nursery

'... yes, it's one of the mums in Gracie's class here... if you see Gracie's mum, could you let her know that I have an emerald and diamond bracelet of hers ...Gracie left it at my home after a sleepover...you could have knocked me down with a feather!.....It's a *genuine* diamond bracelet....if you could... please... I've misplaced mother's number...I think mother picks up little Gracie right about this time ...'

11. Chapter 28, page 178 Letter to Rosemarie Whittington from Bunchee Golding

Dearest Rosemarie....
So sorry. Please not hate me.
You are good friend for me. I think we never meet again after you leave us first time long while. You help me much this last year, and you not well.
He free us because he think we are weak. He does not expect us to do what we do. We tell.
One last help. Please look after her. She deserves peace. She is survivor like us all. I want to say that I did something very bad to her. I am one who writes 'Chastity belt' on her packing list. I am jealous and do not want her to go.
The truth sets us free.
End of shame
Love and love and love

Bunchee Golding.

12. Chapter 29, page 180: Daily Argos Report 'Sex Cult Leader gives the Law the slip' by Crime Correspondent Nathan Chudasamar

"....the prisoner was being transported to hospital with a suspected heart attack...
Lawrence Gibbons, (43) the driver of the prison van, described how, on slowing down at a set of traffic lights, two people with Mickey Mouse masks got out of a silver Lexus and pointed guns at him...

Mr Gibbons stated, "I'm not clear what happened but one of the two men, a stocky individual, assaulted my colleague. I definitely believe he had some sort of military training...The other person was dinky...smaller...soft-like, and I grappled with this person trying to knock the gun out of his hand... and before I knew it the gun went off, hitting me in the buttocks."

... the gun left behind by the shooter was traced back to a safe deposit box, the property of the escapee, Ronald Ewing Partridge'

13. PART 2 Chapter 1 page 189 Peachy-Peach Beauty Remedy
  Peachy-Peach pigment correcting serum*:

gives a rapid glow to the skin and limits the appearance of blemishes and hyper- pigmentation.
Ingredients: Hydroquinone, retinol, Argan oil, Vitamin A, essence of peach, double cream

*skin lighteners may cause damage with overuse

14. PART 2 Chapter 2, page 197: Letter to Sylvie from her father, Bernard DaSouza

Sylvie—
Dear girl! How are you?
How about getting together one afternoon... tea perhaps? Just you, your mother and me?
Name the day, place, and time. You are forever in our hearts.

Your father,

Bernard DaSouza

15. PART 2 Chapter 4 Page 213: Wilbur Partridge's Training Programme

Day	Morning (am)	Afternoon (pm)
Monday	Physical Training	Truth -Telling
Tuesday	Physical Training Assault course	Memory Games
Wednesday	Assault course (timed)	Traps, tying knots, restraint techniques and disguises
Wednesday (cont.)	Intro to martial arts (Beg.)	
Thursday	Intro to martial arts (Beg.)	Surveillance Techniques
Friday	Martial arts (Adv.)	First Aid, resuscitation

16. PART 2, Chapter 7, page 234: Transcript of telephone recording between Ron Partridge and Unchained

(Undisclosed to police by Unchained).

'...Can you do something for 'em? What? No, I don't know about your organisation... I figured you might be able to help because you're supposed to unchain people, aren't you? Well this lot's chained themselves to me...oh, I don't know!—they just keep clinging on like I'm some sort of f***ing mother hen!'

.......Sure I can describe them. They're frail....and not all there... a bit gaga, if truth be told, easily confused...

Oh, come on! I think I deserve a lousy break after forty years...my guts are leaking, and I can't think straight, okay? You do <u>DO</u> that kind of work, don't you? I want to be with my family, but this lot won't leave me alone—they won't fu**ing leave me alone! It's insane! ...I mean, is that too much to ask?'

...Well, okay...if that's what you guys want, that's what I'll say— I've kept 'em hostage for years and years against their will—There! Will that do?'

17 PART 2: Chapter 7, page 235: Extract from Ron Partridges' Pre-Sentence Report, prepared by Mrs. Shirley Helier

"...the New Horizons Project was an idea originally conceived by the defendant to provide a safe house for women facing homelessness, domestic violence, poverty and a general lack of opportunities, particularly in relation to acquiring sustained work, and in meeting the needs of a technologically changing job market. Mr Partridge's submission for funding to the Charity Commission was, however, turned down in 19** and subsequently in 19**, 19**, 19**........
...however, the project became firmly entrenched in Mr Partridge's mind as a fully operational concern, and he...'